D0710115

Also by Michael Baisden

The Maintenance Man
Men Cry in the Dark
Never Satisfied: How & Why Men Cheat

Michael Baisden

GOD'S GIFT TO WOMEN

A TOUCHSTONE BOOK
Published by Simon & Schuster
New York   London   Toronto   Sydney   Singapore

Touchstone
Rockefeller Center
1230 Avenue of the Americas
New York, NY 10020

"God's Gift to Women" by Angela O. Guillory
reprinted courtesy of the author
"Fatally Yours" by D'Ajaneigh Emmanuel
reprinted courtesy of the author
"Moving On" and "Above Average" by B. R. Burns
reprinted courtesy of the author

This Touchstone Edition 2003

TOUCHSTONE and colophon are registered trademarks
of Simon & Schuster Inc.

For information regarding special discounts for bulk purchases,
please contact Simon & Schuster Special Sales at 1-800-456-6798
or business@simonandschuster.com

Designed by Stacy Luecker

Manufactured in the United States of America
1   3   5   7   9   10   8   6   4   2

The Library of Congress has cataloged the hardcover edition as follows:
Baisden, Michael.
God's gift to women / Michael Baisden.
p.   cm.
1. Radio broadcasters—Fiction. 2. Rejection (Psychology)—Fiction.
3. Stalking victims—Fiction. 4. Single fathers—Fiction.
5. Houston (Tex.)—Fiction. 6. Chicago (Ill.)—Fiction. I. Title.
PS3552.A3925 G63   2002
813'.54—dc21   2003269674

ISBN 0-7432-4692-6
0-7432-4997-6 (Pbk)

This book is dedicated
to my beautiful and sweet cousin,
Monica Goree Adams,
who passed away on December 11, 1999.

You were the little sister I never had.
When I think about your warm smile
and the funny way you laughed, I can't help smiling.
You were always supportive of me and my work.
I will never forget your kindness as long as I live.

Love ya', Cuz.

Acknowledgments

It's been eight long years since I sat down to write my first book, and I am more grateful than ever for this incredible gift God has given me. The ability to create stories that touch people's lives is truly a blessing. I appreciate all the love and support all my fans have given me since I sold my first book out of the trunk of my car back in 1995. I promise you I'll always remain humble and remember how much that first ten bucks meant to me.

I want to send a special thanks out to all the African American bookstores for doing such a wonderful job of promoting my work. I can't list them all, but there are a few who have been outstanding in their support: Medu Bookstore in Atlanta, The Shrine of the Black Madonna in Detroit and Houston, Smiley's Books and Malik's bookstore in Los Angeles, Culture Plus in New York, Black Images in Dallas, Books For Thought in Tampa, Karibu Books in Maryland, Apple Bookstore in Detroit, and African American Images in Chicago. It's very important that we continue to support these and other black-owned bookstores. They are the main reason for the success of many self-published authors, including myself.

Of course, I have to thank all the radio personalities across the country who have allowed me to sit in on their show and raise hell over the years. Steve Harvey at the BEAT in Los Angeles; his producer, Hollywood Henderson; and the Angels, Shirley Strawberry, Nautica de la Cruz, and Dominique DiPrima, with whom I've had a love-hate relationship for years. Thanks for always making it hot in the studio and for appreciating how hard my journey was.

A special thanks to Donnie Simpson at WPGC in D.C., crazy Chris Paul, and his producer, Reggie Rouse. And of course, Justin Love and fellow Cancer Todd B. for always inviting me to sit in on *Lovetalk*. To my good friends at WEDR in Miami: James T., Tamara G., and Maestro in promotions. My seminars in Miami have been some of the best I ever had thanks to your support. Thanks to Magic Man and Nikki Thomas at WBLK in Buffalo, New York. I appreciate you packing the crowds in at your expo every year. And I must shout out to the Dream Team in Philadelphia: Donya Blaze; Golden Boy; comedian Dee Lee; Colby Colb (who's now at Power 105 in New York); and the Diva herself, Wendy Williams, who has moved on to WBLS in New York. Congratulations on your success. You go, girl!

To Deneen Busby at Majic 104.9 in St. Louis: thanks for doing such a great job of promoting me and other African American authors. Your Sunday-morning talk show with the book club is off the hook! And last but not least, my homeboy from Chicago, Doug Banks and his cohost DeDe McGuire, J. J. Jackson, CoCo Budda, and his producer, Gary Saunders. Thanks for making me feel welcome every time I walk into the studio at six o'clock in the morning. Hey, Doug, you still got a Dan Ryan head!

Last, I have to thank Je'Caryous Johnson and Gary Guidry of I'm Ready Productions here in Houston. They shared my vision by bringing my novels *Men Cry in the Dark* and *The Maintenance Man* to the stage. It's been a pleasure working with both of you. Looking forward to bigger and better things in the future.

Prologue

Consequences

Houston, Texas
New Year's Day 2002

I WAS FIGHTING to stay conscious as the paramedics rushed me down the corridor of my office building. In the distance I could hear gunfire and horns blowing.

"You chose one helluva way to bring in the New Year, Mr. Payne," the paramedic said.

"Where's my daughter?" I asked while trying to sit up. "And where's Terri?"

"Please lie still. You'll only make the bleeding worse."

The radio station was on the twenty-fifth floor. I didn't feel strong enough to make it to the ambulance—let alone the hospital. The bullet had penetrated my left side and exited through my back. It burned like hell.

"Am I gonna die?"

They both paused, then looked at one another as if to seek the other's opinion. That terrified me. Once we boarded the elevator, they began broadcasting my vital signs into the radio. I didn't know the significance of the blood pressure and heart-rate numbers, but judging by the urgency in their voices, I was in trouble.

"Where's my daughter? And where's Terri?" I asked again.

"Relax, Mr. Payne, your daughter is—"

He stopped in midsentence as the elevator doors opened on the lobby level. Suddenly, a wave of photographers and reporters rushed toward me. I was blinded by a barrage of flashing lights. Although my vision was blurred, I could see the outline of several husky policemen clearing a path.

"Julian, can you tell us what happened?" a reporter yelled out.

"Who shot the security guard?" another shouted while shoving a microphone in my face.

"Fuckin' vultures!" I tried to lift my hand to shield my bloody face, but my arms were strapped down. The yelling was deafening—like a continuous roar. The paramedics tried to move faster, but it was no use. The lobby was packed with policemen, reporters, and nosy fans who had come to watch. The atmosphere was festive, like a circus.

"Get out of the way, please!" the paramedics yelled. "This man is in critical condition! Move, move, move!"

The paramedics fought through the main doors, but once we made it outside we came to an abrupt stop. The crowd was even larger. People were jumping up on the hood of their cars trying to get a better look. As the brisk night air blew across my bloody face, their loud voices suddenly faded—replaced by sirens and the humming of the helicopter blades. I could feel the blood soaking through the bandages.

It was obvious from the paramedics' expressions that we were running out of time. The ambulance was only a few yards away, but the crowd was out of control. When they continued to push, the cops pushed back—violently. People were knocked to the pavement and trampled.

"I love you, Julian!" a woman screamed as she struggled to get off the ground.

"I'm your number one fan!" another woman shouted as she lifted her blouse, exposing her breasts.

Suddenly a woman lunged toward me and ripped the sleeve off my blood-soaked shirt.

"Aarrgh!" I screamed.

"Now I'll always have a piece of you," she said. Her hazel eyes and deranged stare were all too familiar.

"Move back!" the cops yelled as they pulled her away. "Move back, damnit!"

The stretcher seemed to move toward the ambulance in slow motion. I was growing weaker. I fought hard to stay conscious—to stay alive. I gazed up at the flashing lights from the squad cars as they danced across the dark sky and against the nearby glass buildings. It reminded me of the Fourth of July in Chicago.

I wish I had seen the fireworks on Lake Michigan this summer, I thought to myself. And I never did see the view from the top of the Sears Tower. I wish I had gone to Sam's first basketball game when she was seven. I wish I could be with Terri when my baby is born. But most of all, I wish I had never met Olivia Brown. She was the reason I was bleeding to death in Houston, Texas, on New Year's Eve.

How could she go this far? I wondered as they lifted me into the ambulance. *And why did she choose me?*

Part I

Chicago (September 2001)

Chapter 1

JASMINE-SCENTED CANDLES illuminated the studio, creating a spiritual ambiance. I reclined in my chair as I listened to the song "Is It a Crime" by Sade. The candles had become a ritual ever since I started at WTLK back in '89. The flickering light and smell of jasmine were relaxing and made me more introspective—aromatherapy, they called it.

The faint candlelight also served as camouflage for the dilapidated condition of the studio. The carpet was covered with decade-old cigarette burns, the plaster was falling off the ceiling, and the exposed water pipe leaked into an old Folgers coffee can. "Sade, your song is right on time," I said as I glanced around the room. "This place *is* a crime."

Just before the song ended, I put on my headphones and adjusted the volume to the mic. The digital clock on the console read 11:55 P.M. "Five more minutes and I'm outta this dump!" I said with contempt. My producer, Mitch, was in the control booth next door setting up the calls. I could see him through the large soundproof window. I switched on the intercom to get his attention.

"Well, Mitch, in a few minutes it'll all be over," I told him. "The final episode of the Green Hornet and Kato."

"Don't be so dramatic, Julian," he said in his usual smooth tone. "It's not the end of the world, just another phase in life."

"Listen to you, sounding all philosophical. That must be one of the benefits of old age."

"Who you callin' old?"

Mitch had smooth, dark brown skin and short black hair with gray streaks. He looked very distinguished but he had recently turned fifty-five and was getting touchy about his age.

"Look, we can arm wrestle for your Viagra prescription later," I laughed. "Right now, let's get to work and try to wrap up the show on time."

There were five people on hold. Mitch printed their names in bold letters on a piece of paper and taped it to the window. That was our sophisticated communication system. "Five, four, three, two—" I heard Mitch count. Then he pointed at me to signal we were on the air.

"Welcome back to *Love, Lust, and Lies* on WTLK," I said in my deep radio voice. "We only have enough time for two calls, so let's go straight to the phones. Adam, you're on. What's your question or issue?"

"Hey, Julian! I just want to congratulate you on your new show," he said. "I hope you don't get big-headed and forget where you came from when you blow up."

"Negro, please! I've been struggling in this business for fifteen years. I've never been about money *or* fame," I told him. "I've never owned a new car, don't own a nice watch, I cut my own hair, and every night I go home to a ten-year-old girl who's goin' through puberty. Now, if that doesn't keep you grounded, nothing will. Thanks for calling." *Click*.

Mitch was laughing his ass off because he knew I was telling the truth. I drove a beat-up 1994 Toyota Camry, which I bought used in 1996. And my scratched-up Gucci was ten years old. I laughed myself because when I looked down at it, it had stopped working—again.

"Okay, Sharon. You're my last caller!" I said as I pushed the button to line two. "What's your question or issue?"

"My question is about love and commitment." She sounded depressed.

"We don't have much time, sweetheart. What's your point?"

"My point is, when you love someone you should stand by him—no matter what, right?"

"I agree. If you truly love someone, nothing should come between you."

"Well, I thought my husband loved me, until—"

She stopped in midsentence.

"Come on! It can't be *that* serious," I said jokingly, trying to cheer her up. "What happened? Did you gain a little weight, lose your job, get a bad hair weave? What?"

"No, Julian, he left me because I was raped. The doctors said the damage was so severe I'll never be able to bear children," she said. Then she began to cry. "And after going through that hell, can you believe that no-good bastard had the nerve to tell me it was my fault that I got raped? How's that for love and commitment?"

I hit the mute button on my microphone and buried my head in my hands. When I looked up at Mitch, I knew he was thinking exactly what I was thinking. Why tonight—of all nights? The clock on the console read 11:56. We were almost out of time. But I was determined not to end my last show on a negative note.

"Are you all right, Sharon?" I asked. "Do you want me to put you in touch with a therapist?"

"No, Julian, thank you. I'll be fine. It happened a long time ago." She quickly composed herself. "I'm just sick and tired of men using the word *love* at their convenience. The only thing they love is getting pus—"

"Hold up"—I cut her off—"I get the point! And you're right, *love* is a serious word—men shouldn't say it if they don't mean it."

"Have *you* ever been in love, Julian?"

"Hold on a second, who's interviewing who?"

"Sorry, I didn't mean to offend you. But I was just wondering if there's ever been a woman worthy of *your* love."

I paused for a second as I thought of my wife, Carmen. Her picture was right in front of me, the one we took in Vegas on our honeymoon. I never spoke about her on the air since *that* day—it was too painful. But I decided to open up. Maybe I was caught up in the moment or by the vulnerability in Sharon's voice.

"Yes, I've been in love—once," I told her.

"Are you still with her?"

"No, she's gone—cancer took her."

"I guess we have something in common, Julian," she said, then she hesitated. "We're both alone."

Mitch was nodding in agreement. We both knew why. But I wasn't about to go there on the air.

"Like you said, it happened a long time ago," I told her. "You've got to let go of the pain in order to move on. And speaking of moving on, it's time for me to get out of here."

The phone lines were ringing off the hook, but there was no time left for calls. The management at WTLK was strict about ending segments on time, especially since the station was programmed to go off the air at midnight. The clock on the panel read 11:58.

"Before I go, I want to end the show with an inspirational poem, the way I always do on 'Hot Buttered Soul Poetry Friday.' I call this piece 'Movin' On.' I reached for my notebook. "This one's for you, Sharon, and all the ladies out there who are trying to move on." I cleared my throat and began to recite:

every experience
be it bad or good
teaches us a lesson
or at least it should

mr. right
turned out to be mr. wrong

learn from your mistakes
keep the faith
press forward, sista
move on

dry your tears
wipe your eyes
find the strength
look inside
don't call him
don't see him
don't play one sad song
block his cell
delete his email
look ahead, my sista
just move on

love yourself
take care of yourself
and if the need arises
sista, please yourself

do a check up
from the neck up
say a prayer
sista, hold your head up

cause one day you'll have all the joy your heart can hold
and then you'll be glad you pressed forward
and so thankful you moved on

After I finished reading, I felt choked up. I was closing the show for the last time. I hesitated for a second, then I let it go.

"Good night, Chicago," I said emotionally. "Thanks for allowing me into your homes, your hearts, and your minds—peace."

Mitch quickly turned on the studio lights and came running over. He was holding a bottle of Dom Pérignon and two glasses. He shook it up and then popped the cork. Champagne sprayed everywhere.

"Congratulations, Julian," he said, as he poured it over my head. "You're finally escaping this concentration camp!"

"Yeah, it took me over ten years, like *Shawshank Redemption,* but I finally made it," I laughed as I wiped the Champagne from my eyes.

He poured two glasses and handed me one.

"I'd like to propose a toast," he said. "To the most outspoken, talented, and arrogant son of a bitch in talk radio."

"Hear, hear!" I said as we tapped glasses.

"Now, *I* wanna propose a toast. To the man who has given me inspiration, motivation, and die-rection. Here's to you, Mitch."

We toasted again. Then there was an uncomfortable silence. I had dreaded this moment all week.

"You know, Mitch, I'm sorry I couldn't work out a deal to take you with me. You know how much you—"

"Look, Julian," he interrupted, "this is your time—your season. You were born for this. Besides, I've got a big deal I've been working on. I only wish Carmen could've been here to share this moment with you."

"Yeah, me, too." I stared at her picture on the console. "She's the reason I stuck with this raggedy-ass station for as long as I did."

Mitch walked over and put his hand on my shoulder. He was a short man, standing about five six. I towered over him at six three, but he had a charismatic way of speaking that demanded attention.

"It's been two years, Julian. When are you gonna let it go?" he said in that fatherly tone. "You said it in your poem, life goes on! Why don't you stop feeling sorry for yourself and start taking some of your own advice?"

"Look, Mitch, *dating* is not high on my list of priorities!" I said as I pulled away. Then I started packing up my equipment. "I'm moving to Houston in two days. I just want to finish packing, have a farewell drink with Eddie at Club Nimbus, then get the hell outta here!"

"Sounds like a plan, Julian." He poured himself another drink. "But you know as well as I do, Sharon was right; you are alone. You should've asked her out—she's obviously single," he added sarcastically. "Tell you what, why don't we see if she's still on the line?"

Mitch reached for the button on the console. All five phone lines were lit and my microphone was still on.

"Cool out, Mitch!" I grabbed at his hand. But he managed to press the speakerphone button for line two. There was a sudden click, then a dial tone.

"It's best that she's gone, anyway," he said as he backed away from the console.

"And why is that? Not that I care."

"Because Samantha will never allow another woman into her life, or yours, not until she learns to accept that you are *a man*—with needs."

He sat his Champagne glass on the console and headed for the door.

"Where you goin'?" I walked toward him holding my glass. "I thought we were celebrating tonight."

"I'm going home to my woman—what about you?" he said as he opened the door. "I really hope you find what you're looking for in Houston, Julian." Then he turned off the lights and walked out.

As I watched the candle wax slowly melting away, I thought about what my father told me before he died: "Son, money can buy a lot of things in this world, but it can't buy back time." As I stood there in the dim silence of my spiritual ambiance, I had to face up to the reality of what Mitch said. *He's right,* I thought to myself. *Samantha was too possessive and I was only making matters worse by not having a life of my own.*

I gathered up the rest of my things and placed them in my gym bag. Before I put away the picture of Carmen, I looked at it. Then I spoke to it.

"You know I'll always love you, Carmen, but it's time for me to move on with my life!" I said as tears rolled down my face. "My mind needs it, my heart needs it, my soul needs it. And I ain't gonna lie, baby, my body needs it, too." I laughed.

I kissed her picture, then placed it into my bag. "You'll always be my queen."

On the way out the door I blew out my jasmine-scented candles and put them inside my bag. At that moment, I decided it was the only baggage I was carrying with me to Houston.

Chapter 2

SATURDAY MORNING I was awakened by the sound of a horn blowing. I turned over to check the clock on the nightstand. It read 8:15 A.M. When I looked out the window, there was a huge van from the moving company parked in my driveway. The driver was a tall black man. He was wearing white socks, blue jean coveralls, and a straw brim. "Damn, that's country!" I said to myself. The two other men, one black, the other Hispanic, were busy unloading empty boxes.

I put on my robe and slippers then went to find out why my daughter, Samantha, hadn't heard the commotion. "Sam," I yelled. "Where are you?"

I knocked on her bedroom door, the way I always did. We promised to respect each other's privacy. When there was no answer, I went in. Just as I expected, she had on her headphones with the music blasting. She was also wearing my long-sleeve denim shirt; it was her mother's favorite. She must have taken it out of the box, because I had packed it the day before. Her back was to the door, so she didn't see me coming.

"Boo!" I shouted.

She jumped, then spun around with her hand over her heart.

"Daddy, you scared the mess out of me! I hate it when you do that!"

"Well, I hate it when you listen to that rap music. Didn't I tell you not to bring that garbage in this house?"

"What are you talking about?"

"Samantha, don't play the dumb role, you've got the volume turned up so loud I can hear those filthy lyrics a mile away." I pushed the eject button and removed the CD. "Jay-Z? Don't tell me. This is a jazz group—right?"

"It's not mine." She tried to sound convincing.

"I don't care who it belongs to. I don't want you listening to that trash, do you understand?"

"Yes, sir."

"Now, go downstairs and open the door for the movers. And put my shirt back where you found it. I don't want you to mess around and forget it."

As she walked by me, with that pitiful look on her face, I popped her upside the head.

"Ouch! What was that for?"

"That's for lying to me. Now, take your narrow behind downstairs."

As I looked around her room, I thought about all the good times we use to have playing hide-and-seek and one, two, three, red light. It was the only home Samantha had ever known. We moved in back in '93, Sam had just turned three. I smiled as I looked around the room at the posters hanging on the walls. When she was five the walls were covered with Barney the dinosaur and *Sesame Street* characters; a huge poster of Big Bird used to hang over her bed. Samantha thought it protected her from the bogeyman.

When she turned ten the posters had changed. Big Bird and Ernie had been replaced by Usher, Destiny's Child, and Alicia Keys. She really loved Alicia's music. It had rekindled her interest in playing the piano. "Thank God," I said as I looked at the poster of Li'l Bow Wow. "We definitely have enough rappers."

As I was walking out of her room, I heard the phone ring.

"I got it!" Samantha yelled from downstairs. I figured it was one of her girlfriends, so I went back to my bedroom to get dressed. I pulled out a pair of jeans and a Fubu T-shirt. Before I got dressed, I admired my physique in the full-length mirror on the closet door.

"Julian, you need to lay off of those Krispy Kremes." I pinched an inch of my love handles.

It was easy to gain weight in the radio business. Sitting in one spot five days a week, four hours a night had expanded my waistline and everything else. I tried to keep it in check by playing ball and hitting the weights as often as possible.

"Never let your stomach get bigger than your ass." I began doing crunches. "There's nothing a woman hates more than a man whose butt is bigger than hers."

I did two sets of fifty and then I admired my four-pack in the mirror. At thirty-nine I had accepted that my six-pack was gone forever. I flexed one last time by doing my Bruce Lee impersonation from *Return of the Dragon. "Whaa!"*

At that moment, I heard snickering in the background. It was Samantha. She was standing in the doorway watching me flex in my drawers.

"Ahem." She cleared her throat. "Excuse me, Jackie Chan, you have a call."

"For your information, that's Bruce Lee," I said, feeling embarrassed. "By the way, I thought we agreed to knock before entering."

"Yes, Bruce—I mean, Dad." She laughed. "But you were screaming so loud I thought you fell in the shower."

"Just give me the phone, you little comedian. Who is it?"

"It's Denise. She's looking for Uncle Eddie."

"Thank you, my little secretary." I slowly closed the door. "Good-bye."

"Whassup, Li'l Sis?" It was a nickname I had given her after three years of putting up with Eddie.

"Hey, Julian, how you doin'?"

"Everything is great, with the exception of dealing with Sam's preteen hormones. She's going through that stage where she's starting to like boys."

"Judging by our conversation a minute ago, the boys are starting to like her, too."

"Yeah, she's turning into a real fox. If her breasts get any bigger, I may have to break out the shotgun." I laughed. "Now, enough about Sam. Whassup? Don't tell me you and Eddie fell out again!"

"No, we're doing okay. It's just that I came home early from my business trip and he's not here. I called his cell phone and the studio but I can't reach him. Do you know where he is?"

I knew exactly where he was, the Park Avenue Motel. It was one of our hangouts in the old neighborhood. Eddie was still a regular. But coming up with a good lie at eight o'clock in the morning wasn't going to be easy, especially since Eddie was a photographer.

"Oh, yeah, Eddie had a photo shoot on Lake Michigan at sunrise. I believe it was for a magazine ad for sunglasses, sunscreen, or something like that."

"Is that right?" She sounded unconvinced. "Well, you can tell Mr. Sunscreen that he'd better bring his butt home before I *block* him out of this house by changing the locks!"

I covered my mouth to keep from laughing. We both knew that story was lame as hell. But I kept my composure and tried to change the subject.

"Okay, Denise, I'll tell him. By the way, are you coming to Club Nimbus with Eddie tonight? I'd love to see you before I leave town."

"Of course I'll be there. You know I wouldn't miss this for the world."

"Now, you do understand that I only expect to see you and Eddie, right?"

"Oh, lord, here we go again with The Speech."

"That's right, you know where I'm going with this," I said

to her. "Promise me you won't try to hook me up with another one of your strong, independent, corporate-type girlfriends."

"But Julian, I've got the perfect girl for you this time. She's single, no kids, owns her own business, and she's got a great personality."

"Whenever a woman says her friend has a great personality, it usually means she's ugly."

"That's not true, she's a very beauti—"

"Stop right there, Denise. Can we get together for once without you playing matchmaker? Is that too much to ask?"

She paused. I could practically hear her pouting. "Okay, okay. But one of these days I'm gonna hook you up with Ms. Right," she said. "Good things always happen to good people."

"Bad things happen to good people, too—just look at the ten o'clock news." I laughed. "Now let me go so I can finish packing. I'll see you tonight. And I do mean *only* you! Bye, Li'l Sis."

"Good-bye, Julian, you old party pooper."

As soon as I hung up the phone I began looking through the Yellow Pages for the number to the Park Avenue Motel. Once I found it, I dialed the number. The phone rang ten times before someone finally picked up.

"This is the *fabulous* Park Avenue, what's your pleasure?" a man announced in a raspy and familiar voice.

"Old Man Johnson, is that you?"

"Yeah, this is Mr. Johnson, who the hell is this?"

"This is Firebird. Remember me?"

It was a nickname he had given me back in my college days because of the type of car I drove.

"Firebird?" He pondered. "The name sounds familiar, but I can't place it."

"Maybe this will help you remember: I had a burgundy Firebird with a personalized plate that read CHICAGO. My real name is Julian Payne."

"Oh, Julian!" he said excitedly. "How you doin'? It's been

years since that car of yours was parked in front of room one thirty-five."

"I can see you're still just as sharp as ever. You used to memorize every car that drove into your lot—make, model, and license plate."

"Yeah, but you were always one of my favorites. I listen to your show every chance I get. Sorry to hear that you're leaving town."

"Well, life goes on," I told him, then I got to the point. "Look, Mr. Johnson, I'm looking for my friend Eddie, you know, the photographer?"

"I know who you talkin' 'bout, boy. That young man is one of my best customers."

"Is he there now?"

"Oh, yeah, he's here. At least his car is still parked in front of his room."

"Could you ring his room for me?"

"I've already tried three times this morning to give him a wake-up call," Mr. Johnson said. "I was gonna knock on the door but he had the Do Not Disturb sign on. I figured he was still gettin' busy."

Something was wrong. Eddie was a womanizer and a cheat but he was a regimented one. He made it a habit to be home by eight o'clock whenever Denise was out of town on business, just in case she came home early. The only exceptions were when he was sloppy drunk.

"Look, Mr. Johnson, I'm on my way," I told him. "Whatever you do, don't let anyone into that room!"

"Okay, Julian. But are you sure you don't want me to check it out?"

"No, just wait for me to get there."

I quickly put on my blue jeans and T-shirt, then grabbed my car keys off the dresser.

"Sam! Come here!"

"I'm coming!" she yelled while running up the stairs. When she stumbled into my bedroom she was nearly out of breath.

"Yes, Daddy?"

"I've got to make a quick run. I want you to go down to your friend's house until I get back."

"Can I go?"

"Not this time, sweetheart, it's business."

"You're going out on business wearing blue jeans and a Fubu T-shirt?"

"Just do what I tell you, young lady. I'm the parent, you're the child! And make sure your luggage is packed—you're spending the night at your grandmother's."

"But why? I thought we would spend one last night together in our house!" She began to cry.

"Look, Princess, all the furniture will be gone, there won't be anyplace to sleep," I told her. "And besides, I'm going out tonight."

"With who?"

"Don't you *ever* question me about where I'm going!" I said, raising my voice. "You're my daughter, *not* my wife."

Samantha ran off to her bedroom with tears pouring down her cheeks. It really hurt to speak to her that way, especially while staring into those beautiful brown eyes—her mother's eyes. I thought about going after her to apologize but I checked myself. It was time that I started acting more like a parent than a friend.

I was feeling good about myself. So good that I grabbed her Jay-Z CD and my portable player on my way out the door. As I sped off with the music blaring, I was worried less about Sam and more about Eddie. He had a history of sleeping with his clients and picking up strange women at the club. I was praying he hadn't run out of luck and gotten himself killed by some deranged bimbo.

Chapter 3

I ARRIVED AT the Park Avenue Motel late that morning. The place seemed unchanged since my college days. The soda machine had the same dents on the front. I must have kicked that piece of junk a thousand times, trying to get my quarters back. The window shutters and doors were the same dingy lime green color. I doubted they had a fresh coat of paint since '85. I couldn't help laughing as I looked up at the neon marquee. It read WELCOME TO THE FABULOUS PARK AVENUE, and then, in small letters, *hourly rates available.*

"I guess this dump would seem fabulous if you're drunk as hell and horny at one o'clock in the morning," I said to myself.

When I walked into the office, Old Man Johnson was in his usual position, feet propped up on the counter, cigar in his mouth, and holding his remote control. He was a short, chubby man with bad skin and a thick gray beard. If it wasn't for his cranky personality and foul language he would have made one helluva Santa Claus.

"I can see nothin' has changed around this joint."

"Hey, Firebird!" He sprang up from his chair, came from behind the bulletproof glass, and gave me a hug. "Boy, just look at ya, ain't changed a bit. Glad to see ya all grown up and successful!"

"Well, I've been grown up for a while, but the success is brand-new."

"Glad life is treating you so well. Most of the guys you grew up with are either dead or in jail," he said while reaching for a key on the wall. "But I know you didn't come down here to talk about the good ole days. Here's the key to Eddie's room. If you need anything, give me a holla."

"I'm sure everything is okay. He's probably passed out from drinking too much."

I hurried down to Eddie's room, which was at the end of the lot. I tried to see through the window, but the curtains were drawn too tight. I could hear the television playing. I banged on the door with my fist. "Eddie, you in there?" I yelled. "It's me, Julian!" But there was no reply.

My heart raced as I put the key in the lock and slowly pushed the door open. The room was dark, except for the light from the television. I reached over and switched on the lights. To my surprise, the room was empty. The linen on the bed was a mess and liquor bottles were all over the place. A six-pack of Barcardi coolers was on the dresser, a half pint of Hennessy on the night stand, and a forty-ounce bottle of Olde English 800 malt liquor was wasted on the floor next to the bed. There was even a half-smoked joint in the ashtray. But there was no sign of Eddie. No clothes, no shoes, no nothing.

Suddenly I heard a noise coming from the bathroom. I picked up the empty malt liquor bottle and slowly approached the door. "Eddie, is that you?" I said nervously. "Whoever you are, come out! I've got a gun and I'll blow your fuckin' brains out!"

Once I got closer, I put my ear to the door. I heard a muffled sound—*"Mm, mm!"* My heart was beating a hundred miles an hour. I was scared to death, but I had to make my move. I took a deep breath, gripped my malt liquor bottle, and began counting, "One—two—three," then I kicked in the door.

"What the—?" I shouted as I looked down at the floor. I couldn't believe my eyes. There was Eddie, butt naked, handcuffed to the toilet with a pair of lace pink panties on. His mouth was covered with duct tape and his feet were bound with rope. When I removed the tape, I expected him to be hysterical.

"Hey, man, what took you so long?"

"Is that all you have to say? You scared the shit out of me!"

"Can we discuss your anxiety after you take these goddamn panties off me?"

Just then, Old Man Johnson came running into the room, pointing his pistol.

"Is everything all right?"

"Everything is cool, Mr. Johnson," I told him. "Just stay where you are. Don't come in here!"

"You must be crazy," he said as he walked toward the bathroom. "This is *my* establishment. I have a right to know what's going on."

When he looked down at Eddie handcuffed to the toilet seat with the panties over his big butt, he burst out laughing.

"Hey, man, if you wanna get freaky with fixtures it's gonna cost you extra."

"Very funny, you old bastard. Just go get something to take these cuffs off with."

"Okay, I'll be right back," Mr. Johnson said as he backed out the door. "But don't get mad at me, Mr. Plumber. I'm not the one who chained your big ass to the toilet."

I was laughing so hard I almost pissed on myself. Eddie tried not to laugh, but he couldn't hold it in. While we waited for Mr. Johnson to get back, I untied the rope and tore the panties from around Eddie's waist.

"You know I can't wait to hear *this* story." I sat down on the edge of the tub. "What happened?"

"I ran into the wrong women, that's what happened."

"Women? You mean you had a threesome up in here?"

"Stop acting so surprised. It's not the first time."

"Yeah, but it's the first time they jacked you for your draw-ers."

"Don't forget my wallet, jewelry, cell phone, and camera equipment."

"But how in the world did they get your big ass handcuffed to the toilet?"

"The hell if I know. The last thing I remember was lying on my back getting a massage. They must have drugged me with something. I was so high I didn't feel it coming."

Eddie stood six-five, weighed two-hundred-thirty pounds, and was very muscular. His skin was dark brown and his face was smooth, no mustache, no beard. In high school we called him Fast Eddie because he was quick to get into women's pants. I guess he was too quick for his own good that night.

"You want me to call the cops?"

"Hell, no! Are you crazy? How would I explain this to Denise if the case went to court? I'll just take the loss and chalk it up to experience."

Just then Mr. Johnson came strolling in with a laundry bag and a bobby pin. It took him all of thirty seconds to pick the lock.

"Here are some old clothes from the lost and found. Don't worry—they're clean," he said while unpacking the bag. "The shirt should fit, but the pants might be a little tight."

He pulled out a bright orange long-sleeve double-knit shirt and a pair of purple polyester pants. Eddie put them on and then checked himself in the mirror.

"Man, I look like a poor-ass pimp!"

"Beggars can't be choosers."

"I guess you're right. Thanks, old man."

"Don't mention it—Prince."

Mr. Johnson left the room, laughing so hard tears were run-ning down his cheeks. Eddie was getting upset, so I tried not to make matters worse by joining in.

"You know I'm never gonna hear the end of this."

"You got that right," I told him. "We'll be talking about this one for a *long* time."

"Speaking of a long time, I haven't taken a piss in twelve hours. If I don't go soon, there's gonna be a flash flood up in here." He closed the bathroom door.

"By the way, I told Denise that you were on a photo shoot on Lake Michigan with a client who was advertising sunscreen."

"I *know* she didn't buy that weak line."

"No, I don't think so," I said. "But she did say she was coming out tonight to help me celebrate. So I guess she wasn't too upset."

"Don't worry about Denise. She's whipped!"

"I don't know, man, sounds like she's getting fed up."

"That woman's been trying to walk away from me for the past three years," Eddie said arrogantly. "If she had the power to leave me she would've done it a long time ago."

"You need to seriously consider settling down and doing the right thing, Eddie. Denise is a damn good woman."

"Don't start with that again, Julian. I don't want to hear it— not today."

"All I'm saying is, this whorish lifestyle is catching up with you. Can't you see that this incident is a sign that you need to chill out?"

When he came out of the bathroom he had an irritated look on his face. I should have left it alone, but I didn't.

"Eddie, you're thirty-five years old, you have your own business and a woman who's been with you through thick and thin. Denise even co-signed on the lease for your studio because your credit was shot. Why can't you just—"

"That's enough!" He cut me off. "Denise this, Denise that. If you think she's such a great fuckin' woman, why don't *you* marry her? If I'm not mistaken, you don't have a wife!"

The room became silent and tense. I looked him dead in the eye, then headed for the door. Just as I was about to turn the knob, Eddie pressed his hand against the door.

"Wait a minute, Julian. I'm sorry."

"Don't worry about it, you're right. It's none of my business."

"No, I was out of line. I know you're only trying to look out for me. You've been like a big brother to me ever since high school. That's twenty years of blood, sweat, and tears. I'm not gonna throw that away because of an argument over a *woman*! But this is *my* life and I have a right to live it my way. If that means having sex with one woman or one hundred, that's my choice. Denise has always known what I was about and she accepts me. All I'm asking from you as a friend is to do the same."

"You're right, Eddie." I put my hand on his shoulder. "Sometimes friends think they know what's best for each other when all that should matter is their happiness. It's obvious that you're happy living your life the way you do," I said to him. "But I want you to know that the reason I'm so hard on you is because I love you."

"I love you, too, man," he said, then we hugged.

"Just promise me one thing, Eddie."

"What's that?"

"Try to be more careful. This AIDS epidemic is real, not to mention all the crazy women out there. Look at what happened to you."

"Okay, I promise." He raised his hand as if he was taking an oath. "From now on, I'll only pick up women at church and Bible study." He laughed. "Those are the biggest freaks anyway."

"Man, you're hopeless."

Chapter 4

THE CLOCK IN my Camry read 11:30 as I approached Club Nimbus. People were waiting in a line that wrapped around the corner of LaSalle and Lake Street. They looked elegant in their designer business suits and long cocktail dresses. No expense was spared to look the part. Club Nimbus was a popular hangout for the booshie types who liked to flaunt their success. I just liked the old school music and buffalo wings. But the real attraction was the multicultural atmosphere, which basically meant it was a place where white women could flirt openly with black men. That was a rarity in a city as segregated as Chicago.

The club also had a reputation for attracting professional athletes, entertainers, and wannabes. If you flashed an impressive business card or drove a Benz, you were instantly *somebody*. So when I rolled up in my beat-up Camry it was obvious that the women were not impressed. I smiled to myself as I strutted by them and went directly to the front of the line. The entrance was roped off and guarded by two bouncers. One of them was checking IDs when I walked over and tapped him on the shoulder.

"Whassup, Paul?"

"Hey, Julian! I was hoping you wouldn't leave town without saying good-bye to us little people."

"You know me, Paul. I always keep it real."

"Sometimes money has a way of changing a man."

"Having money is just like drinking too much liquor, all it does is expose a person for who he really is."

"That's deep. Let me write that one down." He lifted the rope to let me in. "Have a good time."

"Oh, by the way, Paul, did you get my message about putting Eddie on the VIP list?"

"He's already here. Him and his lady arrived about an hour ago."

"Cool!"

When I walked into the foyer my body began to vibrate to the thumping bass of the music. "To Be Real" by Cheryl Lynn was jammin' in the back room. The atmosphere was electric with the sound of casual chatter and the air was filled with the aroma of perfumes and colognes. Women of all nationalities lined the walls wearing skimpy dresses and heavy makeup—some had hair extensions down their backs. The men, who were mostly dressed in business suits, looked like hungry vultures waiting on something to die. Every woman who walked by was subject to have her ass inspected.

The layout of the club was very stylish. The dining area had two levels with a huge circular bar in the middle. There was another bar that ran the full length of the back wall. We called it the Perch because it had a view of the entire club. It was prime real estate for any man or woman on the prowl for fresh meat. Not to my surprise, Eddie was sitting right in the middle and smiling like a kid in a candy store. I snuck up from behind so he couldn't see me coming.

"Hey, man, stop lookin' at my woman!" I said, trying to disguise my voice.

"Hey, fool, what took you so long?" He stood up and gave me a hug. "We've been waiting for you for over an hour."

"Sorry, I was, uh, all tied up."

"So now you got jokes, huh? Sit your butt down and have a drink," he said while flagging down the bartender. "Give me another shot of Hennessy!"

"So, where's Denise?"

"She went to the bathroom with her girlfriend. You know how women are, they have to do everything together. They even pee in groups. You never see two guys look at each other and go, Hey, man, you wanna go to the bathroom?"

"Wait a second, did you say *girlfriend*? Don't tell me she went behind my back again!"

"Julian, you know Denise is the matchmaker from hell. For some strange reason she thinks you're a good man. I don't have the heart to tell her you were one of the biggest 'hos in Chicago."

"Who, me?"

"Nigga, please! Don't play that holier-than-thou role. Before you got married you screwed more women than Hugh Hefner and Wilt Chamberlain put together."

Just then the bartender set my drink in front of me.

"Okay, I admit it, I was a 'ho." I lifted my glass. "Let's make a toast—to the Twelve Step 'Ho Rehab Program. May I never relapse."

"Hear! Hear!"

As I sipped on my drink, I saw Denise coming down the aisle. She looked elegant in the black halter dress she was wearing. At six-two she demanded attention from every man in the room, which only served to confuse me as to why she had put up with Eddie's nonsense for three years. She was a successful model, very intelligent, and had just turned thirty years old. *Love must do strange things to a woman's self-esteem,* I was thinking.

"Hey, Li'l Sis!" I kissed her on the cheek. "Long time no see!"

"It's great seeing you, too, Julian. You lookin' good for an old man."

"You ain't lookin' bad yourself."

"I'm sure Eddie already told you about my friend."

"Of course he did!" I gave her *that look*. "Denise, I told you—I'm not interested in a relationship, especially not a long-distance one."

"Julian, I promise you, I didn't invite her. I don't even recall mentioning I was coming here tonight."

"Yeah, right."

"I swear to God." She raised her hand. "Maybe it's just fate."

"Fate must be wearing a black halter dress," I laughed. "But I'm not gonna let your matchmaking ruin my evening. I'm gonna enjoy myself tonight, then fly outta here in the morning. That seems to be the *only* way I can get away from Ms. Love Connection."

"Forget you, Julian!"

"I love you, too, Li'l Sis! So, where's this perfect woman with the great personality? And she'd better not be ugly!"

I checked the expression on Eddie's face. He gave me a nod and a slight grin. That told me she was at least a seven and a half or eight.

"Why don't you judge for yourself?" Denise said. "Here she comes now."

I damn near choked on my drink when I saw her walking down the stairs toward us. She had dark, shoulder-length hair, highlighted with light brown streaks. It was silky and full of body, like she had just stepped out of a commercial for Dark and Lovely. The dress she had on was sharp. It was red silk with thin shoulder straps. Her skin was a flawless caramel tone. She reminded me of a young Diahann Carroll as she elegantly glided down the stairs.

As she grew closer I noticed that the dress was a slit way up to her midthigh, which exposed a toned leg. She set it off with a thin gold ankle bracelet. But her most unique attribute was her hazel eyes. They were the kind that could put a man in a trance.

"Olivia Brown, Julian Payne," Denise said formally.

"Hello, Julian," she said in a soft and oddly familiar voice. Then she reached out and shook my hand. "And by the way, they *are* real."

"Excuse me?"

"Eventually the question comes up about my eyes: I just thought I would get it out of the way."

"I see you like to be direct."

"Does that intimidate you?"

"No, actually I admire a woman who speaks her mind."

"Well, in that case, you're lookin' exceptionally fine this evening. And I love the combination of the white mock and French blue jacket. Is that Hugo Boss?"

"I'm impressed! It's rare that you meet a woman who knows men's clothing."

"My father was a designer in Europe. He taught me a lot about fashion"—she paused—"just before he ran off with some twenty-year-old floozie."

Denise and Eddie were sitting there eating it up. It had been a while since I had shown a woman any real interest. Each time Olivia said something interesting, Denise would nudge Eddie as if to say *I told you he'd like her.*

"Well, we're going to leave you two fashion police alone so you can get better acquainted," Denise said. "Come on, Eddie, let's dance!"

"Hold down the fort, partner, I'll be right back." Eddie set down his drink and removed his jacket. "I've gotta go school this young girl on how grown folks party."

"Yeah, right, the last time we went out you tried to moon-walk and sprained your ankle." She laughed as she dragged him away. "Come on, Grandpa!"

I invited Olivia to sit down at the bar and then asked her what she wanted to drink. I assumed she wanted something sweet and girlie, but instead she ordered a Long Island. When she crossed her legs and turned toward me, I instantly got an erection. I quickly grabbed Eddie's jacket and placed it over my lap.

"Are you getting warm?" she said seductively.

"Just a little; alcohol sometimes has that effect on me."

"Yeah, me too."

She took a sip of her drink and moved in closer. She acted as if she was adjusting her seat, but I knew better. That made me even harder. I tried to keep the conversation going, hoping it would take my mind off my dick.

"So, you said your father *was* a designer. Is he doing something else now?"

"No, he passed away a few years ago."

"Sorry to hear that. I lost my father, too. My mother died shortly after. I don't think she wanted to live without him."

"Life is so short," she said. "It's sad that people take it for granted."

"My father use to say money can buy a lot of things but it can't buy back time."

"Money can't buy happiness either. That's why I live in the moment. Tomorrow's not promised."

"So, you're a philosopher, too," I said to her. "It's not often you meet a beautiful woman who is a deep thinker and knows men's fashions."

"I also paint and write music," she said. "I plan to release my first CD in December."

"Ms. Brown, where in the world did you come from? And why are you still single?"

"I was hoping you could tell me," she laughed. "Denise told me you were some kind of relationship expert."

"I'm no expert! I just give advice and try to keep my listeners entertained. Most of their problems are self-inflicted. They're just too afraid to confront them. Sometimes it takes a person on the outside, a stranger, to motivate them to do something about it."

"Okay then, motivate me!" She moved in closer. This time she placed her hand on my knee. I had just managed to get myself under control and she had to go and do that. My crotch became so tight I thought I would burst my zipper. Luckily, I was saved by my cell phone vibrating inside my suit jacket. When I checked the screen I saw that it was Samantha.

"Excuse me," I said to Olivia as I answered it. "Hello?"

"Daddy, I want to watch *The Thomas Crown Affair*, but Grandma said I had to ask you first because it's rated R."

"Yes, Sam, you can watch it. But close your eyes during the sex scenes. Is there anything else?"

"No."

"All right then, I'll see you in the morning. Make sure you're ready at five."

"I thought our flight was at seven."

"It is, but the airports are busy on Sundays and you know I hate to rush."

"Okay, I'll be ready at five. Bye, Daddy."

"Bye, Princess."

When I hung up the phone, Olivia had a wide grin on her face.

"That's so sweet!" she said. "Do you have a picture of her?"

I pulled out my wallet and showed her Sam's photo from her last birthday party.

"She's gorgeous!"

"Yeah, that's my little princess," I said proudly. "I think it was meant for her to be born on New Year's Day."

"That's a good omen, you know," Olivia said. "How old is she?"

"Ten going on thirty. Sometimes I wish I'd had a boy instead. Girls are high maintenance—salon visits, training bras, earrings. They need accessories."

"That's what her mother is for. Doesn't she take care of all the girl stuff?"

"I guess Denise didn't tell you?"

"Tell me what?"

"My wife's been gone for two years."

"I'm sorry, Julian, I didn't know," she said while patting

my leg. "Denise and I only met recently, at the hair salon. She didn't tell me about your wife."

"No need to apologize. I've been doing much better with it lately. A person can't live in the past, right?"

"No, they can't, Julian. Life goes on."

Each time she spoke to me in that sweet sexy tone, my penis throbbed. I wanted her and she wanted me. Although we were perfect strangers, we were connecting on a mental and sexual level. The people sitting at the bar were noticing how close and comfortable we were. They watched as Olivia's hand moved slowly up my thigh but we paid them no mind. We were shameless, like two horny teenagers.

"Look, Olivia, I don't want to lead you on," I said as I gently pushed her hand away. "I'm seriously tempted to go there, but I'm starting a new life in Houston. This affair wouldn't last."

"If I'm not mistaken, airplanes *do* fly to Houston."

"That's not the point. I'm not interested in a serious relationship right now. I've been waiting my whole life for the chance to host a talk show on a major FM station. All of my energies have to go into this. Maybe if we had met at another time things could be different, but right now, my career is a priority!"

"I'm not trying to marry you. I just want to stay in touch, no promises—no commitments."

"I've experienced enough relationships to know there's always expectations and responsibilities."

"Look, Julian, we're both adults. If you don't want a serious relationship, that's fine with me. But don't deprive us of this opportunity. We both know what we want."

"Olivia, I just don't want to start something I can't finish."

"Why can't we start and finish tonight?"

The seductive tone of her voice made me weak. It didn't help that it had been nearly six months since I'd had any. If there was ever a case of the devil being hard at work, this was it. Just as I was about to respond, Eddie and Denise returned from the dance floor. Eddie was drenched in sweat and talking smack.

"Who's the man? Who's the man?" he boasted.

"You are, baby," Denise said nonchalantly. "Can we go home now?"

Denise began pressing her pelvis and wincing. She was bent over like she had been punched in the stomach.

"Are you okay, Denise?" Olivia asked.

"My monthly visitor decided to drop in a little early. These cramps are killing me."

"All right, youngster, let's go!" Eddie grabbed his jacket and put his arm around Denise. "Sorry to ruin your party, Julian, but nature calls. Give me a buzz when you get settled in. I've been dyin' to come to H-Town to see what all the hype is about."

We exchanged hugs, then Eddie and Denise left. Olivia just stood there staring at me. We both knew what she was waiting on.

"So, do you live far from here?"

"No, I have a condo on North Michigan Avenue, about fifteen minutes by taxi."

"Do you need a ride?" We began walking toward the exit.

"Is that an offer?"

"I guess it is, but I want you to know in advance, I can't stay long. I have a plane to catch in the morning."

"Does that mean you accept my proposition?"

"Why not? Like you said, we're both adults."

"Now that we have that established, do you mind if I use your cell phone? I need to let someone know who I'm going home with. A girl can never be too careful."

I pulled my phone out of my jacket pocket and handed it to her. While she dialed the number, I went over to give the valet my ticket.

"What's your license plate number?" she asked.

"Are you serious?"

"As a heart attack. For all I know you could be a mass murderer."

"If anybody should be afraid, it's me."

"And why is that?"

"Because it's obvious that you're a woman who's accustomed to getting what she wants."

She stared at me with those hazel eyes. This time the expression on her face was serious.

"You have no idea."

Chapter 5

THE SHORT ELEVATOR ride up to Olivia's condo seemed like an eternity. All I remembered was admiring her body in that silky red dress and fantasizing about all the sexual positions I wanted to put her in. *Up against the wall and doggy style,* I was thinking. My hormones were raging. I was intoxicated with the thought of laying down with such an erotic creature. I had made love to many women throughout my life, but none had exuded a fraction of the sexual energy that Olivia did. Although she was soft-spoken and very feminine, I could sense that she had a darker side that demanded to be controlled, handled, and dominated.

All that sexual energy erupted the moment we walked into her condo. Olivia unzipped her dress, stepped out of it, and then flung it across the room before the door was even closed. Just as I expected, she wasn't wearing any panties. She pushed me to the floor and frantically pulled my pants and drawers off, then she grabbed my hand and led me onto the balcony. Her condo was twenty-five stories up with a spectacular view of Navy Pier. A brisk breeze was blowing off Lake Michigan. It was chilly, even for September. I tried to pull her back inside, but Olivia's mind was set on what she wanted.

"Fuck me!" she said as she bent over the railing.

I should have stopped and put on a condom, but I didn't. Olivia kept begging for it until I finally gave in. I spread her legs apart and drove myself inside her.

"Oh, baby, that's it!" she screamed. "Push it in deeper!"

I decided to stop playing the gentleman role and allowed the dog in me to come out. I pushed myself deep inside of her until I felt my head touch the bottom.

"Oh Julian, give it to me, baby!" she moaned.

"Is this what you wanted, huh? Is it?"

"Yes, baby, I've been waiting for this big dick all night. Punish me, Daddy, I've been a bad girl!"

Just when I was getting into a groove, she suddenly stopped and dragged me into the bedroom. She flung me onto her king-size bed, which was covered with a white satin comforter, and began giving me head. At first it felt good; she was stroking it gently while flicking her tongue on the head. But then she started getting rough.

"Hey, slow down, baby!"

"Stop acting like a punk and man up!" Her tone was harsh.

I lay back and tolerated the discomfort for a few minutes, then I flipped her onto her back. I drove inside of her as deep as I could. *No more Mr. Nice Guy,* I was thinking.

I slammed into her pussy with the full force of my weight behind it. Her head bounced against the headboard.

"That's it, treat me like the whore I am, you fine mother-fucker," she yelled out. Then she slapped me on the face—hard.

"I can see you need a man to take charge of your wild ass!" I grabbed a fistful of her hair and pulled back on it.

"Show me what you got, poppie!"

For the next two hours we had a nonstop sexual marathon. Our bodies flowed together as if we had been making love forever. We screwed on the bed, on the floor, and against the wall, the way I'd fantasized. We were sweating so profusely a puddle formed in the center of the bed. It was the most exhausting and gratifying sex I ever had.

When it was all over, Olivia rolled over onto the right side of the bed. She placed a pillow between her legs and turned on her side. I thought she had fallen asleep, but a few minutes later I heard sniffling. I thought about asking her what was wrong, but I figured it would only escalate into something dramatic. I wasn't in the mood for that. I lay there for another hour looking out the window and admiring the beautiful view of Navy Pier. I knew it would be the last time I saw it from that particular point of view.

When I was sure Olivia was asleep, I slipped quietly out of bed and went into the living room to find my drawers. After I got dressed, I wrote Olivia a farewell letter. I placed it on the kitchen counter on my way out the door.

I had a wonderful time tonight. The experience was incredible! It's not often you meet a woman who is blessed with so many talents, inside and outside the bedroom. I'm sure you'll find someone who can appreciate all that you have to offer.

Julian

P.S. Thanks for trusting me enough to share yourself. That was the best going-away present I've ever had.

Part II

Houston, Texas

Chapter 6

EARLY SUNDAY AFTERNOON Samantha and I arrived at Bush Intercontinental Airport. It was ten o'clock in the morning and the temperature was already eighty-five degrees. The humidity was so high I worked up a sweat just walking up the jetway. "Welcome to Texas," I said to Samantha. She was sweating so badly her French braid was coming loose. After waiting at baggage claim for what seemed like an eternity, we picked up our rental car from Hertz and headed out to our new house. It was in a suburb called Sugarland, about a forty-minute drive from the airport.

I was impressed by how smooth Houston's roads were. In Chicago, you were liable to hit a pothole every twenty feet. The urban radio stations weren't bad. I tuned in to Magic 102 as we merged onto the Sam Houston Beltway. I was surprised to hear a familiar voice—Funky Larry Jones, who used to be with WGCI in Chicago back in the late eighties. He must have been sitting in for another DJ, because he was usually on during the afternoon drive on weekdays. But who cared? I was just glad he was playing old school music. I was flashing back to the days of basement parties and roller-skating in Markham, Illinois. I almost crashed into the median when he played the song "Bounce, Rock, Skate." That was a roller-skating classic.

Just as we passed the jam-packed I-10 expressway, Sam let out a loud scream. "Look, Daddy, look!" When I saw what she was pointing at, I couldn't believe my eyes. There was a huge billboard of me on the west side of the highway, just before the toll booth. The background was off-white, the text was in bold red and green letters. It read LOVE, LUST, AND LIES WITH JU- LIAN PAYNE—WEEKNIGHTS 10:00 P.M. TO 2:00 A.M. ON 102.3 WBMX.

I pulled over onto the shoulder and stepped out of the car. I didn't know what else to do, so I just stared at it. "Smile, Daddy!" Samantha leaned out the window aiming her camera. "Say 'cheese'!" We took turns taking pictures of each other posing in front of the billboard until a cop pulled up behind us. Instead of giving me a ticket, he asked for my autograph. Samantha was bubbling with pride. It was the first time she ever saw her father give an autograph.

Not long after we got back on the road, we merged onto Highway 59. Three miles from there was our exit onto Highway 6. Samantha was in awe as we passed by all the brand-new shopping malls and parks with tennis courts. I knew she would be just as excited when she saw our house. My real estate agent made sure the new furniture was delivered and set up. Everything had to be perfect for Sam.

When we turned the corner into our subdivision, Sam's jaw dropped. The streets were spotless and the lawns were beautifully manicured. Service trucks lined the streets: Eddie's Pool Service, Merry Maids, and Superior Landscaping. It was a scene right out of *Lifestyles of the Rich and Famous.* I slowed down as we approached our house. It was a beige, two-story brick on the left side of the street. "Which one is it, Daddy?" she frantically asked. "Is that our house? Is it?" I decided to stop torturing her and pulled into our driveway. Sam leaped out of the car and started running around in the yard.

"We're rich! We're rich!" she yelled out.

"No, sweetheart, *we're* not rich, *I'm* rich!" I laughed as I swung her around in a circle. "Let's go inside, I've got a surprise for you."

We ran around to the front of the house like two kids on Christmas morning. I put the key in the lock and slowly turned the knob. "Close your eyes," I told her. I led her by the hand into the living room, then drew the blinds so she could get a good look at what was inside and outside. "Surprise!" When she opened her eyes she was speechless. In the corner sat an ebony baby-grand piano. I had her name engraved on the panel. It read *To Princess, from Daddy.*

"I figured since you listened to Alicia Keys so much, you might wanna learn to play like her."

"I love it, Daddy." She held me as tightly as she could. "You're the best daddy in the whole wide world!"

"Hey, it's hot in here. You wanna go for a swim?"

"Yeah! Let me get my swimming cap and goggles out of my bag." She ran toward the door. "How far away is the pool?"

"I'd say about, uh, fifty feet."

Samantha stopped dead in her tracks. She was so overwhelmed by the piano she never bothered to look out the window at the pool in the backyard.

"Last one in is a rotten egg!" I pulled off my shoes and took off running. Samantha was right on my tail. When we reached the edge of the pool we held hands and jumped in together. We splashed around in our jeans and T-shirts until we were exhausted. I put her on my back and swam into the shallow end, then sat her on the edge. She became quiet all of a sudden. That was a sure sign that there was something bothering her.

"You wanna talk about it?" I asked her.

"Talk about what?"

"Look, if you'd rather not talk about it, it's okay."

She seemed fine at first, then she burst into tears. I got out of the pool and put my arms around her.

"I wish Mommy was here!" she cried.

"Your mother *is* here, in spirit. She's watching over us right now."

"Why did she have to die, Daddy?"

"Only God knows that, sweetheart. But if your mother was here, she would tell you to be strong, carry yourself like a lady, and, most important, always do your best."

"You're right, Daddy. I'm gonna be the best student in my class." She wiped the tears from her eyes. "And you know what else? I'm gonna learn to play the piano *better* than Alicia Keys!"

"That's my girl!" I lifted her up in the air. "Now let's go inside and dry off. We've got lots of unpacking to do, and you have to get ready for your first day of school tomorrow."

As we were walking toward the house dripping wet, Sam looked up at me with those big brown eyes.

"You know, Daddy, I wish Mommy could've lived long enough to give me a little brother."

"I know how you feel. I was an only child. It's hard growing up with no one to play with."

"That's not the reason," she said with a sly grin. "I wanted a little brother so I could have someone to beat up."

Chapter 7

MONDAY MORNING I dropped Samantha off at Clover Junior Academy. Just as we arrived, a convoy of yellow buses pulled up to the main entrance and began unloading students. It was obvious from Sam's expression that she was disappointed by the lack of black and brown faces. For five years she attended Chicago public schools where ninety-nine percent of the students were black. Clover was ninety-nine percent everything but black.

"Am I the *only* black person here?" she said.

"Look, Sam, Clover is a good school and they have the best music program in the city," I told her. "You'll do just fine if you stop worrying about skin color and remember why you're here."

"I know the speech, Dad. I've got to be twice as good as white people if I want to succeed."

She kissed me on the cheek, then nervously stepped out of the car.

"If you have any problems, go see the principal, Ms. Bell. Believe it or not, *she's* black."

"For real?" Her whole demeanor changed and she seemed more relaxed.

"Yeah, for real! Now, have a nice day and I'll be back to pick you up at three-thirty."

"That's okay. I'll take the school bus home like everyone else," she said confidently. "If I can survive Chicago public schools I think I can handle Clover Academy." She slung her backpack over her shoulder, thrust her fist in the air, and yelled, "Westsiiide!"

As I watched her brown skin clash against the sea of whiteness, I realized I was in for a similar experience at the radio station. WBMX was white owned and operated. That was often the case with urban radio in America. One of the few exceptions was Radio One, owned by Cathy Hughes. Most black folks still don't know that the nationally syndicated *Tom Joyner Morning Show* and *The Doug Banks Morning Show* are owned by ABC. But Tom and Doug taught me that you have to play the game in order to get what you want. My real concern was whether or not WBMX would honor my request for a black producer. I wasn't being racist, but we black folks have a unique way of relating that other cultures can't understand. For example, if a white or Hispanic person greeted you by saying, "Whassup, my nigga?" all hell would break loose!

I had all that on my mind as I merged onto the crowded I-59 freeway. I had allowed an hour's travel time to get to the studio, which was located in an office building off I-610 and West-heimer Road, two blocks away from the Galleria mall. But after driving bumper to bumper for fifty-five minutes I was only halfway there. I counted three car accidents between Bissonnett Road and Hillcroft, and that was just on the northbound side. The traffic was made worse by gawkers, which is a polite word for nosy-ass people. "This puts the Dan Ryan Expressway to shame," I said to myself.

By the time I arrived at the studio, the clock on my dash read 9:55. The building was thirty stories high and looked as if it was made completely out of black glass. As I drove into the underground parking, I had to shield my eyes from the sun's reflection as it bounced off the silver WBMX marquee.

Once I found a parking space, I pulled out my organizer to confirm my meeting with the general manager. The notation read: MEETING WITH MR. HARRIS — 10:00 A.M. I took pride in being punctual, so I checked myself out in the mirror, then opened the door preparing to make a mad dash. Just then a white BMW with tinted windows came barreling into the space next to me, nearly knocking my door off. I was pissed. After I looked over my car to make sure there was no damage, I waited at the rear of the BMW so I could curse the driver out.

When the car door opened, a smooth, long brown leg extended outward. The rest of her looked just as good as she stepped out of the car. She had on a fitted beige business suit and wore her hair short but stylish. In her right hand she carried a brown alligator briefcase, in her left, a cell phone. She set off her corporate look with a pair of conservative black-framed glasses that did nothing to take away from her lovely brown eyes and natural beauty.

"Can I help you?" she asked.

"You just about tore my door off when you pulled in."

"I'm so very sorry. Is your car okay?"

"It's fine, but—"

"Sorry to cut you off, but I'm in a hurry. Have a nice day." She began running toward the elevators.

I grabbed my organizer off the passenger seat and took off in the same direction. I caught up with her just as the elevator doors were opening. I wanted to introduce myself, but I had to catch my breath first. Just as I was about to, the doors opened onto the lobby, which was two levels up. She rushed out of the elevator toward the security desk. There were three people already in line waiting to sign in. She stared down at her watch, showing her impatience.

"Good morning, Dr. Ross. I see you're running late again," the security guard said to her.

"Good morning, Joe. Yeah, the traffic on I-10 is a nightmare. If it gets any worse, I'll need a helicopter to get to work on time."

"Well, just give me a second and I'll get you on your way."

I could understand her impatience. Joe was moving so slowly it was irritating. He was a thin, gray-haired white man who looked at least seventy years old. His uniform was pressed to a T and his shoes were spit shined. He wore a thick black utility belt that was cluttered with an assortment of keys, a black nightstick, a pair of handcuffs, and a gun. *Who in the hell is this old fart going to arrest?* I was thinking.

"I'll be right with you, sir," Joe said after making eye contact with me. He must have noticed I was getting impatient, too.

"I don't mean to be rude, but could you hurry it up? I've got a ten o'clock meeting with Mr. Harris at WBMX."

"Mr. Harris, huh?"

"Yes, I'm Julian Payne. My name should be on your list."

"Oh, Mr. Payne, nice to meet you, sir!" He dropped everything and gestured for me to come to the front of the line. "Mr. Harris is expecting you. Let me see your ID and you can go right up!"

He handed me a pass, then directed me toward the tower elevators. Dr. Ross was noticeably perturbed. I guess she didn't appreciate having to wait in line while I was escorted through. I made sure to take my time walking toward the elevator. I wanted to get another look at those lovely brown eyes *and* that tight skirt. I figured I was already running late, so why not make the most of it?

When the elevator came, I held the door open until Dr. Ross was on. Once she was aboard, we both reached for the button for the twenty-fifth floor. Our hands touched.

"Excuse me," she said.

"No problem," I replied. "No problem at all."

There were two other people already aboard. One of them pushed the button for the tenth floor. I assumed they were together because they were standing too close not to be. Sure enough, when the door opened they both walked off in the same direction. When the doors closed, I cleared my throat.

"By the way, I never did get a chance to formally introduce myself. My name is Julian Payne."

"I know who you are, Mr. Payne. I'm Terri Ross." She extended her hand. "Nice to meet you. And may I say, you are the most well-dressed radio personality I've ever seen. And you smell good, too. What is that—Givenchy?"

"I'm impressed. It's nice to meet a woman who can appreciate a fine cologne," I said to her. "But you're not half steppin' yourself, Doc. You're lookin' good in that linen outfit. I'm sure your patients can't wait to see you."

"Just because I have a Ph.D. doesn't mean I have to dress like a librarian."

"So, Terri, I see you work on the twenty-fifth floor, too. Do you work for the station?"

"No, I just sit in with the jock on Monday mornings to give advice on relationships, sort of like Dr. Phil on *Oprah*. But I do work in the building. I have a practice on the fifteenth floor."

"How convenient," I said with a flirtatious smile.

Just then the doors opened on the twenty-fifth floor. We stepped out and began walking toward the studio. Although we were both late, neither of us seemed to be in a hurry.

"So, Terri, would it be okay if I called you sometime? Maybe we could do lunch?"

She paused, then reached inside her purse. I was hoping she was looking for something to write her number on.

"Here, take this." She handed me a card. It read THE GENE-SIS FOUNDATION.

"What is this?"

"It's the number of my foundation. I run a shelter for battered women."

"And?"

"I would appreciate it if you would mention it every now and then during your show. We need all the donations we can get."

"So, what about your personal number?"

"Mr. Payne, I don't *do* celebrities. That includes ball players, entertainers, producers, and especially radio personalities."

"And why is that?"

"Because women throw coochie at them like Frisbees! And like most dogs, they try to catch all of it." She pretended like she was snatching objects out of the air. "Have a nice day, Mr. Payne." Then she walked away.

"There are exceptions to every rule, you know," I yelled at her.

I was disappointed by not getting her number, but I could understand her point. Dating a man in the entertainment industry could be rough on a woman. To this day, I don't know how Carmen put up with it for as long as she did. When we met I was eighteen years old and working as an intern. Every week I had VIP passes to night clubs, concerts, and sporting events. The women were always eager to get to know me. Sometimes they wanted free tickets or to be introduced to the jocks. But many of them just wanted to have sex so they could brag to their friends that they screwed someone who worked at a radio station. We use to call them "radio 'hos."

After I picked my ego up from the floor, I walked down to the studio and pressed the button for the receptionist. Terri must have had some kind of access code, because she entered without any delay.

"WBMX, may I help you?" a soft professional voice inquired.

"Yes, this is Julian Payne. I'm here to see Mr. Harris."

She buzzed the door and I walked in. Right away I was impressed. The foyer was brightly lit with metal-framed posters of the radio jocks hanging on the walls. My picture was the last one on the end. I could smell the newness of the highly buffed hardwood floors and the freshly painted ceilings and walls. Even the receptionist fit in perfectly. She was a young black woman with a bright smile. She wore a peach blouse that accentuated her caramel complexion. She wore locks and had a wrap on her head that reminded me of Erykah Badu's.

"This is a long way from WTLK," I said, loud enough for her to hear.

"We're glad to have you aboard, Mr. Payne." She extended her hand. "I'm Janet Jackson."

"Yeah, and I'm Tito," I laughed.

"I'm serious, my name is Janet Jackson. You wanna see my driver's license?"

"No, I'll take your word for it," I told her. "Look, Janet, would you happen to know the woman who just came in?"

"You mean Dr. Ross. Yeah, I know her. She's been working here at the station for about two years."

"Is she single?"

"Mr. Payne, let me save you some time and energy. You *do not* want to mess around with that sistah!"

"Why, is she married?"

"No."

"Is she involved?"

"No."

"Is she a lesbian?"

"No!"

"Is she a man? 'Cause if she is, that's the best damn operation I've ever seen!"

"No, she's not a man," Janet laughed. "You are so stupid."

"Then what's the deal? I'd like to get to know her. She's beautiful! And she has a quality that most women lack nowadays."

"And what's that?"

"Class!"

"Well, *Mr.* Payne, I'll tell you another quality she has that most women lack nowadays and that's *high* self-esteem and *low* tolerance for game playing."

"What is it with you Texas women? You presume that every man is either a playa or a dog?"

"Because nine out of ten *are,* especially the men in this business!" Janet said. "Over the last two years I've seen more drama at this station than on a *Jerry Springer* marathon."

"But you don't even know me. How could you—"

At that moment her phone rang.

"Yes, sir, he just walked in. I'll escort him down to the studio myself. Bye." Janet came from behind her desk and began walking toward the back offices.

"This way, Mr. Payne."

"Don't be so formal. You can call me Julian," I said as I followed a few feet behind her.

"'Mr. Payne' will do for now. I haven't decided if I like you yet."

On the way to see Mr. Harris, we passed by the studio where Terri was doing her spot. Our eyes met through the soundproof window. I didn't want to appear too interested, so I tried to look away, but I couldn't, and neither could she. I was about to wink, but decided not to. It seemed too childish. So I did what came naturally. I smiled. Once I passed the window I turned around to see where Janet had gone. She was already down the hall watching me watch Terri. When I caught up to her she directed me down a narrow corridor to a corner office.

"Thank you, Janet Jackson."

"You're quite welcome, *Tito*!"

As I was about to head down the corridor, Janet cleared her throat, loudly.

"Is there something else you wanna say, Ms. Jackson?"

"I know this is none of my business, and you were right, I don't know you from Adam." She had one hand on her hip. "But I do know Terri and she's a very special person. Not only is she my mentor, I consider her to be a friend."

"And you said that to say . . .?"

"If you ever hurt her, I'll make your life a living hell! Have a nice day." Then she strutted back to her desk.

I stood there for a second thinking to myself, *Did I miss something?* But I quickly shrugged it off and refocused on my meeting with Mr. Harris. I wanted to find out if his attitude had changed since we signed the contract. Sometimes white folks will kiss your ass to get you to sign on the dotted line, but once you do, they show their true colors. I tried to be optimistic as I knocked on the door.

"Come in," a smooth masculine voice said.

When I entered, Mr. Harris was seated in a high-back leather chair facing away from me.

"Hello, Mr. Harris. Sorry I'm late."

"Well, if you paid more attention to the time and less to Dr. Ross's ass in that tight skirt you wouldn't be so late. I saw you staring at her on the security camera!"

"Excuse me?"

"Surprise!" He spun around in the chair and revealed himself. It was my producer Mitch from WTLK. "Whassup, you outspoken, talented, and arrogant son of a bitch?"

"Mitch! What the hell you doin' here!"

"I told you I was workin' on a big deal. Well, this is it!"

"Man, this is too good to be true, the Green Hornet and Kato in Houston, Texas. Aw, shit, we can't lose now!" I rushed over and put him in a bear hug.

"Just remember, I'm the Green Hornet and you're Kato! Now let me go, boy!"

"I guess these white folks aren't all bad after all," I said. "Check out this studio!"

The room was laid out with stylish furnishings, high-back leather chairs, solid oak countertops, and a console that was state of the art.

"If you think that's something"—Mitch opened the blinds—"check out this view."

The studio was located in the corner of the building, which provided views in two directions through windows that extended from the floor to the ceiling. On one side was the overcrowded 610 freeway. On the other was Westheimer Road where the Galleria mall was located. I could read the Neiman Marcus and Lord & Taylor signs as if they were right in front of me.

"WTLK never had a view like this."

"WTLK didn't have a view, period. Didn't have a microphone that worked or a toilet that flushed, either." Mitch laughed. "I'm just glad I can stop sticking those damned names against the window like Martha Stewart."

"Speaking of Martha Stewart, I can't wait to decorate this place. I'm gonna put my Yolonda Adams poster over here. My Sade poster over here," I said as I walked from wall to wall. "And my jasmine-scented candles there, there, and there!"

"I'm glad you're so eager to get started, because I've got another surprise for you."

"What's that?"

"Instead of starting next week, the schedule's been moved up. We start at ten o'clock tomorrow night."

"Say what?"

"That's right, we going on the air in exactly"—Mitch looked down at his watch—"thirty-five hours and twenty-six minutes."

"Damn, that soon? I've got a thousand things to do. I've got to get my music together, come up with some relationship topics, find a baby-sitter for Sam, and I've got to—"

"What?" Mitch said.

I checked the console to make sure the power was on, then I shuffled through the cassette racks to see if I could find the song I wanted. When I found it, I tried to pull it out.

"Watch out!" Mitch yelled. He ran over and grabbed the rack as it was falling toward my head.

"I knew it, I knew! These white folks spent fifty million dollars to buy a station and couldn't spend five lousy bucks to make sure the damn racks don't fall down and kill a brotha."

"I was gonna warn you, but you didn't give me a chance."

"You better get this fixed before somebody gets hurt and sues both our black asses," I laughed. "Now, where was I?"

I put my headphones on and loaded the music into the console. I pushed a few of the wrong buttons at first, but I finally got it set up.

"What are you up to?" Mitch asked.

"Well, you've been nagging me about finding a nice girl, so I decided to take your advice."

"I hope you're not talkin' about who I think you're talkin' about."

"You saw her, too, huh?"

"You know I did. I met her two months ago when I was here to interview for the job. That woman is fine as wine!" We gave each other a high five. "Boy, if was a few years younger, um, um, um!"

"Well, you can live out your fantasy through me," I told him. "Now, which one of these buttons will put me through to the receptionist?"

"This one." He pointed.

While the phone rang, I cued the song. When Janet Jackson picked up, I turned the music down so she couldn't hear it.

"WBMX, how may I direct your call?"

"Janet, this is Julian. I just called to let you know that I am a good man and I plan on pursuing Terri."

"Mr. Payne, I told you, Terri doesn't need any drama. Why don't you just—"

Before she could finish her thought I turned up the lyrics on the song "Ms. Jackson" by the rap group OutKast.

"Sorry Ms. Jackson—I am for real!
Ne-ver meant to make your daughter cry . . ."

Then I hung up.

"Very creative," Mitch said. "But you're gonna have to do better than that if you expect to get with a lady with that much class and brains!"

"I wouldn't have it any other way, *my brotha*! Besides, I wouldn't want a woman who falls in love at first sight or gives it up on the first date. I need a challenge!"

"Speaking of challenges, we've got a million things to do before tomorrow night." Mitch walked toward the door. "Let's go say hello to Mr. Harris, then we can get to work."

"We're gonna turn this mother out!" I yelled as the door closed behind us. "I hope H-Town is ready for the Green Hornet and Kato."

"Just remember," Mitch said. "I'm the Green Hornet—you're Kato."

Chapter 8

A COOL SUMMER breeze blew off Lake Michigan as Olivia sipped a glass of wine while pacing naked on her balcony. It was her ritual for creating lyrics for the songs she composed. But the inspiration wasn't there that day. Her mind kept replaying what happened Saturday night, the conversation at the club, the elevator ride up to her condo, the great sex, and Julian's letter. And the more she thought about it, the more enraged she became.

"Goddamn men!" she yelled as she slammed down her notepad. "They walk into your life, use you up, then walk out! No guilt, no responsibility, no conscience. I should call his ass right now and curse him out. Yeah, that's what I'll do!"

She gulped down the rest of her wine, then marched into her bedroom to get her cordless phone. Just as she was about to dial the number, the phone rang.

"Hello?"

"Hey, girl! Were you busy?"

"Hi, Denise, I was just about to call you!" She tried to disguise her disappointment. "No, I'm not busy. I was just working on a song for my new CD."

"It must be nice to write music for a living, no office politics, no rush hour traffic, and the freedom to live wherever you want."

"Yeah, it's pretty cool until you have to deal with these nasty producers. When I show up for a meeting they assume I'm there to audition for a video. They think a woman's only talent is shakin' her ass and giving head."

"Men—you can't live with them and you can't kill 'em." Denise was laughing, but Olivia wasn't. "Anyway, I hadn't heard from you since Saturday and I was wondering how your date went with Julian."

"We got along just fine! He drove me to my apartment, we had a couple of drinks, talked for a while, then he left."

"That's it?"

"Well, don't tell him I told you, but he asked me to visit him in Houston."

"And?"

"And I told him I would think about it."

"What's there to think about? Julian's a nice guy! And he really knows how to treat a woman."

"Like a whore," Olivia whispered.

"What did you say?"

"Oh, nothin'. Look, Denise, would you happen to have Julian's home number in Houston? He gave it to me at the club, but I can't seem to find it!"

"No, I don't have it, but Eddie has his cell number. I can have him call Julian and tell him you're trying to reach him."

"No, that's okay. I think I found it. Yeah, here it is on the floor. It must have fallen off the counter while I was cleaning up. Well, it was nice talking to you, Denise. I've got to get back to work. Be sure to tell Eddie I said hello."

"Okay, Olivia. Take care, and I'll talk to you later. Bye."

"Good-bye, and don't bother callin' back," Olivia said after Denise hung up. "I already got what I needed from you."

Olivia poured herself another glass of wine and pulled out

her Rolodex. She found the number for Continental Airlines and dialed while she lay naked on her bed.

"Yes, I'd like to book a flight for tomorrow morning, Chicago to Houston."

"Is this a one-way or round trip?" the agent asked.

"Hmm . . . let me think." She paused. "You can book my return flight for Friday. Three days is all the time I'll need to handle my business."

After her flight was confirmed, she pressed the menu button on her phone to retrieve the list of prior incoming calls. She scrolled down until she reached the numbers from Saturday. The display had Julian's number on it.

"Thanks for allowing me to use your cell phone, Mr. Payne," she said deviously. "You were right, I *am* a woman who's accustomed to getting what she wants."

Chapter 9

ON TUESDAY AFTERNOON I was browsing through the shelves of an African American bookstore on the south side of Houston. My first show was less than ten hours away and I still hadn't come up with a topic. After thirty minutes of looking over several boring titles, I picked up a self-help book by Wayne Dyer called *Wisdom of the Ages*.

When I put the book down at the register, I noticed the clerk was smiling. He was a middle-aged black man dressed in a colorful dashiki.

"That's a good choice," he said while ringing me up.

"It's not exactly what I wanted, but I'm pressed for time."

"May I make a suggestion?"

"Sure."

He reached for a book off the shelf behind him. Right away I recognized the cover.

"*The Maintenance Man,* huh? I think I saw the author on a talk show," I told him. "But I'm not really into fiction."

"Neither was I until I read *this* book. I finished it in one day. It's about a gigolo in L.A. who is from Chicago and—"

"Chicago? In that case, I'll take two! Can't go wrong with a homeboy."

"Yes, sir." He reached for another copy. "Will there be anything else?"

"I'm on a roll; what else you got?"

"Well, we have a line of greeting cards for holidays and that special someone. Do you have a woman in your life?"

The image of Terri stepping out of her BMW flashed across my mind. I smiled as I thought about her conservative glasses and tight skirt.

"Ah, so there *is* someone," the clerk said. "Let me show you what I've got."

I followed him over to the greeting card display. There were hundreds of beautiful cards for every occasion from birthdays to Kwanza. I looked through the sweetheart section and found the perfect card for Terri.

"I'll take this one!"

While he rang me up, I wrote a short poem on the inside of the card along with an inscription. He caught a glance while he was scanning it into the register.

"You think that'll be enough to impress her?"

"I think so." I said. "But to be on the safe side, where can I buy some flowers?"

"I'm your man."

"Don't tell me you're a florist, too?"

"I guess you didn't read the sign outside. It reads 'Afro Books 'n' Things.' That means whatever you need, we got it!"

"So, I guess if I need the flowers delivered, you've got that covered, too?" I was joking, but he was dead serious. He reached beneath his dashiki and pulled out a business card.

"Lonnie's Carrier Service? Damn, brotha, you don't let a dollar out the door, do you?"

"Look, I've got a wife and five kids to feed," he said, "and love don't pay the rent."

"Amen to that!" I gave him a high five. "Now, how much is all of this gonna cost me?"

"Give me seventy-five bucks, a name, and an address, and I'll take care of everything."

"You got yourself a deal!"

I gave him the money and information on where to find Terri. Before I sealed the envelope I wrote a short inscription on the card, then added a little something special.

"I really appreciate your help, my man."

"No problem, Mr. Payne. And I'll be sure to tell all my customers to listen to your show tonight."

"How did you know who I was?"

"Your face is on every billboard in the Third Ward, especially down Martin Luther King Boulevard."

After we exchanged information I rushed to my car, hoping to get home in time to grab a power nap. As I was driving off I noticed the message light on my cell phone was blinking. I checked the voice mail but it was blank and the caller's number had been blocked. It was the fifth time in two days this had happened. That was unusual because only five people had my cell number. "I'm gonna change this damn number first thing tomorrow," I said to myself. At that moment, my phone rang. I looked at the display, but the caller ID was blocked.

"Hello?"

"Hey, Julian! I'm glad I finally caught up with you."

"Who is this?"

"You don't recognize my voice?"

"Look, I don't have time for games."

"Okay, you don't have to be so nasty. It's me, Olivia Brown. Remember me?"

"Olivia? How did you get my number?"

"When I used your phone to call my girlfriend Saturday night, your number was on her caller ID."

"Olivia, I thought we agreed that what happened in Chicago would end in Chicago."

"I understood that, Julian. I'm not trying to harass you. Just so happens I'm in Houston for a couple of days on business. I thought I'd give you a call to say hello."

"Come on, Olivia, you expect me to believe that it's a coincidence that you're in Houston on business just two days after we met?"

"I told you that I was in the music business. I work with producers from all over the country. I decided to meet with one of my clients in Houston rather than fly out to L.A. Besides, I have a girlfriend from college who lives here." She sounded sincere. "Look, Julian, I just called to say hello and see how you were doing. And yes, I was hoping we could at least have a drink. That's all. But if this is the way you're going to act, I will lose your number and never bother you again!"

I had my doubts, but there was no reason for me to suspect she was crazy enough to follow me to Houston. Besides, I did recall her mentioning that she was working on recording a few of her songs. In the entertainment business, flying in and out of airports is as common as flagging down a taxi.

"Look, Olivia, I apologize for snapping at you. I'm under a lot of pressure right now. My first show is tonight and I'm still working on my topic."

"Why don't you let me help? I'm great with coming up with ideas. I *am* an artist, you know."

"I thought you were here on business."

"I am, but my next meeting isn't until later this evening. You know people in the music industry don't do anything until after six."

"I don't know, Olivia."

"What are you so afraid of? All we're going to do is toss around a few ideas over drinks. Who knows, I might actually help you come up with something hot for your show tonight. And you know how important it is to get off to a good start in a new market."

I had to admit to myself that she was right. Getting off to a great start was critical, especially when you're the new kid on the block. But for some reason I couldn't focus. I don't know if I was choking or just excited. Regardless of what it was, I could use some help. My job was on the line and this was no time to be proud.

"Come on, Julian, it'll be fun!"

"Okay, but remember—this is strictly business."

"You have my word. I promise not to take advantage of you." She laughed. "You just make sure to behave yourself, Mr. Payne. I've already seen how naughty you can be."

"What are you trying to say?" I asked. "Don't start none, won't be none."

"You got it, James Brown!"

"Well, I promise to be a good boy." I laughed. "Now, let me run home and get my daughter situated with her new baby-sitter and I'll be right over. As a matter of fact, I can go straight to the studio from your place. By the way, where are you staying?"

"I'm in suite 2205 at the Wyndham Hotel. It's on West-heimer Road next to the Galleria mall."

"What a coincidence. That's right down the street from where I work."

"That *is* a coincidence, isn't it?"

Chapter 10

TERRI WAS IN her office wrapping up a counseling session with an elderly couple. They were her last clients before lunch. She glanced at her watch while she discussed their problem.

"So, Mrs. Adams, why do you need your husband to get down on all fours and bark like a dog in order to become sexually aroused?" Terri asked.

"I don't know. Maybe it's because my father never let me have a dog when I was growing up."

"Mr. Adams, why not bark if it turns your wife on?"

"Because she'll only come up with something even more ridiculous. She's never satisfied! Our love life was fine until she started watchin' that program on HBO about those four nasty women."

"What program is that, Mrs. Adams?"

"He's talkin' about *Sex in the City*. I love that show, don't you, Dr. Ross?"

"I've seen it a couple of times. But let's stay focused on the issue. What's so interesting about that program to you?"

"It gives me new sexual ideas." She blushed. "Did you see

the episode when Samantha had a lesbian affair and her lover squirted in her face while she was giving her oral sex?"

"You see what I'm talkin' about? Every week I've got to deal with this nonsense!" Mr. Adams yelled. "I'm damn near sixty-five years old. I don't want to feel like I'm competing in the Olympics every time we have sex."

Terri stood up and walked behind them. Once she was out of their sight she turned her back and covered her mouth. She laughed so hard tears were forming in her eyes.

"So, Doc, what should I do?" Mr. Adams asked.

She wanted to say, "Let her squirt in your face, you might like it." But instead she composed herself and gave him the clinical response.

"Mr. Adams, does barking like a dog make you feel degraded?"

"No, just stupid. It's hard enough to have sex in the missionary position with a bad back, now I've got to roll around on the floor, too? To hell with that!"

"Wait a second, Mr. Adams, don't you have sexual fantasies?" Terri asked. "There's got to be something naughty you've always wanted to do with your wife."

He sat there with his hand on his chin and looked off into space as if he were painting a picture. Then he leaned back and smiled.

"What is it, sweetheart, come on, tell me!" Mrs. Adams said.

"I'm too embarrassed to say."

"Don't be," Terri said. "I'm a professional. There's nothing you can say that I haven't heard a thousand times."

"Okay, here it goes." He turned toward his wife and looked at her with a serious expression. "I've always wanted you to come to bed dressed up in leather and high-heel boots."

"No problem, sweetheart. I can do that!"

"Wait—there's more. I also want a teenaged girl dressed as a French maid in the bed with us."

Mrs. Adams stood up and slapped him in the face. "You can go to hell, you old pervert!" Then she stormed out of the office.

A few seconds later Mr. Adams calmly put on his dark shades and old gray brim and walked toward the door.

"Well, Doc, I guess you can cancel that appointment for next week. I don't think she'll be asking me to bark like a dog anytime soon." He tipped his hat and backed out of the door wearing a sly grin.

Terri plopped down in her chair, leaned back, and stretched her feet out on her desk. "Talk about reverse psychology!"

Just then the receptionist, Helen, called Terri on the intercom.

"Dr. Ross, Janet is here."

"Send her in."

"Also, there's a carrier here with a package."

"Tell him to leave it with you."

"I think you might want to sign for this *personally*. It's not FedEx."

"Okay, send them both in."

The carrier entered the office carrying a dozen yellow roses and a small white box. Janet made room on Terri's desk. After signing the receipt, Terri sat down and stared at the box.

"You want me to call the bomb squad?" Janet joked.

"Very funny. I'm just not in a hurry."

"Well, my lunch break is over in thirty minutes and I'm curious."

"You mean nosy."

"Whatever," Janet said. "You know who it's from. I don't know why you're trippin'."

"What do you know about him?" Terri asked.

"I'm a single woman with no kids, no man, and no life," Janet said. "I know everything about everybody."

"Is he married?"

"No."

"Does he have kids?"

"A ten-year-old daughter."

"Is he dating?"

"I don't think so."

"Is he gay?"

"I hope not."

"Is he—"

"Stop it, Terri!" Janet cut her off. "I've already been through this interrogation with Julian. Why don't you go out with him and get it over with."

"I don't think so."

"Why not? You know you like him. You were blushing like a teenager when you came into the studio yesterday. I haven't seen you smile like that in over a year."

"He's nothing special. They never are."

"Who is this talking? Not Doctor Terri Ross, the strong, independent, BMW-drivin' superwoman?"

"What are you talkin' about?"

"I can't believe you're still holding on to that shit you went through with Michael. That was more than a year ago. Let it go!"

Terri put her head down on her desk and turned back and forth in her chair.

"You know I hate it when you're right?"

"Yep."

"It's just hard for me to trust again, you know? I wasted two years of my life on Michael. I cooked and cleaned for him, supported him in his career, and paid most of the bills. Then one day, out of the blue, he tells me that he's still in love with his ex-wife."

"Well, like my mama use to say, everybody plays the fool at least once in their life."

"You're right—he was a fool."

"I'm talking about you, Doc!" Janet said bluntly. "You were the one who allowed a grown man to move in with no money and bad credit. You were the one who chose to baby-sit his badass kids. And you were the one who allowed him to play house for a year without putting a ring on your finger."

"It's not my fault! I was in love. He should have told me he wasn't ready to make a commitment. He kept saying he needed more time."

"He needed more time all right, more time to drive your car and spend your money."

"Fuck you, Janet! You don't know how it feels to love somebody and have it all taken away overnight!" Terri yelled. "Get out of my office!"

Janet calmly got up and walked toward the door.

"You don't have a monopoly on pain, Terri. We've all been down that road. But sooner or later you've got to unload the baggage, otherwise you'll never be ready for the right man when he does come along." Then she walked out.

Terri buried her face in her hands and began to cry. When she got up for a tissue she passed by the flowers on her desk. The fragrance and the beauty of the arrangement made her smile.

While she dabbed at her eyes, she opened the box. Inside was a copy of the book *The Maintenance Man* and an envelope. She pulled out the card and opened it and a check fell to the floor. When she picked it up she saw that it was made payable to The Genesis Foundation. The amount was five hundred dollars. The inscription on the card read:

Call me if you need a little maintenance (smile) or just a friend to talk to. Please try to listen to my show tonight. I have a special song I'd like to play for you.

Yours truly,
Julian

P.S. Here's a little something I thought up while waiting in line to buy this card. I call it "Above Average."

Terri leaned back in her chair and cleared her throat. Then she began reading, doing her best to sound poetic.

What do you see
when you look at me

is it just charm good looks
a great personality

do you see another brotha
just like any other
just out to get what he can get
nothing serious just a quick lover
is that all you see
when you see me
then take this opportunity
to get to know me

on a scale from one to ten
i'm a twelve and a half
i'm unlike the brothas you've encountered
i'm unlike any man in your past

i'm not your average brotha
i don't play games
i know you've heard that before
but please—allow me to explain
i don't run from commitment
i face it
i don't look for love
but if it comes—i embrace it

i'm not perfect
i'm no saint
but an average ordinary brotha
no my sista
that i ain't

Terri leaned forward and enjoyed a long whiff of the yellow roses. "Michael never bought me flowers," she said to herself. "And he damn sure wasn't considerate enough to donate any money."

"That's exactly what I thought when I saw the check," Janet said while sticking her head in the door. "I know the carrier from church. He let me take a peek in the box."

"Get your butt in here, girl!"

Terri and Janet met at the center of the office and hugged.

"I came back to say I was sorry."

"There's nothing to be sorry about. You just told me what I needed to hear. That's what true friends are supposed to do."

"True friends should also tell you when it's time to eat," Janet laughed. "Let's go down to the cafeteria and get some of that delicious chicken and dumplings. We probably won't have another soul food day until Black History Month."

Terri grabbed her purse and turned off the lights. Before she walked out the door, she stopped and turned to Janet.

"You know, it's kinda funny how things work out in life," Terri said.

"What do you mean?"

"I make my living talking to couples about their relationships and sex issues."

"What's so funny about that?"

"I haven't been in a relationship or had good sex for more than a year." Terri walked over and picked up *The Maintenance Man* from her desk. "I think I'll look at this during lunch. Maybe I can get some tips on how to get my tires rotated and oil changed. I need a serious tune-up."

"Tune-up?" Janet said. "Hell, I need an overhaul!"

Chapter 11

I WAS ALREADY feeling uneasy as I walked toward Olivia's suite. "This is a bad move, Julian," I said to myself. I didn't want to make the mistake of having sex with her again, especially after that emotional breakdown. That was a dead giveaway that there were some unresolved issues. Maybe I would have been more compassionate if I wanted a serious relationship, but Olivia didn't possess that wholesome appeal that I was accustomed to in a woman. It was purely a sexual attraction. As the saying goes, there's the type of woman you take to bed and there's the type you take home to mama. Olivia was definitely the bedroom type. I made that determination within the first five minutes of our conversation—most men do.

I should have turned my horny ass around and went home, but I was confident that my hormones were under control. After I took a deep breath, I knocked on the door.

"Just a second!" she yelled.

When the door swung open, I knew I was in trouble. Olivia was wrapped in a small white towel that barely covered her breasts. Her hair was dripping wet and slicked back.

"Hi, Julian, it's nice to see you again. Come on in."

She gave me a firm hug that lasted longer than it should have. I practically had to push her away to get free. I sat down at the desk and laid out the books I had purchased along with a notepad and two pens.

"So, let's get to work."

Olivia stood at the door for a moment stunned by my lack of affection. I'm sure she was expecting a repeat performance of Saturday night.

"Sorry I'm not dressed. I didn't expect you to get here so fast," she said while walking toward the bathroom. "Just give me a second and I'll slip something on."

"No problem, take your time."

"So, are you settled into your new place yet?"

"Sort of. We still have a lot of unpacking to do once the movers arrive from Chicago."

"How does your daughter like it?"

"She loves it, especially the swimming pool and the piano I bought her."

"Your daughter plays piano?"

"She hasn't started taking lessons yet, but she seems to have a talent for it. That was the main reason I moved to the Sugarland area. The school she's enrolled in has the best music program in the city."

"I play the piano myself. Maybe I can give her a few tips."

I didn't respond. I just looked out the window admiring the view and kept talking.

"So, how long are you gonna be in town?"

"Just a couple of days," she yelled from the bathroom. "I'm sure I'll get what I came for by then."

When I turned around from looking out the window, I noticed the bathroom door had been left open. I could see Olivia's naked reflection through the closet door mirror as she rubbed lotion over her body. I felt like a Peeping Tom watching her stroking her smooth brown skin. She seemed to be masturbating as she squeezed her breasts one at a time, then let them slide out of her tight grip. She did it over and over until her nipples became flushed and hard. Then she sat down on the toilet and spread her legs apart. She propped her left leg on the edge of the tub and began slowly massaging from her calves up to the inside of her thighs. She moaned as she rubbed against her clean-shaven vagina and pierced clit.

I was so caught up I didn't realize that she was staring back at me through the same reflection. She sucked on her middle finger, then slid it inside of herself. She masturbated for a while, then pulled her finger out and tasted her juices.

"Ah," she sighed, then she smacked her lips together to emphasize how good it was. "You want some of this pussy, don't you?"

I took a hard swallow and shook my head.

"Come on, baby. I'm ready to explode!"

"I'm sorry, Olivia, you're gonna have to explode without me tonight," I told her. "I promised myself to keep this strictly business."

"Strictly business, my ass!"

She stormed out of the bathroom and began frantically unbuckling my belt. I pushed her back halfheartedly, but she managed to get my pants down around my ankles. She pushed me back against the wall and began sucking me. My mind said no but my body was allowing it to happen.

"Ahh!" I moaned as I palmed the back of her head.

"Whose dick is this?" she asked.

I didn't respond.

"Whose is it?" she yelled again, then slapped me on the ass. "Tell me it's mine!"

Olivia had great technique. Her rhythm was perfect and she kept her mouth sloppy wet the way I liked it. But she ruined the moment with her masculine tone and foul language. Dirty talk is stimulating when it's done tastefully. Olivia was just plain old vulgar.

After a few more nasty comments and another hard slap on the ass, I lost my erection.

"What's wrong, baby?" She looked up at me with saliva dripping down her chin. "Don't you wanna come?"

I looked down at her kneeling in front of me and was instantly turned off. There was something about her that wasn't quite right, I could sense it. Suddenly her beauty faded. Nothing about her was appealing, not her long hair, her figure, her flawless skin, not even her hazel eyes. As far as I know, she could've been suckin' on another man's dick last night. I was thinking, *Why should I feel special?*

"Get up, Olivia," I said to her. "I can't do this." Then I bent down to pull up my pants.

"What are you talkin' about?"

"I can't do this, I said!"

"Come on, baby, just relax, I promise I'll suck it better this time." She grabbed my pants and tried to pull them back down.

"Stop it, Olivia!"

"No, I want you! I need you. Don't make me beg!"

When I tried to pull my pants up, she grabbed me by the waist and spun me onto the bed. Then she jumped on top of me and tried to insert my limp penis inside of her.

"What the hell are you doin'?"

"I wanna make love to you, baby. Don't leave me hanging." She sounded like a junkie who needed a fix.

"Make love? You don't even know me!" I said. "Now get your ass off of me. Get off, goddamnit!"

I pushed her off with all my might. She rolled off the bed and onto the floor. I jumped up and quickly pulled up my pants.

"What the hell is wrong with you? I'm not even wearing a condom!"

"A condom? You weren't worried about wearing a condom Saturday night when you were fuckin' me on the balcony! What happened to your morals then?"

"That was in the heat of passion, and it was irresponsible."

"What about what happened a few minutes ago? Was that in the heat of passion, too, or did you just wanna get your dick sucked?"

"Look, Olivia, this was all a big mistake. I never should have come here," I told her. "I'm sorry if I've misled you."

"You're right about one thing, Julian, you are sorry! Now get your sorry ass outta my face! And take your shit with you!"

She began throwing my things at me. Notebook paper was flying everywhere. I dodged most of the objects, but one of the hardcover books hit me squarely on the nose. I began to bleed.

"Oh, sweetheart, I'm sorry. Let me get you a towel."

Her personality instantly changed. In less than five seconds she went from a raving lunatic to Mother Teresa.

"Get the hell away from me!" I shouted as I rushed into the bathroom. I ran cold water over a face towel and pressed it against my nose.

When I came out of the bathroom, Olivia had picked my things off the floor and put them into a bag.

"Give it to me!" I snatched it out of her hand.

"I told you I was sorry. It was an accident."

"This whole damn thing was an accident. I never should have come here. Good-bye!"

"Julian, please don't go!" she yelled. "I said I was sorry! What more do you want?"

I had one foot out the door. I turned and stared deep into her hazel eyes. "Not a damn thing, Olivia!"

While I waited on the elevator I looked at my reflection in the hall mirror. I couldn't believe how ridiculous I looked holding that blood-soaked towel to my nose. I smiled at first, then I laughed, but it wasn't a funny laugh. It was the kind of nervous laugh you make when you're embarrassed and humiliated. "What the hell am I doin' here?" I said as I checked the time on my watch. "I've only got two hours to prepare for the most important night of my life."

Chapter 12

IT WAS JUST after eight when I arrived at WBMX. The building was empty except for the security guard and janitors. I rushed down to my office and laid out the books. I started by reading from the book *Wisdom of the Ages*. Right there in chapter one, page one, was the inspiration I needed: "All man's miseries derive from not being able to sit quietly in a room alone." It was a quote written by French philosopher Blaise Pascal more than four centuries ago. I read it aloud, over and over again. And the more I read it, the more profound it seemed.

At that moment it became obvious why I hadn't been able to think creatively. The pressures of moving from Chicago, getting Sam settled into a new school, and thinking about Terri had caused me to lose focus. All it took was a few minutes of peace and quiet to change my perspective and clear my mind. "Lord, you sure do work in mysterious ways," I said to myself.

In less than two hours I had written ten pages of provocative material, more than enough topics for the rest of the week. "I've still got it!" I cheered.

"You've still got what—VD?" Mitch was standing in the doorway, laughing.

"I can see you still haven't learned how to knock."

"What are you talking about? Your office in Chicago didn't even have a door."

"Oh, yeah, you're right." I laughed. "So, what do you want?"

"I want *you*! It's show time in five minutes. Are you ready?"

"Like Freddy!" I said confidently.

Mitch had the studio set up just the way I liked it. The music carts were stacked in alphabetical order on top of the console, the volume on my headphones was just right, and my jasmine-scented candles were lit in every corner. As I sat down in my high-back leather chair looking out at the Houston skyline, I got a chill.

Mitch was next door in the control room. We could see one another through the large soundproof window. But unlike the raggedy equipment at WTLK, we had a computer system with a monitor. Mitch typed in the callers' names along with their comments. There were ten lines instead of five. I was praying all of them would stay lit throughout the night.

"I hope those billboards and commercials worked."

"To hell with commercials—word of mouth is the best advertising in the world," I told him. "Just get me two frustrated women on the line and I'll turn this motha out!"

"Well, if there's anybody who can piss women off, it's you," Mitch said. "Now get set—you're on in ten seconds."

I put on my headset and took a deep breath. "As Marvin Gaye would say, *let's get it on!*"

Mitch began counting down, "Five-four-three-two-one." When the on-air light came on, I felt a burst of energy.

"Good evening, H-Town, and welcome to the premiere of *Love, Lust, and Lies*," I said in a deep, smooth tone. "I'm your host, Julian Payne, and I'll be with you until two A.M. talking about relationships and the drama they cause. The topic tonight is especially for the ladies. It deals with the lack of satisfaction. That's right, we're talking about women who get maintenance when their man comes up short, inside and outside the bedroom. So, if you're one of those ladies who's neglected and unappreciated, call me up and let's talk about it."

The second I gave out the toll-free number the lines exploded. Mitch couldn't type fast enough to keep up with all the comments, so he started abbreviating. I was laughing my ass off as I watched all the misspelled names coming across the screen. The first three lines were the worst.

Line 1—Karen Smthi—Is there a difference between getting maintenance and getting a tune-up?

Line 2—Lyndah Wilums—Is the size of the tool important?

Line 3—Juanita Johnsin—I'm fifty years old and horny as hell. Where can I find a maintenance man?

Mitch couldn't type worth shit, but he managed to spell the names well enough for me to figure them out. I was anxious to hear their comments, but I had personal business to attend to first.

"Now, before we take your calls, I'd like to kick things off with an old-school dedication. This one goes out to a very sexy doctor. And believe me, fellahs, she's the kinda doctor you can't wait to bend over for. I hope you're listening, Doc, because this one's especially for you. It's a classic by one of the funkiest bands of all time, the Ohio Players. It's called 'Skin Tight.'" When the funky beat kicked in, I could practically feel the entire city snapping fingers and bobbing heads. Then the lyrics set it off:

> "You're a bad-bad miss-sass
> In those skin-tight britches. . . ."

I damn near fell on the floor when I saw Mitch in the control room doing the robot. I joined right in by doing a dance called the Errol Flynn. It was a popular dance back in the seventies. Halfway through the song, we faded the music out and began taking callers. It was obvious by the excitement in their voices that they couldn't wait to vent.

By midnight we were on a roll. Every phone line stayed lit. During the breaks Mitch and I stared at one another and grinned. We knew the show was a hit.

Success is a funny thing. You dream about it all your life, then before you realize it's happening, you're there. Suddenly your thoughts shift from how you're going to make it to how to hold on to what you've worked so hard to obtain. I had come a long way in fifteen years and there was no way in hell I was going back. I didn't uproot my daughter and move all the way down to hot-ass Houston, Texas, only to fail.

I learned a valuable lesson from watching others in my profession: beware of the trappings of success—the money, the fame, and especially the women. All it takes is getting involved with the wrong one, and your reputation and career could be over.

That's what I was thinking as I stared nervously at my monitor. Ever since the opening of the show I had avoided answering line ten. I was hoping she would get disconnected or hang up. But she stayed on the line for two straight hours. The information on my screen read:

Line 10—Olivia—How do I tell my maintenance man it ain't over?

Was I being paranoid? Was it Olivia Brown? I didn't know for sure. But I wasn't about to pick up the phone to find out.

Part III

(October)

Chapter 13

"SAMANTHA, BREAKFAST IS ready!" I yelled. "And don't take all day—the school bus will be here in five minutes!"

When she came downstairs I could tell she wasn't her usual bubbly self. Instead of giving me a hug and kiss, she sat down at the kitchen table and started pouting.

"Good morning, Princess! Why the long face this morning? You look like somebody stole your lunch money."

"I hate school! I wish we'd never moved to this crappy place."

"Watch your mouth, young lady!"

"I'm sorry, Dad, it's just that my music teacher, Mrs. Adams, is getting on my nerves. I've only been in her class a week and she's already picking on me. Then there's this white girl named Melissa who keeps kicking the back of my seat. When I turn around to tell her to stop, I'm the one who gets in trouble. I hate school!"

"Why didn't you tell me about this last week?"

"I didn't want to bother you. I know how busy you are with your new job."

"I'm never too busy for my baby, you know that." I put my arms around her. "Now, let me put some clothes on so we can get this mess straightened out, once and for all!"

"Don't do that, Dad, please!" She grabbed my pajama sleeve as I was headed upstairs. "I don't want to look like a cry-baby in front of the other kids."

"Okay, but if things don't get better in the next couple of weeks, let me know. I might have to come up there and pimp slap Mrs. Adams." I laughed.

"Speaking of slapping, is it okay if I beat up Melissa if she keeps kicking my chair?"

"Absolutely—just make sure nobody sees you."

We laughed and gave each other a high five. Just then the school bus pulled up to the corner. Sam kissed me on the cheek and ran off with her backpack swinging off her shoulder.

"Melissa's gonna get pimp slapped! Melissa's gonna get pimp slapped!" she sang.

As I watched her board the bus, I felt proud of the child I was raising. "Yep, she's a chip off the old block."

While I washed the dishes, I turned on the Weather Channel to check the forecast. The heat was suffocating and I was pray-ing for a cloudy day. But just as I expected, the forecast was for sunny skies and ninety-eight degrees. "No wonder the crime rate is lower in the South; it's too damn hot for the crooks to come out to rob you!" I said to myself. Just then, the phone rang. When I saw the 312 area code I knew who it was.

"Whassup, playa?"

"Whassup, Julian! How's everything in Houston, Texas?" He tried to sound southern. "Are those thick country girls knockin' down your door yet?"

"Eddie, I've only been on the air for a week."

"I figured a big-city boy like you would have a harem by now. I heard all about those Texas and Louisiana girls. They'll put a mojo on you and have you doin' all kinds of outrageous shit!"

"I don't spread myself thin like you. But I did meet a fine

sistah in the parking garage last week. She seems to have it all together—nice body, pleasant personality, real hair, and she's a psychologist."

"Those intellectual types make the biggest freaks," Eddie said. "They listen to perverted sexual fantasies all day. By the time they get home they're ready to break out the whips and handcuffs."

"There you go again with your freak theory. Can you get your mind out the gutter for a second? I really like this woman. I even bought her some roses."

"Roses? Wait a second—is this the same man who, only a week ago, said he wasn't interested in a serious relationship?"

"Who said anything about a serious relationship? I just sent her roses, for God's sake. It doesn't mean we're walking down the aisle."

"Julian, you haven't bought roses for a woman since—"

"I know when, okay? You don't have to make such a big deal out of it," I told him. "Besides, she doesn't seem to be interested. I haven't heard from her since I sent the flowers to her office last week, not even so much as a thank-you. That's why I haven't bothered to mention her until now."

"Have you tried calling her? She could be dead."

"I left two messages at her office the day after I sent the flowers. And I've called the answering service at her foundation twice."

"Lord, help this poor soul. He's lost all of his playa etiquette," Eddie said. "Don't you know a woman can detect a desperate man a mile away?"

"And your point is?"

"Stop callin'! If she's interested, she'll pursue you."

While we were talking, I got another call.

"Hold on, Eddie, my other line is ringing."

"Take your call, Julian. I've got to get down to the studio. I just called to let you know I made reservations to fly in next Saturday."

"That's perfect timing! The radio station is throwing an old-school party at the Hilton next week!"

"Cool! I've been looking forward to checking out some of those thick southern girls," Eddie said. "Oh, and don't forget you promised to throw down on some barbecue."

"I'll have the coals in the grill, hot and ready to go."

"If you play your cards right, that doctor friend of yours will be hot and ready, too. Take it from me, partner—women are all about playing games. Peace!"

I didn't want to accept that Terri was playing games. That would have also meant accepting that she was common, typical, not special. I wasn't ready to admit that possibility. When I clicked over I expected it to be either Carmen's parents or Mitch. I didn't bother to check the caller ID.

"Hello, Payne residence."

"Julian?"

"Yes, who is this?"

"It's Terri Ross, how are you doin'?"

She caught me completely off guard. Although I was happy to hear her voice, my pride wouldn't allow me to show it.

"I'm doin' fine." I tried to sound cool. "And you?"

"I'm fine, too."

There was a pause. I knew she could sense my nonchalant attitude.

"If you're busy I can call you back later."

"Did I say I was busy?"

"No, but you sound like you don't want to be bothered."

"If I didn't want to be bothered, I would've told you. I always say what's on my mind."

"Are you implying something?"

"I'm not implying anything, I'm simply saying that if I felt a certain way about an issue or a person, I would just come right out and say it."

"Look, Julian, I can tell you're in a funky mood. Maybe I should call you another time."

"Call me another time? For what, Terri?" I asked angrily. "You call my home acting as if you haven't received my phone calls or my flowers. You know I've been trying to reach you for over a week. You could've at least extended me the courtesy of a return phone call."

"Now, wait just a minute, Julian. You don't know me well enough to be telling me off, and by the way, I never asked for the stupid flowers!"

"You're right, Terri, we don't know each other that well, in fact, we don't know each other at all. But I assumed, as a gentleman, that an appropriate way of getting acquainted was to send you flowers. But I guess I was wrong." I paused to collect myself. "You know, Terri, I don't know what you've gone through to make you so angry and distrustful toward men, but I'm not to blame. Furthermore, I'm not going to pay for it. Good-bye, *Doctor* Ross. I hope you find what you're searching for."

As I hung up the phone I thought about what Mitch said to me at WTLK in Chicago. He told me to start taking my own advice. In that situation my advice would have been to let it go. If Terri couldn't appreciate a gentleman sending her flowers, if she couldn't give me the courtesy of a phone call, then what the hell did I need her for? Unlike most people who suffer from emotional dependency and low self-esteem, I accept when a person is not for me.

I took a deep breath and headed upstairs to put on my swim trunks. I decided to do a few laps in the pool before hitting the weights. "I didn't like her that much anyway," I said out loud. I was trying to convince myself I didn't care. "Her head was too big and her legs were too skinny. And besides, who wants to date a psychologist? All they do is analyze every damn thing."

Suddenly the phone rang. This time I checked the caller ID. It read ROSS COUNSELING SERVICES.

"Hello?"

"Julian, it's me, Terri. Please don't say anything. I have

something I need to say to you. First of all, I apologize for not calling to thank you for the flowers. It was a wonderful gesture and I truly appreciated it. No one has sent me flowers in over ten years. I also want to tell you how much I loved the poem you wrote. It showed me a tender side of you. Not many men are willing to communicate their emotions in such a romantic way. They're afraid of appearing too soft or weak. Also, you were right about me being hurt in the past. Sometimes it's hard for a woman to move on, even a woman who advises people about their relationships for a living. I guess I have a lot to learn about myself and about how to treat people."

"Can I say something now?" I asked her.

"Not yet, I just have one more thing to say." Her tone was very serious. "I admire you for being the man you are. Raising your daughter after losing your wife must be very difficult. I only hope that I haven't ruined my opportunity to get to know you and find out what kind of man you are—outside of the studio. That's it, I'm done."

"Well, since you're feeling so apologetic, what are you willing to do to make it up to me?"

"I'll leave that up to you, but don't ask for nothin' crazy." She laughed.

"How about a date?"

"Just say when."

"Be careful how you say that. I can be quite spontaneous."

"Like I said, you name the time and place and I'll be there."

"Okay, how about an hour from now at my place?"

"And may I ask what we're going to do at your place, Mr. Payne?"

"Stop trippin', Terri, I'm not trying to seduce you. It's simply an invitation to get better acquainted and have a swim. That is, if a stuck-up, educated sistah like yourself isn't afraid of getting her hair wet."

She got quiet for a second.

"Okay, you've got yourself a date. I'll be there in about an hour and a half. I have to go by the mall and pick up a cute swimsuit. And by the way, don't let my degrees and fancy office fool you, I'm a homegirl from the Fifth Ward and I can throw down with the best of them," she said, sounding cocky. "Now give me the directions to your place so I can embarrass you in your own pool."

Chapter 14

I WAS SO excited about Terri's visit that I mopped the foyer with a bucket of Lysol, vacuumed the carpet twice, and did one hundred inclined push-ups. "You da man!" I admired my physique in the dresser mirror.

At one fifteen I heard Terri's BMW pulling into the driveway. I looked through the blinds as she was stepping out of her car. I wanted to see if she was just as fine as I remembered. She was wearing a white wrap over a two-piece yellow swimsuit and a gold chain that accentuated her slim waist. Her round, tan breasts stood out even more, 36C, I estimated. "That business suit didn't do your body justice," I said to myself. I grabbed a beach towel from the linen closet and wrapped it around my waist to disguise my erection, then I rushed downstairs to let her in.

"Welcome to Club Med, pretty la-dee," I said with a Jamaican accent. "Cu-mon in and take ya shoes off."

"Why thank you, Dexter Saint Jock—don't mind if I do."

"Can I offer ya some soda or tea, are maybe some ganja to relax ya mind?"

"Water will be fine."

"Are ya for sure, now, 'cause I got the good stuff, the Panama Red, the Acapulco Gold."

"No thank you, I'll just have good ole fashion H_2O."

"Comin' right up, child." I said as I went into the refrigerator. "Any ting ya want, just let me know."

Terri laughed as she walked around the living room admiring the house. Her hair was pulled back in a tight bun and she wore tinted glasses that gave her an elegant and sophisticated look.

"I love your place," Terri said. "How long have you been in Houston?"

"It'll be two weeks on Sunday. But it already feels like home."

"Aww, she's adorable. Is this your daughter?" She was looking at Samantha's pictures on the mantel over the fireplace.

"Yeah, that's my baby," I said while walking over to her.

"And this must be your wife. She's very beautiful! Your daughter looks just like her."

"Thank you." I picked up Carmen's picture. "We met back in college when I was working at the campus radio station."

"Janet told me that she passed away." Terri put her hand on my shoulder. "How long has it been?"

"Two years."

"You really loved her, didn't you?"

"There are no words to express how much." I put the picture back on the mantel. "What about you, have you ever been married?"

"Who, me—married? No. I haven't even come close."

"Is that by choice?"

"No, it's by circumstance."

"Meaning?"

"Meaning most men aren't interested in a committed relationship. They lie too much, they don't have any goals, and they will lay up with any hoochie who'll open her legs. Then they have the audacity to expect the woman to be loyal," she said. "At this point in my life, I'd rather collect dust than problems."

"But don't you want to fall in love, have children, and live happily ever after?"

"Do you want the strong, independent woman answer, or the real deal?"

"I want to know what's in your heart, not your head."

"There's not a day that goes by that I don't hope for all those wonderful things. But wanting something badly comes with a price, and that's the disappointment of knowing you can't have it. Every little girl dreams of Prince Charming whisking her off on a white horse, but when you grow up you realize the prince has turned into a toad and the white castle is the basement at his mama's house." She took a deep breath and lowered her head. "I can't even believe I'm telling you this; I don't even know you."

"Why does being comfortable with a man make you so uncomfortable?" I moved in closer and grasped her hand on the mantel. "Maybe you're just afraid of letting someone get close."

"What kind of romantic nonsense is that?" She laughed nervously.

"If it was nonsense, why are you trembling?"

Terri pulled away.

"I've been the only one doing all the revealing—you haven't told me what it is that you want."

"I want everything! A soul mate, a role model for my daughter, and a woman who can make a good pitcher of KoolAid."

"Is that pink lemonade or the red kind?"

"I like mine mixed."

We both laughed. It relaxed the mood temporarily, but we both knew where the conversation was going.

"Look, Julian, there are hundreds of women out there you could choose from. Why me?"

"I wasn't looking to get involved, either. Just two weeks ago I was telling my best friend that I wasn't interested in a serious relationship; then you came along and all of a sudden my attitude changed. Maybe it's fate or just coincidence. All I know is ever since we met, I haven't been able to get you off my mind."

"Julian, I've been down this road before with men who talk about settling down. But after a couple of years, months, or even weeks, they're ready to move on to something new or back to someone from their past."

"I'm not expecting us to get married next week and start having babies. All I'm asking is that you leave the baggage from your previous relationships behind. It all starts with friendship and trust. Don't you remember what I wrote on your card? If you need a friend, I'll be there."

"I also remember you offering your services if I needed a maintenance man," Terri said. "If this is all about sex, I wish you would come right out and say it."

"Terri, I'm not gonna lie and say that sex isn't important. I have needs like any other man. But a relationship is also about being compatible and wanting the same things," I told her. "But you have to admit, if the sex isn't good, you're not stickin' around either."

"You got that right!" Terri said. "You'll never hear me lie and say size doesn't matter. I'll take a cruise ship over a canoe any day of the week!"

"Then why can't we deal with this like adults and move forward. You know, just get to know each other?" I walked over to where she was standing and took her hand. "Like I told you when we met, I'm different, and if you give me a chance, I'll prove it to you."

"Julian, I have no doubt that you're a good man. I admire and respect you for making it to this point in your career and for raising a child on your own. Not many men would do that. But I can't help guarding my heart after it's been stepped on so many times. A woman *has* to be strong just to survive!"

"Terri, being strong doesn't keep you warm at night. And it damn sure doesn't hold you and tell you everything is gonna be all right." I moved in closer. "As strong and independent as you are, you're still alone and incomplete. Why can't you stop focusing on being strong and just be Terri? There's more strength in that than anything in the universe."

She got quiet as if she was contemplating what I said, and then she put her arms around my neck.

"Okay, Mr. Payne. I'm gonna do something I haven't done in years. I'm gonna trust you. And if you can handle my love without getting scared and running away, I will be more than happy to play my role. Hell, I'm tired of being strong and independent anyway; it's too hard," she whispered as she moved in toward my lips. "It's too damned hard." Then we kissed.

Her lips were soft. She moved her tongue slow and smooth, just the way I liked.

"Umm!" we moaned.

When I hugged her around the waist, her wrap fell off, exposing her firm, round ass. I rubbed it gently at first, trying to be a gentleman, but then I grew bold and palmed it. The contours of her hips and the dip in her lower back made me erect. She must have felt it because she backed away.

"I think we'd better stop," Terri said. "I'm not quite ready for that tune-up yet."

She walked over to her bag and pulled out a towel and a pair of goggles.

"Why don't we go get into the pool and cool off. I think we both could use it." She looked down at the bulge in my towel and smiled, then took off running toward the pool. "Last one in is a rotten egg!"

I laughed as I ran after her, because that's a line I always used with Samantha.

For the rest of the afternoon we laughed and talked about all the things we wanted out of life. I could feel her enthusiasm as we engaged in conversation. When she mentioned a city she had traveled to, I had been there. When she talked about ethnic foods, I had tried them or was willing to try them, and when she asked me a question about relationships, I answered it directly.

Terri was everything I wanted in a woman. On the outside she was beautiful and classy, on the inside she was sweet, smart, and vulnerable. Most men would try to take advantage of her past pain, but it only made me even more determined to make sure nothing like that happened again.

Chapter 15

THE THERMOMETER ON my dash read seventy-six degrees as I cruised down Highway 59 on my way to the studio. I had the convertible top down and the music blaring as the warm breeze blew across my face. I smiled as I sang along to "Baby Can't Leave It Alone" by Olu. It was a popular stepper's cut in Chicago. The first time I heard it was at a club called the Fifty Yard Line, a small but classy joint on the south side.

It was the perfect song for a perfect night. Even the humidity was low. Houston may have been hot as hell during the day, but the nighttime was incredible! I felt blessed to be where I was, to have my job, to have a healthy child, and to have Terri in my life.

When I arrived at the studio, I parked in my designated space in the underground garage. It was only nine thirty, so I decided to chill out and listen to one more track off the *Soul Catcher* CD. I pushed the selector to track three, "Sistah Why?" I reclined my seat and closed my eyes while I sang along to Olu's poetic lyrics.

"Sistah why do people fall in love so mad-ly
And then leave each other standin' all alone. . . ."

The symphonic violin interlude echoed through the tiers of concrete like in a concert hall. "Maxwell better watch his back," I said to myself. Just about halfway through the song I felt a light tap on my shoulder. I ignored it until I felt it a second time. When I opened my eyes, I couldn't believe who was leaning over me.

"Olivia, what the hell are you doin' here?" I turned the volume down, then stepped out of the car.

"I just wanted to give you this." She handed me a small box. It was covered with red Christmas wrapping paper. "It's my way of apologizing for the way I acted last week."

"You flew all the way from Chicago to give me this?"

"Who said I ever left Houston?"

Her hair was all over her head like it hadn't been combed in days and she was wearing a long trench coat, which was odd considering it was seventy-six degrees outside. I played it cool, but deep down inside I was scared. I didn't know what she was capable of.

"Olivia, I have to go to work. My show starts in twenty minutes."

"Don't you think I know what time your show starts? I've been listening to you every night."

"Then you should know I don't have time for this drama."

"I didn't come here to bring drama, I just wanted to give you this before I left for Chicago tomorrow."

"What is it?"

"Open it and find out."

I figured the best thing to do was open the box and get it over with. I peeled the paper off and lifted the top. Inside was a small royal blue pillow covered with packing paper. There was a long rope attached that I assumed was used to hang it on a hook or doorknob. On the front were embroidered white letters that read *The Princess Is Sleeping*.

"When we first met, you called your daughter Princess," Olivia said. "I thought she might like it."

"Thank you, Olivia. Now I have to go. I'm running late." I put up the convertible top on my rental car and locked the doors.

"Can't you take a couple of minutes out of your busy schedule to talk to an old friend? I've been waiting around this dump for hours just to see you."

"Well, now you've seen me. Good-bye!" I started walking away.

"Wait, baby, look at what I brought you." She untied the belt on her trench coat and slid it off her shoulders.

When it fell to the ground I damn near lost my breath. She was naked. From twenty feet away I could see her erect nipples.

"Olivia, put on your coat before somebody sees you!" I ran over and put the coat over her shoulders. "What the hell is wrong with you?"

"I just miss you, Julian. Don't you miss me?"

"Go home, Olivia, you're embarrassing yourself."

"Fuck these country-ass people!" she shouted. "I came here to see *my man*!"

"Your man?" I laughed nervously. "Woman, you don't even know me. Now go back to your hotel and sleep off whatever you've been drinkin' or smokin'!"

"Will you come over later and tuck me in?" She put her arms around my neck and tried to kiss me.

"No, Olivia, now get off me!" I pulled away and began walking toward the elevators.

"If you change your mind I'm at the Wyndham Hotel, 2205, remember?"

I didn't say a word, I just kept walking. When I got to the elevator I pushed the button frantically, hoping to escape before she snapped. While I waited, I stuffed the pillow into the garbage can that was nearby. There was no way in hell I was giving my daughter a present from that crazy bitch. Just as I shut the lid, Olivia came walking around the corner.

"What is it now, Olivia? I told you I have to go to work!"

"You can stop being so nasty to me, Julian, I get the message. You don't want to be with me and I have to accept that." She was strangely calm. "I promise you I'll never bother you again. All I want is a hug and then I'll leave."

"How about a handshake instead?"

"No, it's got to be a hug," she said. "Call it—closure."

When the elevator door opened my first impulse was to jump inside and close the door in her face, but for some strange reason I felt sympathetic toward her. Maybe it was my guilty conscience. In an odd way, I needed closure, too.

"Okay, but after I give you this hug, you've got to promise to leave."

"I promise to God and hope to die." She crossed her heart with her hand.

I didn't like the way that sounded, but I let it slide. I gave her a kiss on the cheek and a church hug.

"Mmm," she moaned. "I'm really gonna miss you. I hope we can at least be friends."

"Sure, Olivia, but let's make that long-distance friends. In other words, don't call me, I'll call you."

"I understand, Julian, it won't happen again. Have a great show tonight. I'll be listening."

After I boarded the elevator I held the door open and watched her walk off into the night. As the elevator doors shut, I tried to convince myself it was over. I really wanted to believe that. But Olivia walked away too quietly—too calmly.

Chapter 16

MY TEMPER FLARED as I circled the Delta baggage claim area in my car for the third time. According to the agent at Continental Airlines, Eddie's flight had landed on schedule, but when I arrived outside of baggage claim he was nowhere to be found. I dialed his cell phone three times, but he didn't answer. It was typical of Eddie not to be on time. If I knew him, he was probably trying to get into the pants of some weak-minded female.

The longer I waited, the more frustrated I became. It didn't help that the sun was frying the left side of my face. The high was expected to be ninety-three, but it already felt like one hundred. Even with the air-conditioning on full blast, I was sweating. After another fifteen minutes of circling the terminal, I drove around to the hourly parking area. I hated parking at Intercontinental Airport, especially with all the new construction going on.

Once I walked inside the terminal I checked the monitor for flight arrival information and the carousel number his bags were arriving on. Most of the passengers from his flight had already collected their luggage, but Eddie was still missing. Just as I was about to try him on his cell phone, I saw a tall, light-skinned brotha wearing beige shorts and a tank top coming down the escalator. He had his arm wrapped tightly around the waist of a blond flight attendant. When he saw me walking toward him he waved and pulled her closer to him. "He's got jungle fever!" I sang underneath my breath.

"Julian, meet Cindy," Eddie said cordially. "Cindy, this is Julian Payne, radio personality extraordinaire!"

"Pleased to meet you, Cindy. Do you mind if I talk to my friend alone for a second?"

"*Sure,* go right ahead," she said in a valley-girl accent. "I've got to get going, anyway."

"It was a pleasure meeting you, Cindy." Eddie kissed her hand. "I hope I can ride the friendly skies with you sometime soon."

"Isn't he adorable?" She blushed. Then she strutted down the corridor swinging her behind as hard as she could.

"Don't make me throw up," I said to him. "And by the way, *United* is the friendly skies, not Continental, fool!"

"What difference does it make? As long as I get my face between those creamy white thighs, who cares?"

"Eddie, you have no shame. Why don't you—"

"Hold up, partner." Eddie cut me off. "I thought we had this conversation already."

"Okay, I'll get off my soapbox for now, but one of these days that roaming dick of yours is gonna get you into trouble."

"You might be right, but until then, I'm gonna put as many miles on this bad boy as possible. You heard of frequent flyer miles? Well, this is frequent boning miles." He grabbed his crotch.

"All right, Mandingo, you just make sure to keep your hands off your genitals when we get to Terri's office. She's a classy lady. Besides, things have been going great between us for the last week. I don't want her to get the impression that I'm as trifling as you."

"A whole week, huh? Have you hit it yet?"

"No, I haven't hit it!" I said. "We're taking our time to get to know each other. It's called dating."

"Well, you can call it whatever you want, but what it all boils down to is game playing. A woman knows if she wants to give you some within the first thirty seconds of meeting you. Everything after that is game," Eddie said. "Now, you can try to play the gentleman role if you want, but you and I both know that you would be knockin' the bottom out of that thang right now if it was up to you!"

"I hate it when you read me like that!" I laughed and slapped him five. "You know me too well."

We collected his luggage from the carousel and headed for the exit. Once we were outside, Eddie nearly broke his neck staring at all the beautiful ladies walking by: white, black, Hispanic, Asian, he didn't discriminate.

"Man, Texas has some fine women! I hope your doctor friend can hook me up with one of those intellectual types!"

"Don't you ever turn off?" I said to him. "I'm gonna have Terri give you a psychological examination. You might suffer from some kind of sexual addiction."

"That's cool with me; I love doin' it on the couch. But if she cures me, I'm suing," Eddie laughed. "Now can we *please* get outta this heat!" He wiped the sweat from his forehead. "No wonder they call this H-Town. The H stands for *hot as hell*!"

Chapter 17

"CALM DOWN, GIRL!" Terri said as she paced back and forth in her office. "It's not like you're meeting his mama." Normally Terri didn't care about what people thought of her, but the situation with Eddie was different. He and Julian were like brothers. There wasn't a day that went by that he didn't mention Eddie's name and talk about something funny they had done while they were growing up. It was obvious that Julian valued his opinion about everything, including women.

Just as she finished checking her makeup in her compact mirror for the third time, there was a knock at the door. She quickly put away her purse, straightened her skirt, and took off her conservative eyeglasses.

"Come in, the door is open!"

"Where's the party at?" Janet yelled as she came strutting into the room wearing a snug-fitting pink skirt and matching pumps. "I can't wait to meet Julian's fine friend Eddie."

"Look at you, dressed up like a hoochie mama."

"Whatever," Janet said. "You're just jealous because you don't have these sexy hips." She slapped herself on the butt.

"Like that Klymaxx song says, "The men all pause when I walk into the room.""

"They better pause, before they trip over your big behind. That rascal is so wide you could sit a cocktail table on it and then the drink."

"Well, at least I'm not afraid to show off what I've got. You, on the other hand, try to be slick about exposing your stuff."

"I don't know what you're talking about."

"Okay, then tell me what's up with the two buttons undone on your blouse. I know you're trying to show off a little cleavage."

"Girl, please!"

"And where are those thick Sally Jessy Raphael glasses?" Janet laughed. "I've never known you to take those off, not even for Michael. *Ooo,* somebody's in L-O-V-E."

"You're out of your M-I-N-D," Terri said. "I'm just trying out a new look, that's all."

"Well, if you're not in love you must be whipped." Janet jumped on top of Terri's desk. "So tell me—was it good?"

"Was what good?"

"You know—*it*!" Janet thrust her fist back and forth in a stroking motion.

"I beg your pardon. I would never give it up that quickly. And besides, a real lady would never discuss what goes on in her bedroom."

"Heifer, please. If you were getting good lovin' you would be yodeling butt-naked on top of the Transco Tower."

"Maybe I just keep my business on the down low," Terri boasted. "I could be rockin' Julian's world, for all you know."

"When a woman has gone without sex for as long as you have, it won't be hard to figure out."

"And why is that?"

"Because good dick will have you talking to people you don't even like and laughing at shit that ain't even funny," Janet said. "And you haven't cracked a smile yet."

Just then there was a knock at the door. Janet jumped off the desk and pulled her locks back to expose more of her face. Terri played it cool. She put her glasses back on and slowly walked to the door. When she opened it, Julian and Eddie were standing outside smiling from ear to ear.

"Welcome, gentlemen. Come on in," Terri said while gesturing with her hand.

Eddie barely got one foot in the door before he started laying on the old charm.

"Mm, mm, mm, Julian was right—you *are* fine. And sexy, too." Eddie looked her up and down. "All this body and a mind, too. Man, you hit the jackpot!"

"Eddie, this is Terri. Terri, this is Eddie," Julian said.

"Nice meeting you, Eddie. Julian has told me *all* about you!"

"Well, don't believe everything you hear. I'm actually a very shy person." Eddie kissed Terri's hand.

"I doubt that."

"And who is this lovely young lady?" Eddie said while staring Janet up and down.

"Oh, that's just Janet," Julian said while walking over to have a seat. "You know, the one I told you about who's always giving me a hard time."

"Forget you, Julian." She slapped him on the back of his head as he walked past her.

"Hey, don't hurt those pretty little hands on his hard head." Eddie grasped her hands and kissed them. "A real woman should never resort to violence. Let your man fight your battles."

"I would—if I had a man."

"You're single?" Eddie acted surprised. "These brothas down here in Texas must be blind, crippled, and crazy. How could they allow a fine woman like yourself to walk around unattached?"

"You know what? I've been asking myself that exact question." Janet moved in closer to Eddie as if she were in a trance. "Some men just don't know a good thing when they see it."

"You need to spend more time up north, baby. Cold weather makes for warmer hearts."

"Excuse me, Romeo and Juliet," Terri interrupted. "Do I need to pull out my hip boots, 'cause it's getting deep up in here?"

"Jealous!" Janet stuck out her tongue.

After their hormones calmed down, Eddie and Janet took a seat on the sofa. Julian sat on the love seat opposite them with Terri by his side.

"So tell me, Terri—what is it that you and Janet have in common?"

"Excuse me?"

"Well, you're obviously a mature woman, a professional, and you seem to be very—uh, conservative. Janet is more free-spirited and earthy, and she's very youthful." Eddie gave Janet a very enticing look. She was loving every minute of it. "I guess I'm curious about how two women who seem so different could be such close friends, especially with the generation gap."

"Well, *Eddie*!" Terri sounded irritated. "What you don't know about Ms. Earthy is that she's at the top of her class at TSU and about to complete her master's in psychology. So as you can see, we do have a lot in common, intellectually and professionally. And by the way, I'm not *that* old and she's not *that* young."

"Well, excuse me, *Doctor* Ross, I didn't mean to hit a nerve."

"No need to apologize, I'm perfectly secure with who I am. Besides, there are plenty of men who are perfectly comfortable dating a mature woman," Terri said confidently. "Maybe that's an indication as to how mature and secure they are."

"Touché!" Julian yelled out.

"But since we're on the subject of friendship," Terri continued, "I'm curious about a few things myself, like what it is that you and Julian have in common. Your personalities are total opposites."

"Do you want the grown-folks answer to that question or the PG-thirteen?"

"We're all adults here!"

"Okay, then." Eddie sat up on the edge of the sofa and looked Terri dead in her eyes. Julian put his head down and gritted his teeth. There was no telling how brutally honest Eddie would be.

"Well, when we met back in high school, I would have to say we shared three things in common: our interest in sports, our love of fast cars, and our appetite for chasing pussy. But as we have matured, we've more worthwhile things in common, like love of our career and family."

"I didn't know you had kids," Janet asked nervously.

"I don't, but I would love to have a family someday."

Julian let out a sigh of relief.

"Well, on that note, let's eat!" Julian walked toward the door.

Eddie and Terri were still sitting on the sofas staring at one another like two pit bulls. She didn't like him and he didn't like her, but neither of them wanted to spoil the afternoon, so they let it go.

"Hey, Janet, would you mind taking me on a tour of Houston?" Eddie said while holding her hand. "It's my first time here. I would love to see the sights."

"Sure, if it's okay with Julian."

"Please go. I mean, be my guest, he's all yours."

"Let me have the key so I can get my bags from the car," Eddie said. "You don't mind if I change at your place, do you, Janet?"

"Not at all. I have an extra bedroom—I mean, an extra bathroom."

"All right, partner—I'm outta here." He shook Julian's hand and gave him a hug. "I'll see you and Sam around seven."

"Make sure you're on time. I can't afford to get to the studio late. Before I forget, let me write down the directions."

"No need." He pulled a piece of paper from out of his pants pocket. "I got the directions off the internet. And don't worry, I'll be there on time. I wouldn't miss seeing Samantha for the world. Then he turned to Terri with a sly grin on his face. "Nice meeting you, Terri. I'm sure we'll meet again. After all, we do have *something* in common."

"What's that?"

"Julian."

Eddie and Janet walked out the door hand in hand. After they were gone, Terri lay down on the sofa and covered her face with her hands.

"What's wrong, baby?"

"I don't understand how you could be friends with such a conceited asshole."

"Eddie and I go back a long way. He's always been there for me, through thick and thin. But I'm nothing like him, I promise you."

"For our sake I hope not, because I could never deal with a man like that. He's too slick and arrogant. And worst of all, he's a liar. He had the nerve to say he wants a family someday, knowing doggone well that's the furthest thing from his mind," she said. "I will never tolerate being lied to, Julian. I couldn't handle that."

"Don't worry, baby." Julian walked over and wrapped his arms around her. "I would never do anything to disrespect you. You're my queen."

At first they kissed each other gently on the lips, then it grew into a passionate kiss. Terri spun Julian around and laid down on top of him. She angled her body so that his penis was between her legs. Then she turned his head to the side and began kissing him on the neck.

"Damn, Terri, I've never seen this side of you."

"Who you callin' Terri?" she said in a nasty whisper. "My name is Eve."

"Okay, *Eve,* are we going to grind each other to death or are we gonna take this to the next level?"

"That depends."

"On what?"

"On whether or not you can miss work tonight, because once I get my motor started there ain't no stoppin' me!"

"You know I can't do that."

"Well, I guess this will have to wait." Terri slowly got up and backed away.

"Come on, baby, don't torture me like this! Give a brotha a rain check or something."

"Tomorrow won't work for me—have a visitor comin'."

"A visitor? Who?"

"Aunt Bessie."

"You never mentioned that you had an aunt named Bessie."

"I'm talking about my period, silly. Don't you men know anything?"

"Can't you put it on hold? You know, take a pill, stand on your head, anything, just make it stop!"

"My period is as accurate as an atomic clock. It's never late."

"Maybe we can get together after work."

"Be patient, sweetheart. I promise you it'll be worth the wait. Just enjoy your weekend with Eddie. I'll do something extra special for you next week." She pushed Julian down on the sofa again. "Besides, I'm not going anywhere, not tonight, not tomorrow, not ever."

Chapter 18

"I'M GONNA KILL you, Eddie," I said angrily as I looked out the living room window. "I can't believe you pulled this shit again!"

He promised he would be here no later then seven o'clock, but it was already nine fifteen and I hadn't heard from him. He knew I was expecting him to watch Samantha while I was at work. By nine twenty I gave up and dialed the number for the baby-sitter. Juanita only lived two blocks away, but it was a Friday night and she loved to get her party on. As the phone rang I was praying she would be at home.

"Hello?"

"Hi, Juanita, this is Julian. I know this is short notice, but can you watch Samantha?"

"I thought she was staying with her uncle from Chicago tonight?"

"That *was* the plan, but he hasn't shown up and I've got to be at work in less than an hour."

"Samantha must be terribly disappointed. She's been talkin' about him all week."

"Yeah, I know, so you can just imagine how pissed off I am," I said angrily.

"You know I'm always here for you, Julian, but I do have one problem."

"What's that?"

"I've got my three-year-old grandson with me and he's already asleep, so you'll have to bring her over here."

"I don't care if I have to bring her to the Astrodome! I'm on the air in forty-five minutes and you're my only option."

"Okay, bring her over, but this is gonna cost you extra."

"Just name it."

"I want tickets to the WBMX Old-School party at the Hilton tomorrow night."

"How many tickets do you need, Juanita?"

"Just two, one for me and one for my friend."

"*Friend*? What about your husband?"

"To hell with him! He does his thing and I do mine."

"Sounds like drama to me."

"No drama, just reality. I've learned a lot about getting my needs met since I started listening to your show. I loved your topic about women needing a little maintenance."

"You should have called in for some advice." I laughed.

"How do you know I didn't? There's plenty of fifty-year-old women looking for a little tune-up." She disguised her voice the way she did that night.

"I thought I recognized your voice. And you had the nerve to use your real name."

"As the old saying goes, ain't no shame in my game. What's good for the goose is good for the gander."

"I'm not gonna touch that one," I told her. "But you've got yourself a deal on those tickets. Now let me get Samantha together so I can get to work. It's Friday night, and I can't wait to drop this new poetry."

"You know I'll be listening," Juanita said. Then we both hung up.

"Sam, hurry up and get a bag together," I yelled upstairs. "You're gonna spend the night over at Juanita's."

"I thought Uncle Eddie was staying with me tonight." She sounded disappointed. "I rented *Shrek* and *Spy Kids* especially for him. I got us some popcorn, too."

"I'm sorry, Princess, but Eddie can't make it."

She walked back to her room with her head down and her lips poked out. She had been looking forward to seeing him ever since we left Chicago. He promised her he would be here. Unlike adults, kids take promises very seriously. "Eddie, you'd better have a damn good excuse," I said while grabbing my car keys off the counter. Dissing me was one thing, but lying to my baby was grounds for a serious ass whippin'.

But I knew exactly where Eddie was. He and Janet had been gone for over four hours. That was three hours more than Eddie needed to manipulate her young mind. *He's probably got her in the sixty-nine position by now,* I was thinking. I gave her two months, tops, then he'll dump her and move on to his next victim. That's his M.O.—that's Eddie.

Chapter 19

MITCH WAS ALREADY in the control room taking calls when I arrived at the studio. I waved to get his attention as I sat down at the console.

"I thought I was gonna have to do the show without you," he said over the intercom.

"I haven't missed a show in fifteen years and I'm not about to start now."

"Well, I hope you've got a hot topic tonight because these phone lines are on fire!" Mitch said. "By the way, what *is* the topic?"

"You'll find out soon enough, but I'll give you a hint: look inside the drawer next to your monitor."

When Mitch pulled the CD out of the drawer, he had a curious look on his face.

"*Destiny's Child*? They aren't old school. Hell, they ain't even *out* of school!"

"Trust me on this one, Mitch. It's perfect!"

"How could I question the drama king? If anybody can stir up controversy, it's you," he said. "Now stand by. We're on in thirty seconds."

While I waited for Mitch to begin the countdown, I reclined in my chair and inhaled the sweet aroma of the jasmine-scented candles. The atmosphere was relaxed, peaceful, and cool.

"You know, Mitch, after fifteen years I still get chills every time I sit down in front of the mic."

"That's a good sign. It means you don't take your listeners for granted. Now put on your headphones. We're on the air in five seconds—four, three, two, one . . ."

"Good evening, and welcome to another night of *Love, Lust, and Lies*. I'm your host, Julian Payne, and for the next four hours I plan to stimulate your mind, body, and soul. Or maybe I'll just make you so angry you'll want to throw your radio out the window. Whatever your reaction, don't blame me; I'm just the messenger. And of course this is "Hot Buttered Soul Poetry Friday," so be sure to stay tuned for the end of the show. I promise you it'll be worth the wait.

"Now, let's get on with tonight's topic. It was inspired by three beautiful young ladies from your hometown of Houston. That's right, I'm talking about Destiny's Child, and the song is 'Bug-A-Boo.' " Right on cue, Mitch dropped the upbeat intro:

"You make me wanna throw my pager out the window
Tell MCI to cut my phones off. . . ."

After a few more verses we faded out of the song. Mitch began typing in comments from the callers as fast as he could. It seemed like the entire city of Houston had a story to tell about a bugaboo.

"If you haven't guessed by now, the topic tonight is people who just don't know when to let go! So, if you're being bugged by a stalker, fatal attraction, or just somebody who constantly blows up your cell phone and pager, give us a call. We may not be able to help you get rid of them, but we damn sure want to talk about it!"

The comments that were coming across my screen were outrageous. I decided to take the female callers first. Women are always more dramatic when it comes to relationships.

"Cynthia, you're on the air. What's your comment or question?"

"Julian, you must have been reading my mind when you came up with this topic because I just went to court today over a bugaboo."

"Was he a coworker, a stranger, or somebody you met at a club?"

"No, it was my baby's daddy!" she said, getting loud. "That fool was showing up at my job, following me around to nightclubs, and he even parked outside my house to see if I had company. One night he sat in my driveway from sunup to sundown. I wanted to take his ass some popcorn and tell him to enjoy the movie!"

Mitch was laughing so hard he nearly choked to death on the doughnut he was eating. I turned off my mic while Cynthia was still talking and ran in to the control room to pat him on the back.

"You okay?"

He nodded, then I rushed back to the studio. Just as she finished her story, I switched the mic back on.

"So why did you have to go to court?"

"To get a restraining order! That idiot was trying to control my life. It was getting to the point where I was looking over my shoulder everywhere I went. And what's so funny is that he was the one who walked out on me!"

"I guess some men don't realize they have a good thing until it's gone."

"Well, it's too late now. And you can let all your fine male listeners know I will be at the party tomorrow night and I am single and available!" she yelled. "What about you, Julian, do you need a good woman? 'Cause I know how to treat my man."

"I'll have to take a pass, Cynthia. I don't want your baby's daddy parked outside my studio eating popcorn." I laughed. "But thanks for callin'. Now let's go to Theresa on line two. What's your issue, Lady T.?"

"Boy, do I have a story for you!" she said with a strong southern accent. "I met this guy at Maxwell's nightclub about six months ago, right? He was cute, had good conversation, and he said he was an engineer. What I liked most about him was that he was funny—I mean, he had me crackin' up all night. He also said he had been celibate for two years, which was fine with me, 'cause I'm not the kind of woman who jumps into bed right away. Everything was—"

"I hate to cut you off, Theresa, but it's only a four-hour show. Can you get to the point?"

"Excuse me, Mr. Payne, but I thought this was a talk show and I'm talkin'. You need to be more patient with us southern belles. We're not as fast as those Chicago women, but we do get the job done," she said very charmingly.

"I do apologize. Lady T., please continue."

"As I was saying, everything was going fine for the first two months. He would call once a day, we would get together on the weekends for dinner or a movie. Never once did he pressure me about sex. Then about two months into the relationship I decided the time was right to give him some."

"Some what?"

"You know what *what* is," she whispered. "A little nookie. Julian, after that night his whole personality changed. All of a sudden he was coming by my house unannounced, e-mailing me all kinds of raunchy letters, and calling my house four or fives times a day. If we ended a phone conversation at ten o'clock at night and I said, 'I'll talk to you later,' that fool would call me back at midnight. I had to tell him that 'later' means the next day."

"Damn, Theresa, is the southern stuff that good?" I joked. "You must have really put somethin' on that brotha."

"It had been a while since my last experience, so you know I had to whip it on him. *Whoo-pish!*" She imitated the cracking of a whip.

"So, did this guy finally stop buggin' you, or did you have to get a restraining order like Cynthia?"

"There was no need for a restraining order. He's dead."

"Dead? Don't tell me you gave that poor man a heart attack."

"No, silly! One day after it had been storming outside, he climbed on top of my roof trying to get into my bedroom window. I think he was trying to surprise me by putting a rose on my pillow. Anyway, he braced himself on my DIRECTV satellite dish and it cracked. Next thing I know, I see a body falling past my window to the ground. He broke his neck and died right there in my rose bed."

"Get the hell outta here!"

"I swear to God, it's true. If you don't believe me, I'll fax you a copy of the article from the *Houston Chronicle*," she said.

"Now that's what I call drama! Thanks for callin', Theresa."

"Wait a second. I had one last question."

"What is it?"

"Why would a man with so much going for himself behave that way? I mean, he was good-looking, educated, had a great career, and the sex wasn't too bad either. He had it all! What makes a person like that just snap?"

The image of Olivia immediately popped into my head. I remembered how she cried in bed after we had sex, and the incident at the hotel when she hit me in the nose with the book, and the time she scared me half to death in the parking garage. I had nightmares for a week after that episode. And just like Theresa, I would ask myself the same question. *Why would a woman with so much going for herself behave that way?*

I must have been reflecting on Olivia too hard, because I lost track of the conversation.

"Hello, Julian, are you still there?" Theresa asked.

"Yeah, I'm here."

"So, can you answer my question or not?"

"I guess some people are just emotionally unstable. They appear to be normal on the outside, but they can snap at any time. It's not even about you, it's about timing. Remember Glenn Close in *Fatal Attraction*? Sometimes you can't tell if a person is crazy until it's too late."

"You can say that again. Thanks for your insight, Julian. And by the way, I love your show!"

"Thanks for listening, Theresa," I said to her. "We'll be right back with more drama, so don't touch that dial!"

After Mitch programmed the commercial into the computer, he came running into the studio all charged up.

"Man, if we keep this up, we'll be number one in our time slot by the end of the year!"

I just sat there quiet, staring out the window. I was still thinking about Olivia. I had chosen that topic to deal with my own demons. All I ended up doing was bringing back old memories—bad memories.

"Julian, did you hear what I said?"

"Yeah, number one."

The rest of the night we took several calls on the subject of bugaboos. It never dawned on me how many people were dealing with stalkers and fatal attractions. One woman called from her hospital bed. She had been stabbed in the neck by a coworker who had become obsessed with her. She never showed him any interest, according to her. But that didn't stop him from carrying a butcher knife to work and ramming it into her throat. If this much crazy shit is happening in Houston, I could only imagine what was going on in the rest of the country.

———

The clock on my console read 1:55 A.M. when we went into the last commercial break. I pulled out my spiral notebook and prepared to recite my poetry to close the show. I took a sip of water and cleared my throat. Mitch gave me the one-minute cue and I sat up straight in my chair hoping to cap off the show with something deep. Before I switched on my mic, the light flashed on the hotline. It was a private number for the station managers and special guests. I picked it up, hoping it wasn't Mr. Harris, the general manager, calling to complain about the explicit language on the show.

"Hello?"

"Hey, Julian, it's me, Terri."

"Hey, baby, how you doin'?" I said, feeling relieved. "What are you doin' up at two o'clock in the morning?"

"I couldn't sleep so I tuned in to your show. You had a great topic tonight! And let me tell you, I don't miss out on my beauty sleep for nobody."

"I told you I was the exception to the rule, didn't I?"

"I guess you did."

"Hey, I've got an idea. You wanna go on the air and make a comment about the topic? You know, give us a little expert advice."

"I don't know, Julian; it's late and I'm not in the mood to be technical."

"Come on, it'll be fun."

Before she could chicken out, I connected her call and put her on the air.

"We have one last caller," I said, trying to play it off. "Would you like to give your name, miss?"

"My name is Eve," Terri said seductively.

"What's your comment or question, Eve?"

"Actually I called to find out if you know the difference between an obsessed woman and one who is just—aggressive?"

"I don't understand your point."

"My point is, some women just know what they want. It has nothing to do with being crazy. It's more of a hunger, a craving!"

I swallowed hard. There was a moment of dead air, then she came at me again, sounding even more enticing. I could hardly recognize her voice.

"If you don't know what I mean, I wrote a poem that could probably express it better. Would you like to hear it?"

"You wrote a poem? Now, you *know* I've got to hear this." I was surprised and intrigued. "Go ahead—Eve!"

"I call it 'Fatally Yours,' and it goes like this:

> *It's in your voice—and obvious in your eyes*
> *not even you can pretend*
> *You sense I'll do everything you dream up*
> *including things you can't even imagine*
>
> *It's the initial attraction*
> *That produces a sexual reaction*
> *That stimulates and doesn't hesitate*
> *To guarantee total satisfaction*
> *An insatiable desire—an intangible lust*
>
> *If you touch me—you'll feel me*
> *If you taste me—I'll melt sweetly*
> *And if you penetrate me—I'll fall deeply*
> *fatally—you got me*
> *lover, friend, and everything imaginable—sexually*
>
> *Trembling at thoughts of what I might do*
> *But why continue to wonder*
> *When you can find out for yourself*
> *just how far I will go—for you*
>
> *The thought of you causes my body to applaud you*
> *with a sensual ovation—make no mistake*
> *this is a personal invitation*
>
> *I hope you accept—taking immediate action*
> *Because what I'm feeling can only be described as*
> *a fatal—sexual attraction.*

When she was done, I applauded.

"Now, that was deep!" I said. "Where did all of that passion come from?"

"My soul!" she replied in an erotic tone. "And there's plenty more where that came from."

"So, have you shared these deep feelings with your man?"

"I tried to, but he's too busy working and hanging out with his friend to pay me any attention."

"Why don't you call him up right now? He might surprise you," I said to her. "And who knows, his friend might be out of the picture and he may even have a baby-sitter for his daughter."

"How did you know he had a daughter?"

"Just call me Miss Cleo."

We both laughed.

"I don't know, Julian. I'm a lot of woman. He might be too tired to pull a double shift."

"Trust me on this one, Eve. He'll have more than enough energy."

"So you think I should just go over there right now dressed as I am?"

"What do you have on?"

"A silk nightie."

"Why not? Judging by the message in your poem, you won't have it on long."

"I'm gonna take your advice, Julian. After all, you only live once, right?"

"That's right—Eve."

Terri was playing her role to a T. Mitch didn't catch on until the end. I guess my expression gave it away. He smiled and gave me a thumbs-up, then he raised his finger, indicating we had only one minute left. I tried to think of a provocative way to end the show, but Eve beat me to it.

"Can I say something to my man just in case he's listening?"

"Please do."

"Baby, I'm on my way over to see you. I hope you don't mind being spontaneous." Her tone was smooth and sensual. "Now, you know it's been a long time, so please be patient and go slow, just like in the song 'Tonight Is the Night' by Betty Wright. Remember the lyrics, baby?

"You said you'd be gentle with me
and I—hope you will."

My dick was so hard I could've pole-vaulted down to my car from the twenty-fifth floor. I dispensed with the formalities and got off the air as fast as I could.

"Thanks for listening, everybody. We'll be back with more drama next week. Bye!"

I snatched my car keys off the desk and made a dash for the door. Just as I was grabbing for the knob, I brushed up against the lopsided cart rack and knocked it over. Dozens of tapes fell onto the floor.

"So, you just gonna run off without helping me clean up this mess, huh?" Mitch yelled as I rushed down the hall. "She's probably not even gonna show up!"

"Terri might chicken out, but Eve will definitely show up," I yelled back. "Besides, I told you to get that raggedy thing fixed three weeks ago!"

Chapter 20

I SPED DOWN I-59 at one hundred miles an hour. The highway was empty, as if hastening me to my destination. In the distance I could see bolts of lightning flashing across the sky as a thunderstorm moved up from Galveston. I prayed that it would storm all night, or at least long enough for me to lay down with Terri.

When I arrived at the house I took a quick shower and put fresh linens on the bed. Then I lit twenty tall lavender-scented candles and made a path up the staircase leading to the bedroom. Once the atmosphere was right, I put Maxwell's *Embrya* CD in the stereo and opened a bottle of cabernet. My parents gave it to me on my thirty-fifth birthday. They made me promise to save it for a special occasion. It felt good knowing that I had kept my promise.

Just as I removed the cork, the doorbell rang. I filled the glasses as fast as I could, then rushed to answer the door. When I opened it, Terri was standing there in a pair of thick flannel pajamas and fluffy white house slippers.

"What happened to the nightie? I thought this was supposed to be a romantic evening, not a slumber party."

"Do you want me to go back home?"

"Of course not, come on in," I said, trying to hide my disappointment.

When she walked into the living room, she noticed the trail of candles leading up the stairs to the bedroom.

"You must have really thought you were getting some tonight, huh?"

I was too pissed off to respond. All I could think about was all the trouble I had gone through. I had raced my horny ass home, put my best linens on the bed, opened up a special bottle of wine, and lit all those damned candles. My house looked like a Catholic church. And she had the nerve to be crackin' jokes. While she listened to Maxwell, I excused myself and went back into the kitchen to pour the wine back into the bottle. I wasn't about to waste my special bottle of Clos du Bois on flannel pajamas and fluffy house shoes.

"So, Julian, do you have any movies we can watch?" she yelled from the living room.

"No!" I yelled back. I tried not to sound irritated.

"Do you have any checkers?"

"No!"

"What about Nintendo?"

"No, I don't have Nintendo, either!" I was so frustrated I spilled half the wine trying to pour it back into the bottle.

"Dag, you don't have anything to play with!"

"I've got something for you to play with, all right," I said under my breath while grabbing my crotch.

I was so frustrated, I didn't notice that Terri had crept into the kitchen. When I reached over for the dish towel to wipe up the spill, I got the surprise of my life. Terri was sitting on the counter wearing a black lace teddy.

"I guess we'll just have to play with each other," Terri said in a nasty tone. "Sorry for making you wait, baby, but I wanted to surprise you."

"Mission accomplished."

She led me into the living room then advanced Maxwell's CD to track ten, "Eachhoureachsecondeachminuteeachday: Of My Life." The room was empty except for the stereo and the piano. The thumping bass echoed off the bare walls like in a concert hall. When the prelude started to play, she turned her back and began to dance. I took a seat on the piano bench, anxious to see how far she would go. The candlelight cast a silhouette of her voluptuous body against the wall. When the tempo increased, so did her intensity. She straddled the newel post and stroked it as if she was having sex, then she slowly peeled off her teddy and threw it in my face. Her aureola were the size of silver dollars and the nipples were erect. When she moved in closer, I tried to suck on them but she teased me by moving out of my reach. But the move that impressed me most was when she did a split, then rolled over while slipping her panties off at the same time. I thought I was going to explode. "Do me till I'm done," I sang along with the lyrics.

When the song ended, I lifted her and carried her up the stairs toward the bedroom.

"Right here, Julian," she said.

"What do you mean, right here?"

"I want to do it right here—on the stairs."

"But baby, the bed is more comfor—"

"*Ssshh.*" She put her finger up to my lips. "I want to do it right here, right now!"

I gently sat her down on the top stair, then pushed her backward until she was lying down. I caressed the inside of her thighs with my right hand while massaging her breasts with the other. Her body was perfect in every dimension. Her breasts were just over a handful and her abs were tight.

When I felt that she was relaxed, I spread her lips apart with my fingers and stroked her clit with my tongue. Her insides had a clean, sweet taste that made me want more.

"Ahh," she moaned.

"Is that too rough?"

"No, baby, do it again, deeper this time."

I palmed her ass with both hands and lifted her pelvis up to my face, then I shoved her pussy into my mouth.

"What are you tryin' to do to me?" she said, almost out of breath.

"I'm letting you know where home is."

"Mission accomplished!"

After she climaxed we changed places and she returned the favor. She was a little rusty at first, but after a few strokes she had a nice rhythm. She was enjoying it so much, I wasn't sure if she was doing it for my pleasure or hers. Just as I was about to come, she abruptly stopped.

"Come on!" She grabbed me by the hand and led me down the stairs toward the door.

"Where are you taking me?"

"Outside! I've always wanted to do it in the rain."

"Damn, Terri, you really are a freak!"

"Who you callin' Terri? My name is Eve," she said with a sexy smile. Then she flung open the door and ran into the back-yard.

I wasn't about to be outdone in my own house, so I ran after her, dick swangin' and all. For the next two hours we made love in the pouring rain. Lightning was flashing all around us, but we didn't care. We made love in the pool, on the deck, and in the grass. It was the most incredible sexual experience I've ever had.

By the time we finally made it upstairs, we were exhausted. We took a hot shower together, then collapsed onto the bed. I turned my back and she spooned me from behind. It felt good. Just as I was about to fall asleep, she tapped me on the shoulder.

"What is it, baby?"

"I just want to know if you're going to get scared and run away."

"Why would I do that?"

"Because that's what most men do when they get too close."

"I keep telling you, Terri, I'm not like most men." I turned around and looked her straight in the eyes. "I'm different."

"I want to believe that, Julian, I really do! But men have a way of backing away when they start getting too close. I need a man who's strong enough to be vulnerable."

"You keep forgetting, I know what it means to love," I said, then kissed her gently on the forehead. "Now, stop worrying and go to sleep. I'm not going anywhere—not tonight, not tomorrow, not ever."

Chapter 21

WHEN I WOKE up the next morning Terri was on the other side of the bed snoring up a storm. I slipped out of the tangled sheets and went downstairs to cook breakfast. I didn't bother to put on anything except my drawers. It was the first time in months I had been able to walk around so comfortable on a Saturday morning, and I wanted to take full advantage of the opportunity.

The menu for breakfast was Eggos, turkey bacon, and boiled eggs. I decided to show off my cooking skills by making some of my world-famous hash browns with basil and fried onions. Just as I was pouring the cranapple juice, Terri came dragging down the stairs. Her hair was all over her head and she wasn't wearing any makeup, but she still looked gorgeous. Not too many women can pull that off.

"Morning," she said, with sleep still in her eyes. "I hope you don't mind me borrowing your shirt. Those flannel pajamas were too hot to put on."

She was wearing my old blue jean shirt, the one Carmen used to wear around the house.

"Not at all, baby. In fact, you look kinda cute in it." I gave her a hug and kiss. "Now, I hope you brought your appetite, because I made the bomb breakfast!"

I escorted her over to the dining room table and placed a napkin on her lap.

"Looks like you're feeding an army."

"Well, I figured after that monster workout last night you might need some extra nutrition," I said. "This lovin' is so strong it'll knock the calcium and potassium right out of a sistah's bones."

"Stop strokin' yourself, Julian. You weren't all that great."

"Oh, no? Then what was all this screaming and tremblin' all about?" I imitated her shaking and carrying on. "You were bouncin' around and speaking in tongues like in *The Exorcist*."

"I was just fakin' it."

"Faking it, huh?" I moved in closer to her and slid my hand between her legs. "Well, let's see if you can fake it like that again."

I spread her legs apart and slid underneath the table. I was getting ready to go down on her when I heard someone clearing her throat. I was so startled that I bumped my head on the table.

"Excuse me, Mr. Payne."

It was Juanita. Samantha was standing right beside her, watching us. I stood up as fast as I could and tried to play it off.

"What are you doin' here?"

"I live here, remember?" Samantha said. "Who is that lady, and why is she wearing Mommy's shirt?"

"I think I better be going," Juanita said. Then she rushed out.

"Samantha, go upstairs and I'll be up to talk to you in a minute."

"I'm not going anywhere until she takes off Mommy's shirt!"

"Julian, let me go take it off if it will calm her down." Terri stood up from the table.

"Terri, sit down and eat your breakfast. I'll handle this," I said. "Now, for the last time, Sam, go upstairs to your room, like I told you."

"I hate you, I hate both of you!" Samantha stormed upstairs and slammed her door shut.

"I think I better be leaving."

"You don't have to do that, Terri."

"Julian, you told me your daughter hasn't seen you with any women since her mother died. Given what just happened, I think it's fair to say she's traumatized."

"You're right. I'll go upstairs and talk to her," I said. "Thanks for the advice, Doc."

"Don't mention it. Now, that'll be one hundred dollars and I do accept Blue Cross Blue Shield."

"Very funny."

While Terri gathered her things, I ran upstairs to get her a pair of gym shorts and a T-shirt to wear home. On the way out the door she gave me a passionate kiss.

"And there's more where that came from," she said. "Call me later. Bye."

"Wait a second! I almost forgot! Are you coming out to the WBMX party at the Hilton tonight?"

"I'm sorry, baby, I'm not going to be able to make it. I've got tons of cases to review. And besides, those radio station events are too wild for me. The music is too loud, the men are disrespectful, and there are entirely too many half-naked hoochies."

Right on cue, Eddie comes strolling in the door.

"Did somebody say 'hoochies'?"

"Now I *know* it's time for me to go. Good-bye, sweetheart. And good day to you—Eddie."

Once Terri was out the door, I let Eddie have it!

"What the hell happened to you last night? You know I was counting on you to watch Sam."

"My fault, dog," Eddie said casually. "I got caught up."

"You mean *laid* up."

"I'm sorry, Julian, but Janet wouldn't let me go. After I gave her some of this Chicago-style lovin', she was sprung." He laughed. "I freaked that young girl in so many ways she thought she was in *The Matrix*."

"I don't wanna hear that shit, man! You could have at least called so I could've made other arrangements!"

Eddie noticed the wineglasses on the counter and the trail of candles up the staircase.

"Looks like everything worked out just fine for you," he said while picking up one of the candles. "I guess I'm not the only one who got his freak on last night."

I wanted to kick his ass for not taking me seriously, but I had more important things on my mind, like what I was going to say to Samantha. It was going to be hard to explain why I was on my knees with my head between a strange woman's legs under the table in our kitchen.

Chapter 22

IT WAS STILL raining when Eddie and I arrived at the Hilton. I parked in the area reserved for the radio station employees, then opened my flask of Hennessy. I took a long sip and passed it to Eddie.

"Just like old times, huh, partner?" Eddie said. "Remember when we use to drink Old E and get drunk on the baseball bleachers in Gately Park?"

"I remember all right—the first time you tried to hang with the older boys you got sick as a dog and threw up all over Timothy Redd's brand-new Members Only jacket. You were praying to God to let you live through it." I imitated his whining: "Just let me get through this one, Lord, and I promise I'll never drink again."

"Well, at least Bernard Miller didn't signify on my mama all the way out to Markham skating rink. I'll never forget that joke he told on the bus about your mama's house being so cold that the roaches had to huddle around the toaster to stay warm."

We laughed and slapped five. Those bus rides out to Markham were showcases for neighborhood comedians. It was our version of *Showtime at the Apollo*.

"But what about the time when you showed up at summer camp with those cheap P.F. Flyer gym shoes?" I said. "Everybody followed you around all day singing, 'Don't buy the shoes with the slip and slide, get the shoes with the stars on the side!'"

"How could I forget that torture? I felt so bad I told my mama I wasn't leaving the house until she bought me a pair of Converse All Stars."

"Yeah, those were the good old days." I took another sip and reflected. "We've come a long way since then."

"Yes, we have; especially you." Eddie sounded serious. "Just look at you, a big-time radio personality! You've got a nice crib, a beautiful little girl, and a great career. Damn, Julian, you made it! And just in case I haven't told you lately, I'm proud of you, man."

"Thanks, partner. That means a lot coming from you." We gave each other dap. He might piss me off every now and then, but I loved him like a brother.

"Okay, that's enough of that sentimental stuff," he said. "I don't want to get all misty before I go mack down these southern girls."

"Judging by the caliber of women I've seen going in, there won't be much mackin' going on. It'll be more like herding cattle."

I left the windshield wipers on so I could get a good look at who, or what, was going into the hotel. Most of the ladies were dressed very classy, formal black dresses and pantsuits. But then there were the ghetto queens all decked out in gaudy jewelry with tinted burgundy hair. One woman who was grossly overweight had on a crop top exposing her flabby gut *and* she had the nerve to have a pierced belly button.

"Ain't no shame in her game." Eddie laughed as he took one last sip of Hennessy.

"Terri was right, the hoochies are out tonight." I turned off the ignition. "Come on, let's get this over with."

The minute we entered the ballroom women bum rushed me. Eddie quickly stepped aside to avoid getting trampled.

"Julian, I love your show. Can I have your autograph?" a woman shouted.

"Remember me?" another woman yelled out. "I'm the woman who called in yesterday about the man who fell off the roof and broke his neck."

Several security guards had to come to my rescue and pull them away. I wanted to feel flattered, but instead I felt violated. I had never experienced women grabbing at me like that before. I wanted to be successful and famous, but I didn't know it would be like this. The show had only been on the air for three weeks, and this was the result.

Once I was safely in the VIP section, Mitch came over to make fun of me.

"So, how does it feel to be famous?"

"Damn, Mitch, this is insane! These woman are out of control!"

"That's the price you pay for celebrity. Did you think it was gonna be all fun and games?"

"Hey, man, I'm just a radio personality, not Jesus."

"Do you think that's why WBMX is paying you six figures, to be a radio personality? Think again. You are paid to give advice and entertain," Mitch said. "You may not realize it now, Julian, but these women have come to depend on you, especially the ones who don't have a strong man in their life. When they're alone at night, your voice is their comfort. You are the one who assures them that everything is gonna be all right. And believe me when I tell you, my friend, that's power!"

"And responsibility!" I said as I looked around at all the eyes watching me.

"This is only the beginning, Julian; you'd better adjust yourself to that fact. If I were you, I would get a gun and move into a gated community."

"What about you? You're on the show, too. Why aren't they attacking you?"

"Hey, I'm just a peon! The only reason these women give me the time of day is so they can get to you." Mitch laughed. "But I'm secure enough with who I am to handle that. I'm too old to be chasing around all this young pussy anyway!"

We both laughed. Just then an attractive waitress came over to take our orders. She was wearing a skimpy black miniskirt, a sheer top, and high heels.

"Excuse me, gentlemen. Can I get you something to drink?"

"You're right on time, young lady," Mitch said, trying not to look at her breasts. "I'll have a shot of Seagram's and Seven. And give my friend here a double shot of tequila. And don't forget to bring the salt and lime." Then he sent her on her way.

"What are you tryin' to do, kill me?"

"No, just tryin' to get you to relax and enjoy yourself. This is our night to enjoy the fruits of our labor."

"Okay, I'm with you, Mr. Producer! You set 'um up and I'll put 'um down." I slapped a fifty-dollar bill on the table. "Besides, I have a designated driver."

"Who?"

"Eddie. He flew in from Chicago yesterday."

"You mean Fast Eddie?" Mitch said. "In that case, you'd better get ready for a long night. If I know Eddie, he'll be on the dance floor until the party is over!"

By two o'clock I had put away a glass of white zinfandel, a shot of Grey Goose, and two Coronas. I was drunk as hell and ready to go. Mitch bravely ventured out into the ocean of bouncing bodies to find Eddie. Ten minutes later, he came stumbling back to the VIP section all sweaty and out of breath.

"There must be at least a thousand funky negroes out there,"

Mitch said. "It's dark, the music is loud, and I'm so damn drunk I'm seeing double. There's no way in hell I'm gonna find Eddie out there."

"Okay, that's it!" I said. "I'm outta here!"

I was looking around for the waitress so I could pay my tab when I noticed Eddie making his way toward me. He was dragging some woman by the arm, but I was so drunk I couldn't make out who she was. When he tried to step through the ropes into the VIP section, the huge bouncer stopped him dead in his tracks.

"Hold it right there!" He pushed Eddie in the chest. "This is for VIPs only; do you have a pass?"

"I don't need a pass, I'm with him." He pointed at me.

"It's okay, brotha, he's cool."

"That's right, I'm cool—you big ox," Eddie said under his breath.

When he got closer I saw whose hand he was holding. It was Janet.

"Hey, Julian!"

I was so upset, I ignored her.

"Man, where have you been all night?"

"Getting my groove on with Janet! We did the electric slide, the bump, and danced down the Soul Train line—twice. This party is off the chain!" Then he noticed Mitch sitting across from me. "Whassup, Mitch? I saw you out there on the dance floor a minute ago trying to do the Cabbage Patch. You move pretty good for an old guy."

"So that's why you were all sweaty and out of breath! You were out there getting your groove on!" I yelled at Mitch.

"I'm sorry, Julian. I *was* on my way to find Eddie, but this tender young thang pulled me onto the dance floor. What was I supposed to do?"

"Both of you guys can go to hell! I'm goin' home. Are you comin', Eddie?"

"I'm stayin', partner. The night is still young. Janet can

drop me off at the airport in the morning," he said while looking at his watch.

"That's fine with me." I stood up and pulled out my wallet. "Now, where is that waitress so I can pay my tab?"

Eddie turned to go back out onto the dance floor, then he suddenly turned and came back over to where I was standing.

"By the way, I ran into a friend of yours at the bar," he whispered, then he handed me a business card. "She says hello. Have a good night," he laughed, then he rushed off to get back to the party.

The light was too dim for me to make out the print on the card, so I grabbed a candle off a nearby table. It read OLIVIA R. BROWN—COMPOSER/SONGWRITER. Before I could react, the security guard called out my name.

"Excuse me, Mr. Payne; is she cool, too?"

I lifted my head up and there she was, looking as fine as ever. She had on a red satin tube dress and matching high heels. Her large, round breasts nearly protruded out of the strapless top. Her long hair was full of body; even in the heat and humidity of the club, it was laid. Then there were those mesmerizing hazel eyes. They glared out at me through the smoke-filled air. I tried my best to appear unimpressed.

"Yeah, she's cool," I told the bouncer, "let her through."

Mitch immediately sprang up from his chair to greet her. I was uncomfortable about seeing her here, but there was no reason not to be cordial.

"Mitchell Davis, this is Ms. Olivia Brown."

"The pleasure is all mine, Ms. Brown." He kissed her on the hand.

"Please, call me Olivia."

"Well, Olivia, if you don't mind me saying, you look absolutely stunning this evening. Will you be joining us for drinks?"

"I would love to, but I have a gentleman waiting for me at the bar and I don't want to be rude. But thank you for the offer."

When Mitch noticed I wasn't saying much, he got the hint.

"I guess I'll leave you two alone to talk. It was a pleasure meeting you again, Olivia." He kissed her hand, and gave her one of his business cards. "I hope I'll be seeing more of you. Maybe Julian will invite you by the studio." He saw my expression of annoyance. "Well, good night."

Once he was gone, Olivia sat down and crossed her legs. It was too late and I was too drunk for small talk, so I got straight to the point.

"Don't tell me, you just happened to be in Houston on business again."

"You're being awfully cynical, don't you think?"

"I'm just trying to cut through the bullshit. Why are you here, Olivia?"

"For your information, I came down to help my girfriend move." She put her hand on her hip. "Now, I'll admit, I heard the announcement on the radio station that you would be here, but this is where my friend wanted to go, so I came along. I wasn't even going to approach you until I ran into Eddie." She sounded convincing. "Besides, I have a date."

The fact that she was with someone made me feel less threatened. *Maybe she will start stalking* him *and leave me the hell alone,* I was thinking. Just then the waitress came back. I paid for my drinks and grabbed my car keys off the table.

"Well, it's time for me to go. It was nice seeing you again, Olivia." I stood up and extended my hand. "Take care."

"You do the same, Julian."

I didn't bother asking for an escort to my car. I thought that the crowd would be too busy partying to pay me any attention. I thought wrong. The second I walked out of the VIP section I was mobbed. Women were grabbing at my clothes and kissing me on the face and arms. One woman even palmed my butt and yelled, "Gotcha!" The bouncers immediately stepped in and made a path.

It took me five minutes to get from the VIP section to the ballroom entrance. While we were passing through the lobby, I saw my baby-sitter, Juanita, holding hands with her "friend." They were heading out the side exit. The crowd was too thick for me to reach her. I wanted to thank her for having her sister watch Samantha.

By the time we made it outside, it was pouring down rain. One of the bouncers politely removed his jacket and used it as an umbrella. When the automatic doors opened, we made a mad dash across the lot. Once I was inside my car, I tipped him a twenty to show my appreciation.

"What a night," I said as I turned on the ignition. While I waited for my windows to defog, I turned on my Olu CD to chill out. Suddenly I heard *tap, tap, tap!* Someone was knocking on my passenger-side window. It was still fogged up, so I couldn't see who it was. I let the window down slightly just in case it was some whacked-out fan.

"Julian, it's me, Olivia. Can I get in, please?"

"Olivia? What are you doing out here in the rain? Go home!"

"I can't!" she said sounding distressed. "My girlfriend left me here without a ride."

Reluctantly, I unlocked the door and let her in. She was drenched.

"I'm sorry to inconvenience you, but I didn't know anyone else I could trust."

"What happened to your date?"

"Oh, him? He wasn't really my date, he was just some guy my girlfriend tried to hook me up with. Once he started talking about oral sex, I had to excuse myself."

"Why didn't you call a taxi?"

"Dressed like this? I don't think so."

I understood her point. She was dressed too provocatively to ride alone in the middle of the night with some perverted foreigner. Even though she was a pain in the ass, I never would have forgiven myself if something happened to her.

"Okay, Olivia, I'll give you a lift. But I'm telling you right now, we're not having sex," I told her. "Now give me the directions so I can drop you off and take my drunk ass home."

Chapter 23

THE DRIVE TO Olivia's friend's house took forty-five minutes. It should have only taken a half hour, but Olivia couldn't remember which exit to get off, or at least that's what she claimed. She tried to bring up what happened between us in Chicago, but I ignored her and focused on where I was going. I was so intoxicated that the lines on the road began to blur. It didn't help that my bladder was about to explode from all the alcohol I drank.

When we pulled into the circular driveway, I quickly unlocked the doors to let her out.

"Have a good night, Olivia. Bye!"

"Thanks for the ride." She leaned over and kissed me on the cheek. "You're a lifesaver."

"You're welcome. Now good night."

"You sure you don't want to come in for a nightcap, you know, for old times' sake?"

"I don't think that's a good idea," I said while squeezing my legs together to keep from peeing on myself.

"Are you all right? You seem a little tense."

"I'm fine, I just want to get going. I've got a long drive home."

"Julian, stop acting silly and come inside and use the bathroom. I'm not going to bite you." She got out of the car and ran toward the front door. "Come on!"

I knew it was a bad idea, but I had to go. There were no gas stations in sight and I didn't want to get shot while peeing in somebody's bushes, so I turned off the ignition and rushed out into the rain behind her.

The one-story ranch house was very quaint. The lawn, which was about a quarter acre, was well manicured with rose beds lining both sides of the walkway. The entrance had double glass doors and expensive marble tile, which appeared to be brand-new. There were moving boxes everywhere. I stumbled over one as I walked into the foyer.

"So where's the bathroom?"

"Down that hall." She pointed. "First door to your right."

I walked as fast as I could without running. When I finally made it to the toilet, I let it rip. Usually when a man hasn't been inside a woman's house before he'll try to pee on the side of the toilet to avoid making a loud splashing sound, but I didn't care if it sounded like Niagara Falls. My bladder was so full I peed for two minutes straight. *"Ah,"* I moaned. "That's better than sex."

When I came out of the bathroom, Olivia was in the kitchen drying her hair with a towel. There was a pot of water boiling on the stove and two cups and saucers sitting on the counter.

"I thought you might like a cup of tea to help you sober up."

"No thanks, Olivia, I've gotta go." I was walking toward the door. "I appreciate the use of the bathroom. Take care." Then I rushed out.

The rain was coming down even harder by the time I got back to the car. I was worried about the power going out at home, so I pulled out my cell phone to call Samantha.

"All circuits are busy; please try your call again later," the recording said.

I tried to call a second and third time but got the same message. As I was about to drive off, I noticed that the car was leaning on the front driver's side. I figured it was the alcohol playing tricks on me, but as I drove faster the car pulled sharply to the left.

"What the—" I stopped at the end of the driveway and stepped out to see what was wrong. When I kneeled down to inspect the front driver's side tire, I saw it was flat.

"That's just what I need, a flat tire at three o'clock in the morning in the middle of a fuckin' hurricane! Why me, Lord?" I shouted into the sky.

I popped the trunk and pulled out the jack and spare tire. The lug wrench was small and hard to hold onto. When I tried to loosen the bolts on the tire, my hand slipped off and smashed against the ground.

"Goddamnit!"

I tried again, then again, but each time it slipped off. I conceded defeat and got back in the car to call Hertz's roadside assistance. This time my cell phone read: LOOKING FOR SERVICE.

I dreaded the thought of going back inside the house to deal with Olivia, but I had no choice. I locked the car doors and rushed up the driveway soaking wet. Olivia must have been watching from the window, because the door swung open before I could ring the bell.

"What's the matter?"

"I've got a flat. I need to use your phone."

"It's right there on the end table."

I dialed the number, hoping someone would pick up. When they finally did, I felt relieved.

"Hello, Hertz? I have a flat tire and I need assistance."

"What's your contract number?"

After I gave her my number she put me on hold while she checked to see if there were any tow trucks available.

"Sorry, sir, we're swamped with calls tonight due to the bad weather. We can get a truck out to you first thing in the morning."

"I really need to get home tonight, miss. I'm willing to tip generously."

"We don't work like that, sir. But as I said, if you give me the directions to where your vehicle is located, we'll come by first thing in the morning and take care of it."

"Olivia, what's the address here?"

"Two forty-four Jefferson Parkway."

I repeated the address to the operator along with the other details they needed to get my service set up for the morning. After I hung up the phone, I leaned back on the sofa and put my hands over my face. I was so tired and drunk that the room felt like it was spinning. Olivia came over with a towel and a cup of hot tea.

"Here, drink this. It'll make you feel better." While I sipped the tea, she took off my blazer and began drying me with the towel. When I closed my eyes and started to relax, she lifted my feet and tried to take off my shoes.

"Hold on, slick!" I grabbed her hand. "I'm not *that* drunk!"

"I'm just trying to make you comfortable. You *are* staying the night, aren't you?"

"Yeah, but that doesn't mean I want to get naked. All I need is a blanket and pillow, and I'll be fine."

"You're too tall to sleep on this small sofa."

"I'll sleep on the floor, then."

"Don't be silly; you can sleep in the guest room."

"And where are you going to sleep?"

"In my girlfriend's bed. She'll probably spend the night at her boyfriend's house."

"All right, lead the way. I'm too damned tired to argue."

All I remembered from that point on was the softness of the mattress underneath me and the lights going out.

"Sleep well, my sweet Julian," I heard Olivia whisper. Then she kissed me on the cheek. "I've got a big surprise for you in the morning."

Chapter 24

EARLY THE NEXT morning I was awakened by a loud horn. When my vision cleared I glanced around the room, not knowing where I was. Then it hit me. "Olivia," I said with disgust. I staggered over to the window and saw a muddied tow truck parked in the driveway. The driver was an elderly white man wearing a cowboy hat. He was already at work changing the tire. "Better late than never!"

I didn't want to be in Olivia's presence any longer than I had to. I hurried into the bathroom and began washing underneath my arms. That's when I realized my shirt was gone, along with my pants, shoes, blazer, car keys, and cell phone. Then I noticed a bruise on the right side of my neck. I thought it was some kind of rash, but when I turned on the lights I realized it was a hickey.

"I don't believe this shit," I said while rubbing it. "Now I know she's crazy!"

I tiptoed down the long narrow hallway in my boxers, hoping to find my clothes and get out before Olivia woke up. The floor was covered with moving boxes and wrapping paper, and I saw a piano covered with a drop cloth. I figured Olivia's girlfriend must have moved in recently, because hardly anything was unpacked.

I continued down the hallway until I came to the master bedroom. The door was slightly open. I peeked inside to make sure Olivia was still asleep. To my surprise she wasn't there, but I did spot my cell phone on her nightstand. I quickly grabbed it and headed for the front door.

Just when I thought I was home free, I heard what sounded like a woman singing. It was coming from the room adjacent to the foyer. I crept up and peered inside to see who it was. It was Olivia. She was sitting naked on a stool with her back to the door. I noticed her hand moving in a stroking motion. As I leaned in further, I saw that she was painting on a canvas. From what I could see, it was a picture of a little girl holding hands with her mother. It was very detailed—down to the yellow barrettes in the girl's hair.

As I glanced around the room, I realized that it had been converted to an art gallery. Colorful paintings covered the walls from top to bottom. There were abstracts, portraits, and even a couple of expensive-looking sculptures. As I continued to admire the paintings they took on a more disturbing tone, especially the ones in the corner. There was a painting of a man's tongue with a bullet hole in it. There was another with a penis being nailed to a crucifix. The testicles, which had fallen to the ground, were being eaten by jackals. Right next to it was a bloody painting of a man hanging upside down with his heart being ripped from his chest and tossed into hell.

Suddenly my cell phone started to vibrate. Olivia stopped singing and turned around. I jerked my head back and prayed that she hadn't heard me. "Julian, is that you?"

I waited for a few seconds to see if she would come out, but she didn't. When she began singing again, I looked around the corner to see if her back was still turned. When I saw that it was, I crawled on my knees until I was past the door. Once I was clear, I quietly walked toward the door. I was about to go outside with nothing on except my drawers when I spotted my clothes on the kitchen counter. I rushed over and started getting dressed as fast as I could. While I was slipping on my shoes, I lost my balance and grabbed the kitchen counter to break my fall, accidentally knocking over a stack of mail. Olivia was still singing, so I was sure she didn't hear me.

The first two letters I picked up were an electric bill and a bright yellow envelope with a clover symbol on it. When I looked closely at the name on the electric bill I was horrified. The type in the address window read:

Olivia R. Brown
244 Jefferson Parkway
Houston, Texas 77000

"Oh my God, this is *her* house!" I quickly slipped on my shoes and headed for the door. Just as I grabbed the knob, Olivia walked out of the room.

"You're not leaving without saying good-bye, are you?"

She was naked and holding a palette and brush. A few drops of red paint fell off the brush and onto the carpet.

"I was just goin' outside to see what's happening with my car."

"Stop worrying about that stupid car and sit down. I've got something to show you!" She ran past me into the kitchen and pulled something out of the top cabinet. "Remember that surprise I told you about last night? Well, here it is!"

She stuffed a small jewelry box into my pants pocket. "Promise me you won't open it until you get home."

"What's the special occasion?"

"It's our four-week anniversary, silly!"

"Olivia, I can't accept this."

"Julian, I don't take rejection well." She grabbed my hand before I could take the box out my pocket. "Please take it. I insist!"

There was a large box cutter on the table next to her, and I didn't want her to get any crazy ideas. I figured the fastest and safest way to get out of there was to go along with her little presentation.

"Fine, Olivia." I pushed it back into my pants. "Now I've got to get going."

"Why do you have to leave all of a sudden? Can we at least go out for breakfast?"

"The only place I'm goin' is home!" I told her. "I've been out all night and I have to pick up my daughter from the baby-sitter's."

"That's perfect! I'll get dressed and go with you. I've been dying to meet her!" She rushed toward her bedroom, leaving a trail of paint. "It'll only take me a couple of minutes."

"Olivia, stop it! Just stop it!" I yelled. "You're not going anywhere, especially not to meet my daughter! Now, I've tried to be polite because I know you mean well, but this shit has got to stop!"

She walked toward me slowly with a deranged expression on her face.

"So, I'm not good enough to meet your nappy-headed child, huh?"

"What did you say?"

"You heard what I said, you arrogant bastard. I'm not good enough to meet your precious little princess, but I am good enough to suck your dick?" She was waving her brush vio-lently. Red paint splattered onto the carpet and her face. She was so enraged she didn't even flinch.

"Look, Olivia, we had an understanding. No expectations—remember?"

"That was *your* understanding, not mine!" She began to cry. "When a woman allows you inside of her, she's emotionally in-volved, damnit! You of all people should know that—Mr. Rela-tionship Expert!"

"Olivia, this conversation is over. Good-bye! And don't ever call me again." I headed for the door.

"Don't turn your back on me, you son of a bitch!"

She picked up the box cutter and threw it at me with all her might. I shielded myself with the door just as the blade embedded itself in the oak frame.

"You could have killed me, you crazy bitch!"

"If I wanted to kill you, you'd already be dead!"

"You need help, Olivia," I said as I walked out the door. "And I mean professional help."

"You think you're God's gift to women but you're nothing but a conniving dog, just like all the other men in my life. But every dog has its day—and your day is comin'!" Then she slammed the door shut.

As I walked down the driveway, my hands began to tremble. I covered them with my jacket as I approached the tow-truck driver. He was sitting on the trunk of my car filling out paperwork and listening to country music. When he saw me coming he stood up and handed me a clipboard.

"Here, sign on the dotted line," he said with a strong Texas accent.

I wrote my name as fast as I could to conceal the shaking.

"So, what was wrong with the tire? Was it a slow leak?"

"A slow leak?" he laughed. "Down here in Texas we call that a *fast* leak." He opened the trunk, where he had put the tire. There were jagged slash marks on the side, mostly near the rim. "I know this is none of my business, but if I were you, young fella, I'd get as far away from that gal as possible."

He climbed into his truck and turned up the volume on his radio.

"Have a nice day!" He smiled. Then he sped off.

I closed the trunk and got into my car. I struggled to put the key in the ignition, because my hand was still shaking. As I was about to drive off, I noticed something stabbing me in the right side. It was the jewelry box Olivia had given me. I pulled it out of my pocket and opened it. Inside was a Rolex watch and a piece of paper that read:

Here's the watch that you never could afford when you were struggling to make it. I hope you'll always think of me each time you wear it.

Love,
Olivia Brown
—a.k.a. Sharon

It all began to make sense. Olivia was the woman who called in during my last show in Chicago. When I thought back on it, I never did disconnect her line before reading my poetry. Olivia was listening the whole time Mitch and I were talking. That's how she knew I would be at Club Nimbus.

I tossed the watch onto the lawn and burned rubber out of her driveway. As I sped off down the street, I saw my pathetic reflection in the rearview mirror.

"Damnit, Julian! What the *hell* have you gotten yourself into?"

Part IV

(October)

Chapter 25

THE DOOR SLAMMED as Samantha left for school. I watched from my bedroom window as she boarded the bus. I tapped on the glass and waved good-bye, but she didn't wave back. It had been five days since the incident with Terri in the kitchen, and she still wasn't speaking to me. Every time I asked her a question she answered me casually with yes sir or no sir. Her attitude had begun to affect her conduct at school as well. Her homeroom teacher said that she hadn't turned in a homework assignment all week. I decided to give her another week to get over it before I put my foot down.

After the bus pulled off I slipped into my gym shoes and prepared to get some exercise to relieve the stress. I had converted the spare bedroom into a mini gym, complete with a treadmill and universal weight machine. I set the treadmill to seven miles per hour and began jogging. Just as I was working up a good sweat, the phone rang.

"Hello?" I sounded irritated.

"Well, excuse the hell outta me! Maybe I should call back when you're in a better mood."

It was Denise. She never called me so early in the morning. I knew something had to be up.

"Sorry about that, Li'l Sis. I didn't know it was you. Whassup?"

"Oh, nothing. I just thought I would call to see how things were working out."

"Everything is fine. The show is doing great, the house is nearly furnished, Samantha is adjusting to her new school, and, believe it or not, I'm dating again."

"So I've heard. Eddie told me about your sexy doctor friend. She sounds like a real keeper."

"I'm not going to pop the question anytime soon, but she's definitely special. Now that we've gotten the formalities out of the way, you wanna tell me why you really called?"

"I don't know what you're talkin' about."

"Denise, I've been knowing you for three years and you never call me this early in the morning unless something's wrong."

"You're not gonna let me slide, are you?"

"Nope!"

"Okay, here it is. Maybe you should sit down for this one."

"Stop with all the drama and just spit it out!"

"Okay—Eddie proposed to me."

"Excuse me?" I said while tapping on the receiver. "We must have a bad connection."

"Stop acting silly, Julian. You heard what I said. Eddie asked me to marry him. It happened right after we got home from dinner last night."

"Well, congratulations! It's about time that knucklehead woke up and realized he had a good thing! Now, put him on the phone so I can curse him out for not letting me in on the big surprise."

"He's not here. He left out early this morning for a photo shoot in Hyde Park."

"Wait a minute, you mean to tell me that the most commit-

ment-phobic man in the universe proposed marriage and he
couldn't take five minutes to call his best friend last night or
this morning? That doesn't sound right."

"Neither does this engagement," she said, sounding upset.
Then she began to cry. "It wasn't supposed to be like this."

"Calm down, Li'l Sis, and tell me what happened."

I should've known this was too good to be true. Eddie was
the last man on earth who needs to be married. He had just laid
up with Janet five days ago, and I knew for a fact that he had
two women in Chicago he was sleeping with. But I tried to keep
an open mind and give him the benefit of the doubt.

"We had a big argument last night when we were on the
way back from dinner," Denise explained. "I caught him in a lie
about some woman who called the house. I told him that if he
couldn't keep his dick in his pants he had to go. After we exchanged a few more unpleasant words, we went home and he
started packing his stuff. Just before he walked out, he said he
loved me. I told him that wasn't enough—I couldn't continue to
play house without a commitment. That's when he got down on
one knee and proposed."

I just sat there shaking my head while I listened. I knew Eddie was just doing what was expedient.

"Are you still there?"

"Yeah, I'm here," I said as I exhaled. "I really don't know
what to say."

"Julian Payne, speechless? Now that's a first," she laughed.

"Denise, Eddie is my best friend. I don't want to get involved in his personal business."

"I thought you were my friend, too. All I'm asking for is
some friendly advice."

"Don't you understand? It's impossible to do one without
being guilty of the other."

"Please, Julian, you're the only person in the whole world I
can talk to. My father's gone and my two uncles are just as bad
as Eddie. You're the only decent man I know."

"Denise, I told you I—"

"Julian, please!" she cut me off in midsentence. "I really need your help!"

I took a deep breath while strolling over toward the window. I looked up into the sky as if seeking guidance from a higher power.

"Okay, Li'l Sis, you asked for it! Ever since you and Eddie met, I tried to understand what you were doing together. He was irresponsible and reckless, you were organized and ambitious. He liked to be out in the streets, you were a homebody. He never wanted kids, and you always talked about having a family. Now after three long years of getting in and out of his bed, washing his dirty drawers, and handling his business, you get the proposal you've been waiting for. The only problem is, you only got it after you threatened to walk out of his life."

"So what are you trying to say, Julian, that Eddie isn't sincere and that I should leave him?"

"It's not my place to tell you to stay or to go. But I will tell you this: When a man loves a woman, and I mean, really loves her, she won't have to wait around for years or beg him to marry her. He'll feel so blessed to have found her that *he'll* be pursuing *her,* not the other way around. I know this because it happened to me when I met Carmen. I couldn't wait to put a ring on her finger and let the whole world know she belonged to me!"

"Since we're being so open and honest—I have a confession to make. I've always envied what you and Carmen had. The way you held her, the way you spoke to her, and the loving way you looked at each other. Your love for her was so strong, *so real*! So many times I thought to myself, 'Why can't Eddie be more like him?'

"I appreciate the compliment, Denise, but I'm not perfect. I make mistakes, too."

"Like what, not paying your taxes on time?" she joked while trying to hold back the tears.

"No, my mistake was having sex with Olivia the first night we met in Chicago. I didn't want a serious relationship, but I slept with her anyway. That's not how a good man should behave. Now I have to deal with the consequences. Like I always tell Eddie, if you wanna play, you have to pay."

"What do you mean by that?"

"Denise, your friend Olivia turned out to be a real psycho! She used my cell phone to steal my number, and a few days later she shows up in Houston claiming to be in town on business. Then last week I found out that she bought a house and moved to Houston, expecting us to be together."

"Julian, I'm so sorry. She seemed like such a nice person."

"It's not your fault. I'm sure she manipulated you to get to me," I said. "Hopefully it's all over with."

"I'm just surprised that Eddie never mentioned it."

There was a short pause.

"Eddie *does* know about what's going on with her, doesn't he?" Denise asked.

"We've all got skeletons—even me. Like I told you, I'm not perfect. I've tried to set a good example for Eddie, being older and all. If he knew about what happened between me and Olivia, I'd never be able to check him when he steps out of line. So, if you don't mind, I'd like to keep this strictly between us."

"If you can keep my little secret, I'll keep yours."

"Thanks, Li'l Sis, and I do wish you the best no matter what decision you make. Just remember, it's okay to be a woman in love, but it's more important to be a woman who loves herself. Don't ever forget that!"

"I promise you, I won't," she said. "And you promise me that you won't beat yourself up over this situation with Olivia. Sometimes even a good man makes bad choices."

"I'll do my best, Li'l Sis. You take care."

"You too, Julian, and thanks for being a true friend. Bye."

A second later my sky pager went off. I ran into the bedroom to read the text message. It was from Mitch.

I tried to reach you at home and on your cell phone but there was no answer. Meet me at the studio at noon. I've got a big surprise for you!

I looked at the message and shook my head. "I don't think I can handle any more surprises!"

Chapter 26

SAMANTHA WAS SITTING at her desk in music class waiting for Mrs. Adams to arrive. While looking over her homework assignment she felt a bump to the back of her chair.

"Stop it, Melissa," Samantha whispered as she turned around.

"Stop what?" Melissa replied.

"Don't play dumb; you know what I'm talking about!"

"And if I don't, what are you gonna do about it, you African booty scratcher?"

Samantha jumped out of her chair with her hands balled into fists. The entire class gathered around to watch the fight. Just as Samantha was about to pop Melissa in the mouth, the principal, Ms. Bell, walked in. Everyone quickly ran back to their seats.

"Good morning, class."

"Good morning, Ms. Bell," they responded in unison.

"I'm here because I have some bad news to tell you. Mrs. Adams will not be here today."

"Why not?" Melissa asked.

"Mrs. Adams had an accident yesterday while shopping for new instruments. A piano top fell on her wrist and broke it."

The class gasped.

"When will she be back?" Melissa asked.

"Probably not for a while," Ms. Bell explained. "In the meantime, I want to introduce your substitute teacher. Her name is Ms. Randall and I want you to be on your best behavior, understand?"

"Yes, ma'am."

"Now, please give her a warm welcome."

When the children began to applaud, an attractive black woman entered the classroom. She had brown eyes, caramel brown skin, and long black hair that was pulled back into a ponytail. Most of the class was happy to see her, especially the boys. They were blushing so hard their faces turned bright red. But Melissa was wearing a frown. She didn't want to lose her position as the teacher's pet.

"Good morning, everyone. My name is Ms. Randall and I'm looking forward to teaching you the art of music," she said. "Now that you know my name, let's find out who you are, starting with the front row."

Samantha was in the middle of the second row, directly in front of Melissa. She wasn't hard to miss, being the only black child in the class. When it was her turn to introduce herself, Ms. Randall smiled at her. Melissa noticed and kicked the back of Samantha's chair again.

"Stop it, Melissa!"

"Is there a problem?" Ms. Bell asked.

"Why don't you let me handle this?" Ms. Randall whispered to Ms. Bell.

"Okay, but if you need me, I'll be in my office." Then she walked out of the classroom.

Once the door was shut, Ms. Randall walked over to where Samantha and Melissa were sitting and stood over them.

"So, what seems to be the problem, young ladies?"

"Melissa keeps kicking the back of my chair."

"Is that true, Melissa?"

"No, ma'am, she's a liar!" Melissa shouted.

"I'm telling the truth, Ms. Randall. She even called me an African booty scratcher."

All of the kids laughed.

"So, you don't like black people, huh, Melissa?"

"I like some black people, like Halle Berry, Michael Jordan, and Will Smith."

"What about the black people you see every day, like the garbage man, the janitor, or your black neighbors?"

"I don't have any black neighbors."

"Maybe that's your problem," she said to her. "You need to be exposed to black people who aren't dribbling basketballs or dancing in videos."

"She said white people are better than black people," Samantha said.

"Did you say that, Melissa?"

"No, I just said that white people are smarter than black people."

"Is that right?" Ms. Randall walked back to the front of the class. "Well, since you're so smart, tell me who invented the traffic signal and the telephone transmitter."

Melissa's eyebrows raised as if she was contemplating an answer.

"Or maybe you can tell the class who the first self-made female millionaire was?" Ms. Randall continued.

When Melissa didn't answer, Samantha raised her hand high into the air.

"I know the answer, Ms. Randall!"

"Okay, Samantha, what is it?"

"Garrett A. Morgan invented the traffic light, Granville T. Woods invented the telephone transmitter, and Madam C. J. Walker was the first self-made female millionaire."

"And what do all these people have in common?"

"They're all black!" Samantha said proudly.

"So I guess you're not as smart as you think you are," Ms. Randall said while grabbing a piece of chalk. "Now come up to the front of the class and write one hundred times on the blackboard 'All people are created equal.' Come on, let's go!"

Melissa pouted as she stood up from her desk. As she started toward the front of the class, Samantha covered her mouth and whispered, "Welcome to Africa."

Chapter 27

IT WAS ELEVEN THIRTY when I arrived at the office building. The lobby was buzzing with activity as the men rushed to eat lunch and the women hurried down to the Galleria mall to go shopping. As I approached the security desk, I saw a familiar face. It was Joe, the security guard. He was looking sharp in his spit-shined shoes and pressed uniform.

"Good afternoon, Joe."

"Good afternoon, Mr. Payne. I see you're here for the big meeting."

"Big meeting? I didn't know about any big meeting."

"Well, I just assumed it was important, since all the bigwigs were in town from New York and Los Angeles. That only happens two times a year, usually after the Arbitron ratings books come out for the fall and summer."

"Joe, you really know what's going on around this place, don't you?"

"Don't let this tough exterior fool you, young fella," he said while sticking out his skinny chest. "I'm not just a well-trained fighting machine, I'm a customer service rep."

"Well, at ease, soldier," I said, trying not to burst out laughing. "I'll rest a lot easier knowing you're on the job." Then I started walking toward the elevators.

"Wait a minute, Mr. Payne. Do you mind signing this picture for me? It's for my daughter-in-law. She listens to your show every night."

He pulled out a picture of a middle-aged white woman in a hospital gown holding a newborn infant. There were two younger children standing in the picture beside her.

"I took this picture two weeks ago in the hospital after she gave birth to my third grandchild. Isn't she adorable?"

"She's sure is, Joe. Congratulations," I said while signing the picture.

"By the way, Mr. Payne, I'll be seeing you on the midnight shift starting next week. My daughter needs help with the kids during the daytime until my son returns from his tour of duty overseas." He whipped out a photo of a man wearing an army uniform. He looked exactly like Joe, only younger.

"I can see G.I. Joe runs in the family," I said while rushing toward the elevators. "See you on the graveyard shift."

"Good luck with the meeting, Mr. Payne!" he yelled to me. "And by the way, I hope your neck is okay."

While riding up to the studio, I remembered that I still had the bandage on my neck to cover up the hickey. "I hope Terri doesn't find out I'm here." I peeled back the bandage and looked at the hickey in the elevator mirror. Most of it had faded, but there was still a small spot on the right side of my neck. "Just two more days," I said to myself. I had been avoiding her all week to give the bruise a chance to heal. As the elevator doors opened onto the twenty-fifth floor, I pressed the bandage back on and prayed that she wouldn't show up.

The moment I entered the studio lobby, I could feel the tension in the air. The employees were rushing around the office trying to look busy. Even Janet Jackson was at her desk answering calls during her lunch break. I knew something major had to be going down if that sistah wasn't eating.

"Good afternoon, Mr. Payne."

"Excuse me?"

"I said—good afternoon." She was whispering and gritting her teeth. "Don't make this harder than it already is."

"Oh, now I get it. You're on your best behavior today. Now I know there's something major going on," I said, teasing her. "How about a cup of coffee, Ms. Jackson?"

"Don't press your luck, Julian," she said under her breath in an evil tone. "The bigwigs will be gone tomorrow and you'll be all mine!"

Just then Mitch came running out from the back office with a frantic expression on his face.

"Come on, man, everybody's waiting for you!" He grabbed me by the arm and pulled me toward the door.

"Who's everybody?"

Mitch dragged me into the conference room where Mr. Harris and several men and women were engaged in deep conversation. They were all conservatively dressed with leather business planners placed neatly in front of them at the long oak table.

"Whassup with the power meeting, boss?" I asked.

"Glad you could make it on such short notice, Julian," Mr. Harris said as he stood and shook my hand. "Have a seat. We were just talking about you."

Suddenly all the attention was directed at me. The eleven men and women in the room, mostly male *and* white, were staring at me as if they were expecting a speech. I felt uncomfortable because I was wearing dingy blue jeans and I had a huge bandage on my neck.

"Ladies and gentlemen, this is Mr. Julian Payne, the man responsible for us being here today," Mr. Harris announced. "Julian, these men and women are the program directors for our top ten urban markets. The gentleman at the head of the table is Mr. Ron Stevens, president and CEO. I'll let him take it from here."

Mr. Stevens was the poster child for white corporate America. He was in his mid fifties, with dark brown hair that was graying around the edges. He appeared to be in fairly good shape and had a very distinguished face, sort of like Robert Redford.

"Mr. Payne, have you checked your e-mail on the station web site?"

"To be honest with you, sir, I didn't know I had an e-mail address or that the station even had a web site."

"Well, take a look at this and tell me what you think."

Mitch passed a folder over to me. It contained several pieces of paper with dates and numbers.

"What's this?"

"On the left side of the page is a list of e-mail addresses from every listener who logs on to the station site. On the right are those who e-mail you directly."

"I'm sorry, I still don't get it."

"Look at the number on the bottom right side of page one."

"Wow, seventy-five thousand addresses. Not bad for a month, huh?"

"Mr. Payne, that information is processed weekly."

I slowly turned the pages while checking the total numbers at the bottom. It read:

> Week One 75,000
> Week Two 81,889
> Week Three 99,563
> Week Four 120,901

"We estimate that over half a million listeners will log on to the web site by the end of October to get advice or to curse you out. Either way, they're listening. And that's all that matters to the advertisers."

"So now what?"

"'Now what,' is why we're all here. We want to take *Love,*

Lust, and Lies national. We'll start with Chicago and Atlanta," he continued. "If the ratings show the same trend by the end of November, we'll be on coast to coast by the new year."

"This is all so sudden. I'll need a couple of days to talk this over with my lawyer before I make a decision."

"We figured you might want to do that, so we took the liberty of flying her in from Chicago. She should be here within the hour," Mr. Harris said while staring at his watch. "Why don't you think it over. Let's meet again at three o'clock. That'll give you time to look over the contract."

"Yeah, that's a good idea."

He handed me a brown folder and patted me on the back. I walked out of the room in a daze, Mitch trailing closely behind me, clapping and laughing like we had just hit the lottery. Once we were inside my office I sat down at the desk and stared off into space.

"What just happened?" I asked Mitch.

"Your dream just came true, that's what."

"But this is happening way too fast. I thought maybe a year from now, maybe two, but not this soon."

"Julian, snap out of it! This is the opportunity of a lifetime!" Mitch yelled. "Don't even think about blowing it!"

"I need a few minutes alone, Mitch. Do you mind?" I said calmly.

"Take all the time you need, partner," he said with his hand on my shoulder. "But remember what I told you back in Chicago. It's your season. Don't be afraid to claim it." Then he walked out.

While I sat there in deep thought, I reflected back on all those frustrating days in Chicago at WTLK—the low pay, the raggedy equipment, the leaking ceilings, and the weak radio signal. Now I had a chance to be heard nationwide. But instead of celebrating like Mitch, I was trippin'.

"Mitch is right. I need to claim what's mine!" I said, trying to pump myself up.

While I was working up the courage to take that next step, there was a knock at the door.

"Mitch, I told you I needed a few minutes alone."

"It's not Mitch, it's me—Terri. Can I come in?"

"Oh, shit!" I said under my breath.

I quickly sat down in my chair with my right cheek turned away from the door.

"Come on in."

When she opened the door I could see the look of disappointment in her eyes. I had been avoiding her all week.

"I was hoping to see you for a couple of minutes just to say hello." She sat down in the chair directly in front of my desk. "Why didn't you tell me you were coming over? I could have rearranged my appointments."

"This meeting was called at the last minute. As you can see, I didn't even have time to change clothes."

"Is something wrong, Julian? You seem a little tense."

"No, I'm fine. I just have a lot on my mind lately—the situation with Samantha, and this syndication deal. It's a little overwhelming."

"Mitch told me about it. In fact, the whole office knows about it. Congratulations."

"Thanks, baby," I said while making sure to keep my head turned. "Well, I've got to read over this contract before my lawyer gets here. Why don't we get together this weekend to celebrate?"

"Sure, that sounds like fun!" She stood up and began walking toward the door, then stopped. "Can I at least have a hug before I go?"

"Of course."

I approached her from the right side of my desk while doing my best to keep the bandage hidden. I leaned over to her left side and gave her a firm hug.

"Mmm," I sighed. "I had forgotten just how good you feel."

"Is that right?" She said in a curious tone. "Then why don't you hug me on the other side to see if it feels any better?"

I knew I was busted, but like any man who's guilty as sin, I tried to play it off.

"What are you talking about?"

"I'm talking about this!" She pulled the bandage off my neck with her left hand and threw it on the floor. "You must think I'm a damn fool! Now I see why you've been avoiding me!"

"If you just calm down, I can explain."

"Don't even waste your time, Julian! I saw the bitch get in your car at the Hilton Saturday night!"

"So now you're spying on me!"

Smack! She slapped my face. Then tears began to roll down her cheeks.

"How dare you accuse me of doing something so trifling! I came because you asked me to be there. I wanted to surprise you, but I guess I was the one who got the surprise."

"Terri, I swear to God, this is not what you think. I can explain everything if you'll just give me a chance."

"I don't want to hear it, Julian!" she yelled. "I never want to see you again. Don't call me, don't send me any flowers, and don't you dare write me another damn poem about how different you are, because you're as typical as they come!"

As she turned to leave, I grabbed her by the arm.

"Terri, please!"

"Let me go, goddamnit, before I forget I'm a lady!" Then she jerked away and rushed out the door.

A few seconds later Mitch came rushing in.

"What the hell is goin' on?"

"I fucked up, Mitch!"

"Let me guess. She's not the one who gave you that hickey."

My sad expression said it all as I walked over to the window and peered out.

"Julian, you know I try to stay out of your personal business." He put his hand on my shoulder. "But you can't carry around this burden forever. It's been affecting your performance on the air for the last few days and now this!"

I turned around and stared at him, surprised by how transparent I was.

"How did you know?"

"Come on, man, I've been dealing with your drama for over fifteen years! I was there when you got cold feet at your wedding, I was at the hospital when Sam was born, and I was crying right along side of you at Carmen's funeral. Hell, I know you better than you know yourself!"

"Mitch, you wouldn't believe this crazy shit even if I told you."

"Try me!"

I was embarrassed about telling him, but I needed to talk to someone who would listen without passing judgment. Mitch was mature and open-minded. After fifteen years of working together he had proven to be more than a mentor, he was a friend—even more so than Eddie. Funny how I never realized that until that moment.

"All right, Mitch. Close the door." I took a deep breath. "Pull up a chair and have a seat."

"I'm cool right here." He was leaning against the wall.

"Trust me, Mitch, you'll need a Snickers for this one—it's a *long* story."

Chapter 28

DAYS QUICKLY TURNED into weeks and I still hadn't heard from Terri. I respected her privacy by not calling or writing letters. The one time I saw her at the studio she walked right past me without saying hello or even making eye contact. I guess the old saying is true: Once a woman is through, she's through.

I put all my energies into the show, hoping it would distract me from missing Terri. I came to work an hour earlier than usual and stayed an hour later. When I was asked to make personal appearances around town to promote the show, I hit every spot I could think of. I spoke at Texas Southern University and Wheatley High School, and passed out flyers at the after-work party at Maxwell's nightclub. I even signed autographs at Mikki's Café off Highway 59 and W. Belfort. I never saw so many black folks licking their fingers and arguing about relationships at the same time.

All that extra effort paid off. By the end of October, *Love, Lust, and Lies* was the number one radio show in Houston. WBMX billboards went up all over town, even in the white suburbs. They ran full-page ads in the *Houston Chronicle* and did an article on my career in the Sunday entertainment section. It was a real ego trip seeing my mug on the front page. The caption underneath my photo read:

THE BAD BOY OF RADIO
NEW PERSONALITY STIRS UP CONTROVERSY
ON HOUSTON AIRWAVES.

But all the media exposure came with a price. It wasn't long before I couldn't even pump gas without being approached for relationship advice. When I stopped at the grocery store, the cashier asked if he should take his wife back after she slept with his best friend. When Samantha and I went to Katy Mills mall to see the movie *Monsters, Inc.,* a teenage girl selling popcorn asked if giving a blow job was considered having sex.

The public appearances and long work hours also began to affect my relationship with Samantha. It was already strained because of the incident with Terri. It had been nearly a month since she had seen me on my knees in the kitchen giving Terri head, and she still wouldn't talk about it. *Maybe I should be more stern and press the issue,* I was thinking, but my guilty conscience wouldn't allow it. For the first time in her life she didn't see me as Superman. I was just *a man.*

I tried to rebuild our relationship by taking her to the studio, but she got bored within the first fifteen minutes. She spent most of the night downstairs playing checkers with Joe the security guard. She was much better when we went to Astro World amusement park. She laughed and screamed on the roller-coaster and water rides. We ate cotton candy, played games, and took silly pictures in those little photo booths. But as soon as we got home she went back into her shell again.

At least she seemed to be enjoying music ever since the substitute, Ms. Randall, took over for Mrs. Adams. I was grateful for that. But I couldn't help feeling like a failure as a father. For the first time since Carmen was gone I questioned whether

I had what it took to raise a little girl into a healthy woman. Many nights I stared at Carmen's picture on the mantel searching for answers. "What would you do, baby?" I was so desperate that I considered calling Terri for professional advice, but each time I picked up the phone something told me—*bad idea*.

The only good news was that I hadn't heard from Olivia. That was four weeks ago. There's no way I could have dealt with her insane ass while going through these changes with Samantha. I guess the old saying is true: The Lord never puts more on you than you can bear.

Chapter 29

MS. RANDALL WAS writing the homework assignment on the blackboard when the school bell rang. The children jumped to their feet and rushed toward the door.

"Don't *even* think about it! Sit down and copy this homework assignment before you leave my class! You'll be quizzed on Thursday."

"But Ms. Randall, it's Halloween!" Melissa whined. "Can't we wait until next week?"

Ms. Randall slapped the eraser down hard on her desk and gave Melissa an evil stare. Melissa quickly opened her notebook and began copying down the assignment along with the rest of the class. Samantha laughed when she saw Melissa being put in check.

"Do you have something funny you'd like to share with the class, Ms. Payne?"

"No, ma'am."

"Then why are you disrupting my class?" She walked over to Samantha's desk and stood over her. "I can see you need to be taught a lesson."

Samantha stared down at her desk, afraid to look Ms. Randall in the eye. She was more intimidating than old Mrs. Adams.

"I want you to stay after school and practice playing the piano and holding a note," she said. "If you're going to run off at the mouth in music class, you may as well do it singing."

"But Ms. Randall, I didn't do anything!"

"Don't play me for a fool, Samantha! Now go to the front of the class and start playing."

"What do you want me to play?"

"I don't care, 'The Star Spangled Banner,' 'Lift Every Voice and Sing,' or 'Wade in the Water,' it doesn't matter to me. But you *will* play until I tell you to stop, and you'd better hold your notes."

Samantha sat down at the piano and began playing the Destiny's Child song "Independent Woman." As she pressed down on the keys, she sang along.

"The shoes on my feet, I bought it
The clothes I'm wearing, I bought it. . . ."

"Very funny, Samantha. Now try again. This time choose a song with lyrics you can sing, not rap."

As the rest of the class filed out, Melissa stuck out her tongue at Samantha. She was about to give Melissa the black eye and busted nose sign but Ms. Randall was watching her. Once the room was empty, Samantha nervously bit down on her lower lip, trying to think of a song she knew the lyrics to. Then it came to her. She took a deep breath and hit the high note of the Alicia Keys song "Fallin'": "I keep on fallin' in and out of love with you."

As she continued to play, Ms. Randall was amazed by how well she played and how strong her voice was. She listened for a while and then joined in on the piano. Samantha grew confident and sang even stronger. "That's it, hold that note!" Ms. Randall shouted while waving her hand like an orchestra leader. "Relax; now breathe."

Samantha sounded just like Alicia when she hit the high

notes. She sang with emotion and passion. Ms. Randall couldn't believe this sound was coming out of a ten-year-old child. When the song was over she gave Samantha a hug and rocked her back and forth.

"That was great! Where did you learn to sing like that?"

"I listen to a lot of radio."

They were so excited, Samantha missed the school bus. It drove off while they were talking.

"Now how am I supposed to get home?"

"Don't worry, I'll take you. But I think you should call home and tell your father you'll be a little late."

Ms. Randall gave Samantha her cell phone to call her father. When he didn't pick up, she left a message. After gathering up her books, Samantha flung her backpack over her shoulder and followed Ms. Randall out to her truck.

"Hey, I've got an idea! Why don't we stop by the mall before I drop you off?"

"I don't know, Ms. Randall. My daddy gets really mad when I go somewhere without telling him first."

"Come on, Samantha, you're a big girl. Besides, men don't always need to know what we girls do, right?"

Samantha was starving for attention. She saw Ms. Randall as someone she could relate to. She was young, intelligent, beautiful, and hip, just like her mother. Samantha thought about the offer for a second, then gave in.

"Okay, let's go!"

"Great!" She opened the door to her truck and strapped Samantha into her seat belt. "I've always wanted a little girl I could take shopping."

"You don't have any kids, Ms. Randall?"

"Not yet," she said with a smile. "But I'm thinking about adopting a little girl." Then they drove off.

First Colony Mall was only a short drive from the school. Ms. Randall held Samantha's hand and led her around the mall as if she were her own daughter. They took a photograph together and bought matching outfits. While she was in the dressing room trying them on, Ms. Randall left her with the store clerk and went to have a key made.

By the time she returned, Samantha was all decked out in her new outfit and ready to go.

"This is fun! Where to next?"

"Home!"

"But I don't wanna go home yet! Can we at least go down to Foley's and sniff some perfume?"

"Okay, just one more stop," she agreed. "But before we go, you have to do me a favor and put your school uniform back on."

"Why can't I keep my new clothes on?"

"Because your father may not approve of you taking gifts from strangers."

"But you're not a stranger, you're my teacher."

"I know, Samantha, but still, I think it would be best if we kept this between us girls," she told her. "I'll keep your things at my house. You can come over anytime you want and pick them up. You can even practice your singing if you want—I have a piano."

"For real?"

"For real!"

"Thanks, Ms. Randall!" She gave her a firm hug. "You're the best teacher I've ever had!"

"And you're my favorite student," she said as they walked down the mall holding hands. "Now let's go sniff some perfume at Foley's, then I have to get you home—Princess."

"Hey, that's what my daddy calls me."

"Isn't that a coincidence?"

Chapter 30

THE VIEW FROM the twenty-fifth floor was still as awesome as it had been the first time I saw it back in September. During the commercial break I stared out of the oversized windows onto the 610 freeway watching the cars as they zoomed by. In the distance I could see the flashing lights of a state trooper's cruiser as he pulled over a shiny red Corvette. I could just imagine how pissed off the driver must have been to be getting pulled over at two o'clock in the morning. "I guess that cop had his doughnuts to go!" I laughed.

It was one of the few times I smiled during the entire month of October. Although the radio show was number one in Houston, I wasn't happy. Every night I stared at the studio phone hoping Terri would call to recite another erotic poem, but a month had passed since we fell out and still there was no call. I knew it was time to resign myself to the fact that she never would.

As I prepared to go back on the air, I took a deep breath and inhaled the aroma of the jasmine-scented candles to refocus. Mitch gave me the ten-second countdown from the control room, then faded back into the show with "Masquerade" by George Benson. It was the perfect song for Halloween night.

"Welcome back to *Love, Lust, and Lies,*" I said smoothly into the microphone. "It's Halloween night and we're talkin' about people who hide behind masks, or, as Chris Rock would say, you don't really meet the true person, you meet their representative. Let's take one final caller before we wrap it up. Gloria from the Third Ward, what's your question or comment?"

"My question is, how can a woman ever know who a man truly is? Men are always putting on facades, especially at the nightclubs."

"Give me an example."

"Okay, I met this gentleman at Maxwell's nightclub. He was very attractive, well groomed, and had good conversation. When I asked him if he was married or had kids, he said no. Then he went on to tell me about a successful cleaning business he owned. Well, the following weekend we're driving down Richmond Avenue in his Navigator. Out of nowhere this woman with two kids in the back of her car pulls up next to us, screaming at the top of her voice. She sideswiped us a couple of times, then cut us off in the middle of the street."

"Don't tell me, it was his wife!"

"Oh, no, it's much better than that; it was one of his three babies' mamas. Turns out the car he was driving was hers. She cursed him out so bad I almost felt sorry for him."

"What about his cleaning business? Don't tell me that was a front, too?"

"Chile, please! Two days before that incident I talked my boss into hiring him to clean our office building. Can you believe this clown shows up with a wet vac from Sears, three plastic buckets, and two Mexicans? I was so embarrassed I took two weeks' vacation just to avoid my coworkers."

"It's obvious that he was a real busta," I said. "But what about the good men out there who are misjudged?"

Mitch's head sprung up from the control board. He knew I was about to vent.

"What do you mean?" Gloria asked.

"I'm saying that sometimes women have a tendency to jump to conclusions without all the facts. For example, I have a friend whose girlfriend saw a woman get into his car. Should that affect her trust?"

"Not necessarily!"

"And let's say that the next day that man has a hickey on his body, maybe on his neck; does that make him a cheater?"

"Hold up a second, Julian. Your friend needs to put the shoe on the other foot," she said wisely. "If his woman came home with a mark on her neck, back, ass—whatever, he'd drop her in a split second," Gloria asserted. "And besides, what kind of explanation could he possibly have, that his neck accidentally fell against her mouth while she was sucking? Give me a break!"

"But what if—"

"What if nothin'." She cut me off. "Now, I listen to you give advice five days a week, and to your credit, it's pretty good," she said. "Now, take some advice from a fifty-year-old veteran—perception *is* reality. If a man puts the wrong perception out there for his woman to see, then he must deal with the reality of the consequences."

I had to pause for a second to let that marinate. She broke me down and read me like a Dr. Seuss book. Even if I wanted to play it off, I couldn't.

"You're right," I sighed. "Thanks for the honesty and the insight—*veteran*!"

"Anytime, Mr. Payne," she said graciously. "And I hope everything works out for *your friend*. Sounds to me like he's got a little drama in his life."

"Don't we all?"

Mitch was frantically waving his hands. When I checked the clock on the console I realized why: it read 2:02.

"That's it for me tonight, Houston. Thanks for allowing me into your homes, your hearts, and your minds—peace."

Mitch hurried out of the control room and into the studio. He switched on the lights and came over to where I was sitting.

"What the hell is wrong with you?" he said while getting in my face. "You know better than to air out your personal issues on the air!"

"Whatever."

"*Whatever*? Is that all you have to say?"

"Back up off me, man!" I stood up and stepped toward him. "You work for me, not the other way around, remember?"

"Boy, if I was ten years younger I'd wipe the floor with your sorry ass!" He put his hand in my face. "Now I know you're hurting over this thing with Terri, but don't you ever allow it to affect *our* show. That's right, I said *our* show because I help put this together. When the day comes that you forget that, it will be the day you can do this by your damn self."

As he turned to walk away he knocked over the wobbly cart rack. Hundreds of tapes scattered on the floor. "Damnit, not again!" he yelled out. We both bent down and started picking them up. While stacking the tapes on top of the console, I looked into his eyes and saw the pain that I caused him. I knew I had made a terrible mistake.

"Mitch, I'm sorry, man. I don't know why I'm trippin'. I know I wouldn't be here without you."

He didn't say anything at first; he just looked at me with that fatherly expression of disappointment. Then he stood up and spoke to me in a firm tone.

"You know, Julian, it's not always easy working in the shadow of a celebrity. It takes a man with a lot of confidence to handle having women pass by him to get to the *star*. But I've had my moment in the spotlight and I'm secure enough to play my role in this relationship because that's exactly what it is, a relationship. And there're not too many couples who make it five years, let alone fifteen." He paused. "What I'm trying to say is, I've always seen your success as my success. My job was to put you in the best position to win! And I take a lot of pride in what I do and I'm damn good at it. So the next time you even think about putting another person down, remember—no man is an island. We all need help to get to where we want to go."

"I hear you, Mitch. What can I say? It's another lesson learned." I extended my hand. "Still friends?"

He tried to play stubborn, but Mitch was always a sucker for a genuine apology.

"Yeah, still friends," he said under his breath. "But don't ever disrespect me like that again! Next time, I'll turn up the voltage on your mic and shock your big ass to death!"

"Deal," I said as we shook hands and embraced. "Now, go home to your wife. I'll pick up the rest of these tapes."

"Are you sure? The last time you knocked over this rack it took me a half hour to put them back in alphabetical order."

"Yeah, I'm sure. Now get the hell outta here!"

After Mitch programmed the station for the morning crew, he grabbed his things and left. I sat down on the floor and got comfortable while I put the tapes in order. There was no need to rush. I didn't have anyplace to go.

A few minutes into stacking the tapes, I noticed that some had fallen underneath the console. I got down on my stomach to reach them. Suddenly I heard the studio door swing open. I knew it couldn't have been Mitch, because I'd seen his car pull out of the underground parking. As I turned over onto my side, my heart pounded like a drum. Before I could twist completely around to see who it was, I heard a voice.

"I love the smell of those candles; what is that, jasmine?"

"Terri? You scared the shit out of me!"

"Who did you think I was—Olivia?"

I paused for a second, then went back to stacking tapes.

"I see you've been talking to Mitch. How much did he tell you?"

"Everything! Even the part about the hickey—which I still find a little hard to believe." She laughed, then she bent down and joined me on the floor. "Can I give you a hand?"

"Terri, I know you didn't come here at two o'clock in the morning to help me stack tapes."

"I was already downstairs in my office catching up on some work. Maybe that's where I wanted to be. It was the excuse I needed to see you."

"You still haven't told me why you're here," I said with attitude.

"Don't be like that, Julian. You know I came here to tell you I was sorry. Sorry for not listening to your explanation, and most of all, sorry for not trusting you."

"It took you four weeks and a visit from Mitch to finally open up? And what if he hadn't come to see you? Would we be talking right now?"

"Baby, what difference does it make? What's important is that I'm here."

"I'll tell you what's important. What's important is that I expected you to be more open-minded."

"Come on, Julian, how did you expect me to react when my man shows up with a big hickey on his neck like a teenager?" she said. "I was hurt!"

"I was hurt, too! My sleep is all messed up, I'm snapping at Mitch every night, and my issues with you are starting to affect my show."

"Yeah, so I heard. Gloria sure broke you down." Terri laughed. "For a minute, I thought she was hosting the show."

I laughed, too. Although I didn't show it, I missed the sound of her laugh and her bright smile. And she was looking good, too. She had on a tight blouse and a pair of those spandex pants that showed every curve. While she was kneeling down, I couldn't help looking between her legs. Terri was slightly bow-legged, and she had a gap that was sexy as hell. I had to hand it to her, she knew how to get a man's undivided attention.

"So, where do we go from here, Mr. Relationship Expert?" Terri reached over and grabbed my hand. "I really do miss you, you know?"

"I miss you too, baby. But I've got to know that from now on you're going to trust me to do the right thing."

"I promise." She stood up and walked toward me. "And baby, just so you know, you were always in my thoughts. I just needed time to get my head together. Like I told you, I'm not going anywhere. Not tonight, not tomorrow, not ever."

We held one another. I was holding her so tight I could feel her heartbeat. She stroked the back of my head while kissing me gently on the neck. "I missed you, Julian," she spoke softly into my ear. "God, how I missed you!" Then we kissed.

We were so into each other we didn't notice we were crushing the tapes on the floor.

"This raggedy-ass rack is gonna get somebody killed one of these days," I said.

"Yeah, I know. I knocked it over yesterday while I was on the air."

As we continued to pick up the tapes, I sensed that Terri had something she wanted to say. I knew what it was, so I broke the silence.

"The answer is no."

"No, what?"

"No, I haven't heard from Olivia," I said. "I think she's finally got the message."

"Julian, I deal with these types of obsessive disorders every day. There are cases where patients receive treatment and then years later kill the person they've been stalking. I'm not trying to scare you, but you need to understand that Olivia could still be dangerous."

"Thanks for the warning, Doc," I said nonchalantly, "but I have this under control."

Chapter 31

WHEN I MADE it home later that night, Juanita was asleep on the sofa. She still had the remote in her hand with the television tuned to NBA TV. I shook her by the shoulder to wake her.

"Hey, Julian. What time is it?"

"It's three thirty."

"Time flies when you're watchin' hoops." She stood up and grabbed her purse off the counter. "There must have been eight different games on at once."

"So, how did Houston do tonight?"

"Steve Francis dropped thirty-six points on the Lakers."

"All right, Rockets!"

"Yeah, but they still lost. Kobe Bryant hit another last-second shot. That bucket cost me twenty bucks!"

As I escorted her to the door, I handed her a crisp one-hundred-dollar bill.

"Well, here's a little something extra for staying late for the past few weeks," I said to her. "Now go home and get some sleep—Laker Hater."

"Why thank you, *Mr. Payne*," she said. "And by the way, I'm not a Laker Hater, just a Rocket Lover. See ya tomorrow!"

I went upstairs to check on Samantha. I was so caught up with my work that I had hardly laid eyes on her in two days. When I opened her bedroom door she was diagonal on her canopy bed, nearly hanging off the edge. She looked precious all twisted up in her pink comforter with her arms wrapped around a stuffed animal. Just looking at her little brown face melted my heart.

But it was my unconditional love that blinded me to my responsibilities as a parent. Ever since the incident with Terri, Samantha had been walking around with an attitude and giving me the silent treatment. I should have dealt with that issue right after it happened, but instead I let weeks go by. That only made me appear ashamed and guilty. Now that Terri and I were back together, I had all the incentive I needed to put my foot down. If that didn't work, there was always the good old-fashioned ass whippin'.

"Get your rest, Princess," I whispered while closing her door. "Tomorrow morning, we're gonna have a *long* talk."

Instead of going to bed, I threw a few items in my gym bag and went downstairs to get my groove on while I showered. I lit two scented candles and placed one inside the shower door and the other on the counter. Then I dragged the stereo speakers in from the living room. I turned the radio dial to Magic 102, hoping they would play something smooth and relaxing. Just as I was taking off my drawers, "Smooth Operator" by Sade came on. "Now that's right on time!" I turned off the lights, peeled off the rest of my clothes, then stepped into the steamy shower.

As the water ran over my head and down my back, I closed my eyes and sang along to the lyrics. "He's a smooth operator . . . Smooth . . . operator." The tempo was so smooth, so relaxing, so—Sade. *What would it be like to get with a woman so classy and deep?* I was thinking. But Sade was only a voice, Terri was real. She's my fantasy come true.

I chilled out in the shower listening to one cut after another. "Portuguese Love" by Tina Marie, "Devotion" by Earth, Wind & Fire, and the classic, "Strawberry 22" by The Brothers Johnson. I turned the lever until the water was so hot I could hardly bear it. Steam filled the small room, fogging the mirrors and the glass shower doors. *"Ah,"* I sighed. "If only Terri was here to wash my back."

I was jammin' so hard I completely lost track of time, but when the skin on my fingertips began to wrinkle I knew it was time to get out. I turned off the water and stepped out onto the floor mat. After putting on some lotion I walked over to turn the light switch on—that's when I saw something that shocked me.

The words TRICK OR TREAT? were written in bold letters in the middle of the fogged mirror. Time stood still. The sound of the radio faded into complete silence and my heart pounded so hard it echoed in my ears. I tried not to panic as I slipped on my drawers. I turned down the volume on the radio, then reached underneath the sink for my pipe wrench. I grasped it tightly and stepped out into the living room.

When I saw that she wasn't there, I checked the living room, then the kitchen and pantry, but there was no sign of her. Then I remembered. "Oh, shit, Samantha!" I said out loud. I rushed up the stairs so fast I fell down twice. All sorts of horrible visions flashed through my mind as I came closer to her bedroom door. *Was she dead, kidnapped?* I thought to myself. I stopped short of the door and cocked the pipe wrench back so I would be ready to deliver a blow. I pushed the door open slowly and looked inside. "Thank God!" I sighed as I lowered the wrench. Samantha was still sound asleep.

Suddenly I heard the sound of screeching tires. I rushed down the stairs, out the front door, then into the street. I caught a glimpse of a dark-colored SUV as it turned the corner. It was too dark to make out a face or a license plate number, but I knew who it was.

As I stood in the middle of the street at four o'clock in the morning wearing nothing but my drawers, I knew I would never have peace in my life again, not until Olivia got what she wanted—or one of us was dead.

Part V

(November)

Chapter 32

I WAS PEELING a bag of potatoes when I saw smoke coming from the grill in the backyard. I grabbed a bottle of water off the counter and rushed outside to pour it over the fire. "Mitch will never let me hear the end of this." Just then I heard a car pulling into the driveway. When I heard Luther Vandross blaring from the speakers, I knew who it was.

"Daddy, Daddy, it's Uncle Mitch!"

"Aw, hell, it's Chef Boyardee himself," I said, then I quickly put the lid over the grill.

On my way out of the backyard, I fanned the smoke with both hands.

"Hey, Princess," Mitch said while lifting Samantha into the air. "How's my little Beethoven?"

"Bay who?"

"Never mind, just give your uncle a big hug!"

"Can I have a kiss, too, Uncle Mitch?" I joked as I walked up to the car.

"No, but you can help Betty with the bags while I go check on the meat. I can see you still can't barbecue worth shit."

"Samantha, forget you heard your uncle Mitch say that bad word," I said.

"What bad word?" Samantha smiled as Mitch carried her into the backyard.

"Betty, how did you stay married to that brotha for twenty-five years?" I said while giving Betty a hug.

"I don't know. How did you stay married to him for fifteen?"

"Beats the hell out of me, but it damn sure wasn't his warm personality."

I began unloading the groceries from the trunk while Betty lifted a large pot from the backseat.

"So, where's Fast Eddie? Mitch told me he was bringing Denise down to celebrate their engagement."

"He should be here any minute. He called about an hour ago to let me know they landed on schedule."

"It's about time he made a respectable woman out of that beautiful girl! I don't know why she stayed with his cheating behind *this* long!"

"Stop hating on Eddie, Betty."

"I'm not hatin'. I'm just keepin' it real! I've known that boy since you and Mitch started working together, and he's still the same slick-talking playa."

"Well, you and Terri should have a lot in common, 'cause she can't stand him, either."

"I like her already."

After I dropped the bags off in the kitchen, I called Samantha inside to give Betty a hand so me and Mitch could talk. He must of sensed I had news about Olivia, because he brought her up before I could.

"So, what's the latest with that crazy broad?" Mitch asked.

"So far, the police haven't been able to prove anything. I didn't catch her in the house. I couldn't make out her face when she was driving away. Hell, I didn't even get a license plate number!"

"Wait a minute! You mean to tell me that she's gonna get away scot-free with breaking and entering? That *is* still a crime, isn't it?"

"She entered, all right, but she didn't break anything."

"Meaning what?"

"Meaning there was no sign of forced entry. She either picked the lock, or she had a key. I'm sure both doors were locked."

"How is that possible?"

"Man, I don't know!" I said in disgust. "Every week I give my keys to valets at restaurants, parking attendants, and God knows what other strangers. For all I know, she could have sweet-talked some horny young kid into giving her the keys long enough to make a copy."

Mitch glanced through the kitchen window to where Samantha was helping Betty.

"Do you think—"

"I already asked her," I cut him off. "She hasn't been approached by any strangers, especially black women with hazel eyes."

"Okay, so now what?"

"I guess I'll have to wait for her to make another move. But she better think twice before she comes creepin' around here. I bought a .38 the other day."

"I don't blame you! If some deranged female snuck into my bathroom while I was buck naked in the shower, I would sleep with a 3-57 under my pillow!"

"Well, all the locks have been changed, and Samantha knows to keep the alarm on at all times. And of course, I already told Terri what was goin' on," I said to him. "By the way, I never did thank you for butting into my business and getting me and Terri back together."

"Hey, what are friends for?" Mitch laughed. "Besides, I got tired of looking at your pitiful face around the studio every day. You deserve to be happy, and it's gonna take a woman like Terri to put up with your arrogant ass."

"I would tell you to go to hell, but you're right!"

We laughed and slapped each other five. Mitch knew me all too well. He was a true friend and he was always on time. That's what I was thinking as I looked down at my watch and realized Eddie still hadn't made it in from the airport.

"Where is that fool?" I said to Mitch.

"Who?"

"Eddie!"

"Well, if he's driving a car with a white top, he just pulled up." Mitch was looking over the top of the gate.

But it wasn't him, it was Terri. Samantha must have thought it was Eddie, too, because she ran toward the door.

"Samantha, slow down before you break your neck!" I yelled through the window. "It's not your uncle Eddie, it's Terri." She stopped dead in her tracks. "Now remember what we talked about."

"Oh, I remember, all right," she said, while rubbing her behind.

The long talk I had with Samantha didn't work out, so I had to resort to Plan B, the good old-fashioned ass whippin'. It was the first time I had spanked Samantha since she was seven and it was long overdue.

I intentionally waited for Terri to knock on the door so Samantha would have to greet her. She took a deep breath, then opened the door wearing a phony smile.

"Hi, Miss Doctor Ross, come on in."

"Hello to you, Samantha. You don't have to be so formal. Just call me Terri. Now where can I put these bags down?"

Samantha led her into the kitchen and helped her put the bags down on the counter. Then Terri politely introduced herself.

"Hi, I'm Terri."

"Hi, Terri, I'm Betty, Mitch's wife. Nice to meet you." They exchanged hugs. "Julian says we have a lot in common."

"Oh, really!"

Just as I was headed out to the backyard, another car backed into the driveway. The windows were heavily tinted. I walked around to the driver's side expecting to see Eddie behind the wheel. When the door opened, I couldn't believe who stepped out.

"Janet, what are you doin' here?"

"Eddie asked me to meet him here at five." She checked her watch. "Am I too early?"

Before I could tell her about Eddie's engagement, a blue Ford Taurus drove up to the front of the house. Denise came bolting out of the passenger side and rushed across the lawn toward me.

"We're here, we're here!" She jumped into my arms. "Pop the champagne, roll out the red carpet, roll up a blunt!"

"I missed you, too," I said while gasping for air. "Now, can you please loosen your grip? You're choking me."

"Sorry, I guess I got a little carried away. It's just so good to see you again, Julian!"

"Okay, step back so I can check you out, make sure you haven't blown up since I last saw you."

Denise was wearing fitted black jeans and high heels. She walked up and down the driveway doing her runway model imitation.

"Notice anything different?" she asked.

"Well, your butt's gotten a little wider."

"No, silly, I'm talking about this!"

She lifted her hand and flashed an impressive diamond ring.

"Congratulations, Li'l Sis. I'm really happy for you." While I was hugging Denise I looked over her shoulder at Eddie and gave him a disappointed glare. Eddie ignored me and began taking the luggage out of the trunk.

"Why don't you go inside and let Sam show you around the house?" I told her. "Mitch and Betty are inside, and so is Terri."

"Finally! I get a chance to meet Doctor Love," Denise laughed. "And she better be cute, too. You know we can't have any ugly women in the family."

As Denise began walking toward the house she noticed Janet standing in the driveway. "Julian, aren't you going to introduce us?"

"Oh, yeah, my fault. Denise, this is Janet, Terri's friend. Janet, this is Denise—Eddie's *fiancée*!"

"Pleased to meet you, Denise. I've heard a lot about you."

It was obvious by Janet's casual reaction that she knew who Denise was. That only made me even more upset as I walked over to confront Eddie.

"Man, you must be outta your damn mind inviting Janet here!"

"Hold on, partner, I've got it all under control."

"Don't try to play me, Eddie! I'm not one of your dizzy broads! What you're doing to Denise is flat-out *wrong*! You're disrespecting her, me, and my house!"

"So what you gonna do, Julian? Make a big scene and ruin Denise's engagement party?"

I despised him for using Denise to get his way. It took everything I had to keep from whipping his ass. Eddie continued to pull luggage out of the trunk. He was whistling and smiling like he didn't have a care in the world.

"I guess this conversation is over," Eddie said. "Now, let's go have a drink and enjoy the rest of the evening—like one big, happy family." He handed me a suitcase and began walking toward the house. "Like I said, I've got it *all* under control."

"Yeah, right," I said. "That's exactly what I said a week ago before all hell broke loose."

Chapter 33

BY FIVE O'CLOCK the party was in full swing. Mitch was blending daiquiris and Julian was playing his old-school CDs. Juanita and her boyfriend, Charles, who had arrived earlier, were dancing to the song "Oops Upside Your Head" by the Gap Band. Terri dragged Julian into the middle of the living room and started a Soul Train line. Mitch and Betty joined in, then Eddie and Denise got into the act.

"The roof—the roof—the roof is on fire!" Juanita yelled as she strutted down through the line.

"We don't need no water let the mothersucker burn—burn mothersucker—burn!" they all sang.

"What's wrong with the roof, Daddy?" Samantha asked.

"Nothin', sweetheart, that's just something old folks shout when they think they're getting down."

When the James Brown song "Payback" came on, Julian cleared the floor so he could give Terri lessons on how to do the Chicago step. Everyone gathered around to watch and make fun.

"Okay, give me your hands, and try to follow," Julian directed.

"I told you, I can't do this."

"Come on, baby, just close your eyes and pretend like we're at the Fifty-Yard Line on the south side of Chicago."

Terri went the wrong way and stepped on Julian's foot. When he tried to spin her around, she smacked him in the face. Everybody covered their mouth to keep from laughing, except Mitch.

"I think you better stop before you get a knot upside your head," Mitch laughed. "These country girls can cook, but they can't step worth shit."

"Who you callin' country?" Terri had her hands on her hips.

"I'm callin' *you* country, Ms. Green Acres!"

"I beg your pardon. I've been to Chicago many times and those black folks are country with a capital K, with their lime green suits, white shoes in December, and those ghetto-fabulous hairstyles. Hell, half the south side is from Mississippi!"

They all broke out laughing. Even Mitch had to give her a high five for that comeback.

After they wiped the tears from their eyes, Terri suddenly excused herself to go to the bathroom.

"You all right, baby?" Julian asked. "You don't look so good."

"I'll be fine. I think it's something I ate." Terri rushed to the bathroom holding her stomach. "Samantha, honey, could you please bring me my purse?"

"Okay, Terri."

"Maybe it's that time of the month," Eddie said.

"Man, shut up and come take this ass whippin' on the card table. Who wants to play bid whist?"

"I'm in!" Denise yelled.

"Me, too," Janet said.

Julian got a brand-new deck out of the kitchen drawer and marked the jokers—one with a large *B* and the other with an *L,* for little.

"Okay, rookies, who wants to play with the master?" Julian boasted.

Janet sat opposite him at the dining room table.

"Wise choice, Ms. Jackson," Julian said to her. "Now, let me tell you my house rules. Don't ever cut me out when I'm running a Boston. Don't lead without purpose. And rule number three, no swearing at the table unless you hear me swear first. Got that, damnit?" Julian laughed.

"Okay, I can see right now I'm gonna need a drink before I start playing with you, 'cause you're already getting on my nerves."

"That's a good idea," Mitch said as he reached under the counter. He pulled out a bottle of tequila, the brand with the worm inside it.

"What the hell is that?"

"This is the good stuff from Juarez, Mexico. Don't be *scurred*."

Betty sliced three lemons and set them on the table with the salt shaker. Mitch was already busy filling their glasses with shots.

"What about Terri?" Denise asked.

"I don't think she can handle this poison," Julian said. "We'll celebrate later with a glass of two-percent milk."

"I want to propose a toast," Mitch said while raising his glass. "To the future Mr. and Mrs. Eddie Harris. May you be blessed with many years of peace, prosperity, and frequent sex!"

"Hear, hear!" they said in unison, then gulped down the first shot. Mitch quickly gave them a refill and raised his glass again.

"And last, I'd like to propose a toast to our host and my partner, Mr. Julian Payne, for having the courage to pursue his dreams. As of December first, *Love, Lust, and Lies* will be on the air, coast to coast!"

"Hear, hear!" They all raised their glasses, then gulped down another shot.

While everyone was playing cards and getting drunk, Terri

came out of the bathroom and joined Samantha at the piano. She sat down next to her on the bench.

"Are you okay?"

"I'm fine, Sam. Thank you for bringing my purse."

"No problem."

"So, can you play this thing, or is it just for show?"

Samantha felt awkward being with Terri one on one, but she wasn't about to pass up an opportunity to show off to her.

"What song do you want to hear?"

"Why don't you create your own groove? You know, be original like Jill Scott and India.Arie."

Samantha was surprised by how down-to-earth Terri was.

"Aren't you supposed to be a doctor?"

"Yeah—and?"

"Well, I didn't think doctors were so cool."

"Girl, please—I can bust a move and get my swerve on with the best of 'em, so don't get it twisted!"

"You're funny!" Samantha giggled. "I thought you would be stuffy and, well, kinda boring."

"I'm still young, chile. Now, your daddy on the other hand, he's old as dirt."

"I *know*!" Sam agreed. "When I told him I was watching Big Tigger on BET, he thought I was talking about the character from Winnie-the-Pooh."

They both laughed.

While Terri and Samantha were talking, the card game in the dining room was beginning to heat up. "You're set!" Julian yelled as he slammed the big joker on the table. It was just a card game, but Julian saw it as revenge against Eddie for disrespecting Denise. Up until that point Eddie had managed to keep his secret on the down low, but as the shots of tequila began to take effect he and Janet became more relaxed and careless.

While Denise was dealing cards, Janet picked up the Corona Eddie was drinking and took a sip. At first no one paid attention except Julian. But when it happened a second time,

Denise caught it. Her happy expression changed as she and Julian made eye contact. Julian gave her a look of reassurance, letting her know he had her back. Denise tried to compose herself and continued to deal out the rest of the cards. Eddie was so busy flirting with Janet, he didn't notice the change in Denise's attitude.

"It's your bid, Janet," Denise said.

"Five no trump."

"What about you, *sweetheart*?" Denise glared at Eddie.

"I pass!"

"I pass, too," Julian said. "It's on you, Li'l Sis."

"I'll take six, down-town!"

A few minutes into the hand, Janet reached for Eddie's beer again. But before she could take a sip, Denise snatched the bottle out of her hand and poured it over her head.

"Maybe that'll cool you off, bitch!"

"What the hell is wrong with you?" Janet yelled.

Terri and Samantha came rushing in from the living room.

"What's goin' on?" Terri asked.

"Your girlfriend is fuckin' my fiancé!"

"I don't know what she's talkin' about."

"Don't play the innocent role, you tramp!" Denise shouted. "You must be *real* comfortable with each other sippin' out of the same bottle."

Eddie just sat there with a silly smirk on his face, looking down at his cards.

"I guess your whores in Chicago weren't enough, huh, Fast Eddie?" Tears began to roll down her face. "I can't believe you had the audacity to bring one of your women around me, especially today of all days."

"Look, baby, you know what kind of man I am," Eddie slurred. "Now, why don't you sit down and finish the card game. Later on maybe we can all get together and have a good time."

"That's it? That's all you have to say to me after three long years of supporting your business and washing your dirty drawers?"

"Look, goddamnit!" Eddie stood up and got in her face. "I never promised you a damned thing! You knew I had other women, you knew I didn't want kids, and you knew I never wanted to be married! Now, you can either sit your emotional ass down and play cards or get the hell out!" Then he sat down.

"Now I see what this is all about. You set this whole thing up to get out of our engagement. Well, baby, mission accomplished!" Denise threw her ring in Eddie's face. "When we get back home, I want all of your shit out of my house. Now, if you will excuse me." Denise began walking toward the stairs.

"Thanks for the memories, *Li'l Sis,*" Eddie said sarcastically.

Denise stopped dead in her tracks.

"No, sweetheart, thank *you* for the lesson. Sometimes it takes someone like you to make a woman realize she's wasting the most valuable thing she's got—her time." Then she walked upstairs.

There was a tense silence. Juanita and Charles excused themselves and left through the back door. Janet was so embarrassed she rushed out right behind them. "I'm sorry, Terri," she said on her way out.

"Terri, take Samantha upstairs," Julian said in a serious tone. "Betty, you need to go with them."

"Can a brotha get a drink around this joint?" Eddie slurred.

Mitch walked over to the table and sat down next to Eddie. Julian, who was already sitting on Eddie's left side, moved his chair in closer to him.

"Can you believe that woman?" Eddie continued. "I guess she's gonna have to catch a cab and find a place to stay tonight, huh, Julian?"

"I don't think so, *partner,* you're the one who's leaving."

"Excuse me?"

"You heard what the man said!" Mitch's tone was hostile. "Get to steppin'."

"Oh, so it's like that?" Eddie drank the last sip of his tequila and stood up from the table. "Fuck both of you—especially you, Julian." He staggered toward the door. "You ain't nothing but a hypocrite. I know you fucked Olivia in Chicago, and you probably hit it again after the party at the hotel. You ain't no better than me!"

"That's where you're wrong, Eddie. There's a big difference between you and me. I appreciate a good woman and I'm not afraid of commitment. You, on the other hand, can't separate your dick from your manhood, and it's gonna get you in serious trouble one of these days."

"Save your sermon for the radio," Eddie said as he picked up his garment bag. "I told you, I live life on my terms and I'm willing to pay the price for my sins. What about you?" Then he walked out the door.

Julian walked over to the window and watched as Eddie drove off. He covered his face with his hands and exhaled. He knew it was the end of their friendship.

"It's never easy letting go of your friends." Mitch placed his hand on Julian's shoulder. "Some people just have to learn the hard way."

"Twenty-five years, down the drain," Julian replied. "Why can't he just grow up?"

"The real question is: Why can't you accept that he won't?" Mitch said.

As he walked toward the pantry to get a mop to clean up the beer, the phone rang.

"Hello, Payne residence." Mitch paused. "It's for you, Julian. Sounds like one of those annoying telemarketers."

When Julian picked up the phone he checked the caller ID, but the number was blocked.

"Hello, this is Julian."

"Nice party—why wasn't I invited?"

"Olivia?"

"How did you like my little message?" She laughed. "I thought it was appropriate for the occasion."

"Where are you?"

Julian peeked out the window nervously. When he didn't see Olivia's truck, he rushed outside to look down the street.

"*Mm,* I love those tan shorts, they show off your hairy legs."

"Look, you psycho bitch, I'm telling you for the last time, stay away from me and my family, you understand!"

"Don't raise your voice at me, Julian. You know how sensitive I am," she said in an evil tone. "I might really get mad and carve my next message into your chest with my box cutter. You remember my box cutter, don't you?"

"What do you want, Olivia? And why are you doing this?"

"I want respect, damnit! I want love, and I want you!" Suddenly, her tone was soft and polite. "Why can't we go back to the way it was that first night in Chicago, remember? The good conversation, the great sex?" She sighed. "Now, I know I scared you away, and I'm sorry. But the only reason I act this way is because I love you and I don't want to lose you."

"Olivia, I don't want you—hell, I don't even know you. I suggest that you get some professional help before somebody gets hurt."

"The only person who's gonna get hurt is you!" She went back to her hateful tone. "Like I told you, every dog has its day, woof-woof, motherfucker!" Then she hung up.

Chapter 34

A PROCESSION OF yellow school buses stood idling outside the entrance of Clover Junior Academy. The principal was staring impatiently at her watch as she waited for Samantha and Ms. Randall to come down. After a couple of minutes, she rushed back into the building to find out what was holding them up. When she arrived at the music class, Samantha was holding her stomach and moaning.

"Samantha, why aren't you on the bus with the rest of the kids?" Ms. Bell asked her.

"My stomach hurts. I think it was something I ate for breakfast."

"Ms. Randall, could you please take her downstairs to see the nurse? I've got to get these buses moving."

"Don't worry, she's in good hands."

"Sorry you're going to miss the field trip. If you feel better, Ms. Randall can drive you to the zoo later on."

As soon as Ms. Bell was out of sight, they burst out laughing.

"Well, I guess we have the rest of the day to ourselves," Ms. Randall said. "Are you ready to go?"

"Yeah, where to first?"

"Well, we're going to get a pedicure and manicure, then we're going shopping."

"Good, I love shopping!"

"First we have to stop by my house so I can change out of these boring clothes."

"While we're there, can I change into the clothes we bought at the mall?"

"Sure, I don't see why not."

"Can I play your piano, too, like you promised?"

"Yes, Samantha. But you have to swear not to tell anyone that I took you to my house; not your baby-sitter, not Ms. Bell, and definitely not your father!"

"Don't worry, Ms. Randall, I won't tell. Like you said, it's just between us girls."

———

When they arrived at Ms. Randall's house, Samantha was overwhelmed by how beautifully the rooms were decorated. The living room was furnished with a peach-tone leather sectional and black granite tables with matching lamps. In the middle of the table was a hand-painted lavender vase with freshly cut roses inside. The kitchen wallpaper was a bright floral design with bright green borders.

"Wow! Now, this is what I call a girl's house," Samantha said. "My daddy decorates everything in our house in black, or gray, or green. Yuk!"

"That's men for you. They'll decorate the entire house with beer cans and wine bottles if you let them." Ms. Randall laughed. "I bet your dad has that poster of Malcolm X with his hand on his chin hanging up somewhere."

"How do you know?"

"Experience, sweetheart. When you grow up you'll realize

that all men are basically the same. They want to eat, watch basketball, and sleep. Of course, there's a few other things they like to do, but you're not old enough to know about that yet."

"Oh, I know all about sex," Samantha replied wisely. "I watch the Discovery Channel."

Ms. Randall laughed as she walked into the kitchen. She pulled out a pot and began boiling water.

"Well, why don't you discover that piano while I make us some tea?"

Before Samantha sat down at the piano, she peeked into the room that was adjacent to the foyer. It was dim inside, so she turned on the lights.

"Wow, this is great!" she said as her eyes scanned the paintings on the walls. She walked up closer to the painting she saw on the easel. It was a portrait of a young girl holding hands with her mother. They were dressed as if they were going to church. Samantha noticed that the girl in the picture looked just like her.

"What are you doing in here?" Ms. Randall shouted.

"I was just looking at your paintings. Is that me?"

"No, it's not you. Now get out!"

She grabbed Samantha by the arm and jerked her out of the room, then she turned out the lights and closed the door.

"I'm sorry, Ms. Randall, I didn't mean to—"

"No, sweetheart. You don't have to apologize. That was my fault. I shouldn't have overreacted. It's just that I have your birthday present in there and I didn't want you to ruin your surprise."

"But my birthday isn't until—"

"January first," Ms. Randall finished her sentence.

"How did you know?"

"I'm your teacher—I know *everything*," she said as she walked back toward the kitchen. "Now, why don't you play something for me on the piano while I finish making us some tea? And remember, hold that note."

Samantha began warming up on the huge piano. She had

never played on one so big. The piano her dad had bought her was smaller and less intimidating. Ms. Randall could hear her hesitation.

"It's no different than any other piano, Samantha. Just let yourself go and be creative," she called out from the kitchen.

"That sounds like something my daddy's girlfriend, Terri, would say."

Ms. Randall suddenly stopped washing dishes and pulled her soapy hand out of the water. She was holding a wineglass full of water.

"What did you say?"

"I said, my daddy's girlfriend told me to be different and create my own style. I hated her at first, then I found out she was kinda cool," Samantha said cheerfully. "She's smart, and pretty, and she writes poetry just like my daddy."

The more Samantha boasted about Terri, the more Ms. Randall tightened her grip on the wineglass.

"Oh, yeah, and she's a doctor, too!"

Finally, it shattered. A large gash opened in the palm of her right hand and began to bleed profusely.

"You all right?" Samantha sprang up from the piano bench.

"I'm fine, Samantha; sit down and finish playing!" She spoke calmly as she pulled another dish towel out of the drawer and wrapped it around the wound.

"You're sure you don't need a doctor?"

"How many times do I have to tell you, I'm fine!" she snapped. "Now, let's get back to your lessons. Sit down!"

Ms. Randall sat down next to Samantha on the piano bench. As she began to play, the blood from her wound soaked through the towel.

"So, tell me, where did your daddy meet this smart and pretty *doctor*?"

"They met in the parking lot at his building."

"Does she work in the building, too?"

"I think so." Samantha's voice was trembling. "Ms. Randall, I'm ready to go home now."

"In a while, Princess, but first we have to practice your singing. Now remember to breathe." She pressed down hard on Samantha's hand, smearing it with blood. "And you'd better hold that note!"

Chapter 35

"WHERE IS SHE?" Terri said to herself while pacing frantically in her office. "Julian is gonna kill me if I'm late again." After a few minutes, she called the receptionist, Helen, on the intercom to confirm the appointment.

"Yes, Doctor."

"Helen, have you heard from my four o'clock?"

"She called about fifteen minutes ago and said she was running late."

"Okay. When she arrives, escort her into my office and make her comfortable. I'm going to the rest room to freshen up."

"Another hot date with Mr. Payne, huh?"

"Listen to you, getting all in my business," Terri laughed. "But since you asked, Ms. Nosybody, we have a dinner date."

"I didn't mean to pry. It's just nice to see you so happy."

"It's okay, Helen. Thanks for noticing." Terri blushed. "By the way, you can go home after you check the patient in. Just leave her folder on my desk."

After Terri hung up, she rushed out the rear door to the employees' rest room. No sooner did the door close behind her than there was a knock on the lobby door. Helen checked to see who it was and then buzzed her in.

"You must be Ms. Johnson," Helen said while trying not to stare at her outfit.

The woman was wearing a black tuxedo dress, fishnet stockings, and three-inch heeled pumps. Her hair was pulled back into a tight bun revealing her pearl choker.

"Sorry I'm late; the traffic was horrible and the elevators were out of order. I thought I was going to faint walking up those fifteen flights of stairs," she said, nearly out of breath. "Is the doctor still in?"

"Yes, she's been expecting you. Now, if you would just fill out this paperwork, we can get you set up in our system."

"That's not necessary. I'm paying cash."

Helen was in too much of a hurry to worry about formalities, so she signed her in, collected one hundred fifty dollars, then escorted her into the office.

"Have a seat. Dr. Ross will be with you shortly."

The second Helen closed the door, Ms. Johnson walked over to Terri's desk and began going through the Rolodex. She scrolled through the letters J and P looking for Julian's new home number. When she didn't find it, she opened Terri's laptop and was about to log on when she noticed a picture underneath a transparent desk pad. It was a five-by-seven of Terri and Julian at a nightclub. Terri was wearing a low-cut dress that showed off her cleavage. "Fuckin' lovebirds!" she cursed, then she spit on it.

Just then Terri came in from the back entrance snapping her fingers and singing "I Shot the Sheriff." Ms. Johnson rushed back over to the sofa and sat down.

"Oh, my goodness!" Terri put her hand over her chest. "I didn't realize you were here."

"Sorry, Doctor, I didn't mean to startle you." She stood and extended her hand. "Thanks for seeing me on such short notice."

"No problem. Have a seat," Terri said, then sat down at her desk. "What happened to your hand?"

"It's nothing; just a little domestic accident."

Terri reached for the folder Helen had left on her desk and unknowingly wiped the wad of spit on her blouse sleeve. Ms. Johnson smiled.

"It says here that you're suffering from depression," Terri said. "Do you know what's causing this?"

"I've got so much drama in my life, I don't know where to start."

"Why don't we start with your childhood."

"Now, that's classic!" she laughed. "I guess you're expecting me to tell you a story about my daddy molesting me when I was seven."

"Well, did he?"

"My father wasn't at home often enough to molest me, or even raise me, for that matter."

"Do you resent him for not being there for you?"

"Resentment isn't a strong enough word. I hate the bastard!" she said. "A father is supposed to be your hero, your first love. But my father was nothing but a cheating dog. Instead of being my first love, he was my first heartbreak." She paused briefly to compose herself. "What about you, Doctor, do you resent your father?"

"My father was a very affectionate and responsible man. I was blessed to have him in my life until he died five years ago."

"Good for you," she replied sarcastically as she reached for her purse. "Look, can we change the subject? I didn't come here to talk about my father."

"We can talk about anything you want. It's your time."

Ms. Johnson reached into her purse and took a cigarette out of a gold case, then leaned back on the sofa.

"Do you mind if I smoke?"

"I'd rather you didn't, but if it will help you to relax, then—"

Before Terri could finish her sentence, she lit the cigarette.

Terri handed her an ashtray.

"Thank you, Doctor."

"Why don't we dispense with the formalities? It makes it easier to communicate." Terri pulled her chair closer to the sofa. "From now on, call me, Terri. What's your first name?"

"Evelyn, but my friends call me Eve."

"Okay, Eve, let's get down to business." Terri began taking notes. "What are you depressed about?"

"Like most women, I'm depressed over a man."

"Can you be more specific?"

"I want to be with him, but he doesn't want to be with me," she replied. "I've called him a thousand times, left him messages at his job, I've even followed him."

"Is this a former boyfriend, husband, or lover?"

"He's just some guy I like to fuck."

"Why not go fuck someone else and save yourself all this time, energy, and drama?"

Evelyn laughed at Terri's blunt retort.

"Because."

"Because what?"

"Because I don't have a damn thing else to do, that's why!"

"Are you in love with him?"

"Of course I am! Why else would I be here talking to you?"

"Does he love you?"

"What difference does that make? A person once told me that if you truly love someone, *nothing* should come between you!"

"Look, Eve, letting go isn't easy. And it's even more difficult when the sex is good—believe me, I know. It's like a crack addict going through withdrawal. But like any drug, it ultimately destroys you." Terri put her hand on her shoulder. "From one woman to another—let it go. A situation like this can only get worse."

"You got that right, worse for him!" She yelled as she sprang up from the sofa. "I'm sick and tired of these arrogant-ass men using women like doormats then throwing us away like garbage. They've got to learn that there's a price to pay for toying with a woman's emotions!"

"So, I guess this isn't the first time you've been hurt?"

Evelyn calmly walked back over to the sofa and sat down.

"Everything I tell you will remain just between us, right?" she whispered.

"I'm bound by law not to divulge my patients' secrets."

"What if I told you I killed someone?"

Terri squirmed in her seat, trying to disguise her discomfort.

"Relax, Doc, I haven't gone that far—not yet," she said with a sly grin.

Suddenly Terri felt dizzy. She put her hand on her stomach and rushed over to the trash can next to her desk and began vomiting. Evelyn rushed over with a Kleenex.

"Are you okay?"

"I'm fine. It must have been something I ate for lunch."

Evelyn happened to glance over at the photo of Julian and Terri on the desk. She noticed how much smaller her breasts were in the picture.

"Are you sure it's not morning sickness?"

Terri looked up at her with a shocked expression as she wiped her mouth with the Kleenex.

"What made you say that?"

"I was a mother myself—well, almost." She went back to the sofa and sat down. "The first time I got pregnant I was in high school. I was so afraid of my father finding out that I rushed to the clinic and had an abortion."

"And the second time?"

"It was six months ago—I was married then. But three months into the pregnancy I had a miscarriage."

"I'm so sorry, Eve. I'm sure you and your husband were devastated."

"He was devastated, all right, when the police came and arrested his ass," Eve said as tears rolled down her face. "I lost the baby because he was beating the shit out of me. I'll never forget the silly grin on his face when the doctors told him I could never get pregnant again. I should have killed that mother—"

She stopped abruptly. Terri passed her the box of Kleenex.

"Look, Evelyn, I know this is very difficult, but I can't help you if you don't open up and face your problems."

"Is that what you want, Doctor, you want me to open myself up to you? Okay, how's this?"

She slid up to the edge of the sofa and spread her legs. As Evelyn continued to cry, Terri noticed that her right eye began to change colors. The more she rubbed it with the Kleenex the more it changed from brown to hazel. Her contact lens had fallen out.

Suddenly all the pieces began to fall into place. There was the story about Evelyn being beaten by her husband and not being able to bear children. Mitch told her about the radio interview in Chicago when Olivia claimed she became sterile after being raped. But the dead giveaway was when she called herself Eve. It was the same name Terri used when she seduced Julian on the radio.

Terri's hands were shaking as she stood up from her chair and walked over to her desk.

"Maybe you should come back when you're not so agitated. Why don't we get together next Wednesday, Ms. Johnson?"

"Ms. Johnson? I thought we were on a first-name basis," she said. "Don't you want to know why I hate my father and the rest of these goddamn men?"

"I think you need to take a deep breath and relax."

"You've gotta lot of nerve calling yourself a doctor! You can't cure me! And you damn sure can't erase a lifetime of pain and misery. You don't have the slightest idea of what it feels like not knowing if your husband is going to come home with a hand full of roses or a balled-up fist. After so many years of abuse, all the anger builds up inside you until it erupts like a volcano." She picked up her purse and began walking toward

Terri. "Do your college textbooks and sophisticated degrees teach you about that kind of hell?"

Terri was terrified as she pretended to write in her appointment book.

"You sure you can fit me into your *tight* schedule?" she said, while reaching inside her purse. "I know how busy you are nowadays."

"Please sit down."

"Why—am I making you uncomfortable?" She was lifting her dress above her waist, exposing her vagina. "I thought you wanted me to—*open up.*"

Just then, the buzzer rang. Terri sprang up from her desk and rushed toward the door.

"Excuse me, Ms. Johnson, I'll be right back."

"Take your time," she said with a conniving grin. "Like I told you, I don't have a damn thing else to do."

Once she was outside the office Terri rushed over to Helen's desk and pushed the buzzer to let Julian in.

"What's the matter?"

"She's here."

"Who?"

"Olivia! She's in my office half-naked!"

Julian laughed, thinking Terri was kidding, that is until he saw the distress in her eyes. Terri quickly jumped in front of him, blocking the door.

"I've had enough of that psychotic bitch. Let me by."

"Wait, Julian, she's got something in her purse. It could be a gun!"

Julian broke away from her and burst into the office, but when he looked around there was no one there.

"She must have gone out the back. I'll call security."

"To hell with security! This ends today!" Julian said as he rushed out the door after Olivia.

Julian charged down the hall toward the stairway. Just as he thought, Olivia was racing down the metal stairs with her high heels in her hands. He bolted after her. There were fifteen flights of stairs between him and the garage exit. Olivia was already on the tenth floor and moving fast.

Julian narrowed the gap by jumping down a flight at a time. He nearly caught up to her as she passed the third floor. He could see the top of her head as she sped down the flight directly below him. Just when he was close enough to grab her, he fell and twisted his ankle.

"Aaargh!" he screamed.

Olivia stopped on the lobby level and quietly put down her shoes. She pulled a box cutter from her purse and tiptoed back up the stairs toward him. Julian was bent over holding his ankle and never saw her coming. She extended the blade as far out as it would go, then lunged toward him.

"Miss me, baby?" she whispered as she began slashing him.

The first blow grazed his forehead, but the second one caught him flush on the right side of the face, just below the cheek.

"Let's see if you can talk on the radio with your throat cut!" she yelled.

Julian grabbed her arm and twisted it until she dropped the box cutter. It fell through the space between the metal stairs and landed two stories down. Olivia fought wildly, scratching, kicking, and biting until she finally broke away. She was about to go after the box cutter to slash Julian again when she heard Terri coming down the stairs.

"I'll be back!" she said with a deranged look in her eyes. "I'm not through with you—or your uppity whore!"

She took off down the stairs and ran out the garage exit. By the time Terri reached Julian, his white shirt was covered with blood.

"Oh, my God! Let me get you to the hospital." She bent down and helped him to his feet.

"Terri, did you make that call to security or the police?"

"No, I was too busy running after you."

"Good, because I'm gonna handle this myself."

"Are you outta your mind? This woman is insane!" she said. "I'm going straight to the police!"

"If you do, the press will have a field day," he told her. "The show goes national in two weeks. Two weeks! I've been waiting all my life for this opportunity and I'm not about to blow it, not even over this!"

"Damn you, Julian! You can't just let her get away with this!"

"She won't—that I promise you," he said with conviction. "But right now I'm more concerned with getting my face stitched before I bleed to death. I've got a show to do tonight."

Chapter 36

OLIVIA WAS LYING on the floor in her living room eating stale pizza and sipping from a bottle of champagne. Her radio was tuned to WBMX and the volume was turned up. She was listening to Julian's show. It was Thanksgiving Day and the topic was Why can't men be thankful for what they've got?

"Fuckin' hypocrite!" she screamed at the radio.

She gulped down one glass after another, working herself into a rage.

"I didn't move all the way down here from Chicago to be left out, goddamnit!"

She stumbled over to the mirror and admired her reflection. She had on a pair of cutoff blue jean shorts and a tight halter top.

"Julian must be blind as Ray Charles and Stevie Wonder put together! I'm much finer then that bony-ass doctor!"

She pulled her hair on top of her head and turned from side to side; then she went into an act.

"Hi, my name is Olivia Payne, nice to meet you. And this is my lovely daughter, Samantha." She pretended to shake hands.

"Oh, Julian? I'm sorry he couldn't make it. He's very busy with his new talk show. I'll be sure to let him know you asked about him."

She suddenly stopped acting and rushed into the kitchen for a pen and piece of paper to write on.

"Olivia Payne, Olivia Payne," she said to herself over and over. "That has a ring to it!"

Then she began writing it down, slowly at first then faster. But as she continued to write, the thoughts of Terri having Julian's baby overwhelmed her. The words gradually changed as she went down the page.

Olivia Payne
Olivia Payne
Olivia Payne
Terri Payne
Terri Payne
Payne
Payne
Payne
Pain
Pain
PAIN!!!!

She pressed down so hard on the pen that it snapped.

"If you think I'm gonna let you live happily ever after, you've got another thing coming!" she yelled.

Olivia picked up the empty champagne bottle and threw it at the radio, then she stormed into the bedroom looking for her business card holder. When she found it, she removed three cards and laid them out on her dresser. The first card was from Terri's office, the second was the one Mitch gave her at the club, and the third was Eddie's photography card. They'd exchanged cards at the Hilton.

"If I can't hurt you, I'll hurt someone close to you," she said to herself. "Now, which one will it be?" She closed her eyes and shuffled them around. "Eenie, meenie, minie, moe!"

After she made her choice, she picked up the phone and dialed the number. While the phone rang, she glanced over at the photograph that she and Samantha took at the mall.

"I'm gonna give you a birthday present you'll never forget—Princess!"

Part VI

God's Gift to Women
(December)

Chapter 37

MY HANDS WERE shaking as I turned onto Jefferson Parkway. I parked just short of Olivia's driveway and checked my .38 one final time. I took a deep breath and tucked the gun into my pants. As I stepped out of the car, a brisk breeze blew a pile of leaves through the air and into a swirl. It was symbolic of what Olivia had done to my life. It had been weeks since I slept peacefully and I looked nervously out the window every time a car drove by. It was hell on earth, and I wanted it to end.

I looked around to make sure the coast was clear, then ran across the lawn. I was so busy watching out for the neighbors, I didn't see the For Sale sign. I tripped over it and fell flat on my face. "Lord, are you tryin' to tell me something?"

I brushed myself off and approached the door. The back of the porch was spray painted with graffiti that read, *The Witch is Gone!* When I peeked inside the window I saw that the house was empty.

"Yo, mister!" a voice said out of nowhere. "You lookin' for that lady who use to live here?"

I turned around and saw a white kid in baggy pants sitting on a bicycle.

"Yes, I am. Where is she?"

"She moved out two weeks ago."

I walked over to him and extended my hand.

"What's your name, young man?"

"Randy, but my friends call me G-Money."

I tried my best not to laugh at his hip-hop dialect. He was a rich white boy living in the suburbs of Houston, Texas, and had the nerve to call himself G-Money.

"Nice to meet you. My name is—"

"I know who you are. Me and my homies listen to you every night."

"So, Randy, I mean G-Money, would you happen to know where she moved to?"

"Nope! I'm just glad she's gone! I hated that witch, all the kids did. If one of our baseballs landed in her yard, she kept it," he said. "But the whole neighborhood turned against her when she poisoned her next-door neighbor's dog for crapping on her lawn."

"That sounds like Olivia, all right."

"So, are you her boyfriend?"

"No, just an associate," I replied. "I was dropping by to, uh, pay her back for something she gave me."

I unconsciously rubbed the bandage on my cheek where she'd cut me.

"The way you were creepin' up to her house, I thought you were the police."

"I was just trying to surprise her."

"Yeah, right. I guess that's why you needed this."

He pulled my pistol out of his pocket and handed it to me. "You dropped it when you tripped over the sign."

"That's just a little something I carry around for protection."

"Whatever, Mr. Payne." He laughed, then he pulled out a piece of paper. "Can I get an autograph for my mom?"

I signed it and then began walking toward my car.

"Nice meeting you, G-Money; and if you don't mind, I'd like to keep this between us."

"No problem, Mr. Payne. And don't worry, I won't tell my homies that you fell on your ass." He laughed as he pedaled away. "Have a merry Christmas!"

Chapter 38

IT WAS CHRISTMAS Eve and I was lying in bed waiting for Samantha to come rushing into my room. I could see the outline of her feet outside my bedroom door as she waited for six o'clock. At five fifty-nine, the countdown began. I pulled the comforter over my head and pretended to be asleep. As soon as the digital clock on my nightstand read 6:00 A.M., she came flying through the door.

"Wake up, wake up! It's time to go shopping!" She jumped up and down on my bed.

"Later, sweetheart! Daddy is tired from work."

"But we always go shopping on Christmas Eve," she said as she pulled the covers off me. "Come on, Daddy, let's get going before all the good stuff is gone!"

"I said later, Samantha! Don't make me get my belt!"

I peered through a small opening in my comforter and saw her walking out of the room with her head down and lips poked out. As soon as she was out of sight I hopped out of bed and rushed up behind her.

"Surprise!" I lifted her over my head.

"That was mean, Daddy! You almost made me cry. That's gonna cost you a pair of diamond earrings *and* a Coach purse."

I got dressed as fast as I could and met her downstairs. She was already waiting at the door with a two-page shopping list in her hand. "I hope you brought your platinum card."

When I opened the door I was surprised to see Terri standing there with three large boxes in her arms.

"What are you doin' here?"

"I was invited." She smiled and gave Samantha a wink. "Here, put these underneath the tree and we'll meet you in the car. Girl, that's a nice outfit."

"Why, thank you," Samantha replied, sounding prissy. "And may I say you look quite lovely yourself."

I stood there looking confused as they walked toward the SUV in the garage. They were holding hands and chatting like bosom buddies.

"Two women in a mall—on Christmas Eve!" I shook my head. "I should've rented an eighteen-wheeler!"

We fought through heavy traffic and frustrated shoppers driving from one mall to another. First Colony to West Oaks, Town & Country to Sharpstown, Memorial City to the Galleria. I've never seen so many hyper women in all my life. They rushed in and out of stores like roaches trying to find the best deals. I sat in the food court with the rest of the men who had been forced to be there. We all had the same pitiful expression that said, "I'd rather be at home sipping on a brew and watching the game."

By seven o'clock, Samantha and Terri were shopped out.

During the ride back home, they talked nonstop. I thought my head was going to explode. When we pulled into the driveway, they grabbed their bags, rushed upstairs to Samantha's bedroom, and shut the door.

"That's right, just use me for my money then forget about me!" I yelled at them.

"Thank you, *Daddy!*" they both laughed, then shut the door again.

I was just relieved to be home again. I had a refrigerator full of beer, and the Sacramento Kings were playing the Dallas Mavericks. I grabbed a Bud out of the fridge and opened the window in the den. It was late December, but the temperature outside was in the low seventies. I turned to the Weather Channel during the commercial to see how cold it was in Chicago. Just as I figured, the high was thirty-three degrees. I took a long sip of my brew and kicked my feet up. "So much for being homesick."

Later that evening while I was in the kitchen cooking dinner I heard giggling coming from Samantha's bedroom. I crept up the stairs and looked through the crack in the door. Terri and Samantha were sitting on the floor eating popcorn and watching my wedding video.

"There's Daddy waiting at the altar with the preacher," Samantha said. "He looked young back then."

"Yeah, he looked scared, too." Terri laughed. "I can see the sweat beading up on his forehead."

"That's Grandma and Grandpa, and that's my auntie Joyce." Samantha stood up and pointed. "And there's Uncle Eddie standing next to my daddy. He was the best man!"

I went back and forth from watching them to watching the video. I hadn't seen it in five years. I had almost forgotten how happy we were then.

"That's Mommy coming down the aisle, see?" Samantha pointed.

"I see, sweetheart. She was a beautiful bride."

"Sometimes I miss her so much my heart hurts."

"I know how you feel. I lost my mother when I was about your age."

"When did the pain of losing her go away, Miss Terri?"

"It still hasn't. I think it will always be with me. But I had to learn not to let it get me down." She was holding Samantha's hand. "I knew my mother wanted me to be happy, and your mother would want the same for you."

I shut the door quietly and went back downstairs thinking about Eddie. Weeks had passed since the incident with Janet, and we hadn't spoken since. It was the longest span of time we ever had gone without talking. I didn't want to miss him, but I did.

While I was seasoning my red beans, I decided to call him in Chicago to wish him a merry Christmas. As his phone rang, I was a little nervous about what I would say. I was still upset with him, but I wanted to make sure he was okay. His phone rang five more times, then his answering machine picked up. I decided to leave a message.

"Eddie, this is Julian. I just called to wish you a merry Christmas. Well, take care and—"

I stopped to check myself from sounding too formal. I knew what I wanted to say.

"I hope you're taking care of yourself, Li'l Brother. I'm still mad and disappointed, but I love you. Peace."

As soon as I hung up, the phone rang. I was hoping it was Eddie.

"Hello, Payne residence."

I heard light breathing, then silence, then the dial tone. The number came up OUT OF AREA. I turned off the lights in the kitchen and stared out the window. A few seconds later, the phone rang again.

"Who is this?"

"It's me—Mitch. You all right?"

"Yeah, man, I'm fine," I said, trying to play it off.

"Don't tell me that crazy broad is still stalking you."

"I'm just a little paranoid." I kept my voice down and carried the phone into the bathroom. "Everything is under control."

"That's what you said right before Olivia showed up at

Terri's office and nearly killed you. You need to stop worrying about your reputation and go to the police."

"Now you're starting to sound like Terri."

"Somebody needs to talk some sense into your hard head. That woman is dangerous!"

"Yeah, so am I," I said while pulling my pistol down from the top shelf of the linen closet. I had hidden it underneath a stack of old towels.

"This is not a game, Julian. It's for real. And Olivia is playing for keeps."

"For your information, Olivia is history!"

"What are you talking about?"

"Last week I drove out to her house with my pistol, you know, just to scare her."

"You did *what*?"

"Calm down and let me finish. When I got there the house was empty and a For Sale sign was on the lawn."

"That doesn't mean she left Houston."

"Well, if she's still here she must be sleeping on the floor, because her furniture was shipped back to Chicago."

"How do you know?"

"Let's just say celebrity has its privileges."

"That still doesn't prove she's gone," Mitch said. "If I were you I'd hire a private detective to find out *exactly* where she's at, just to be on the safe side."

Suddenly, there was a knock at the door. It was Terri.

"Julian, open up!"

"Hey, Mitch, I'll talk to you later," I said, loud enough for Terri to hear. "Tell Betty I said merry Christmas. Bye."

I put the pistol back underneath the stack of towels and opened the door.

"Hey, baby; you and Sam finished wrapping gifts yet?"

"Where is it?"

"Where's what?"

"The gun, Julian, I heard what you said to Mitch."

"Now you're eavesdropping?"

"I was getting something to drink from the kitchen when I heard your big mouth. Now, where is it?"

"Look, Terri, there's nothing to worry about. Like I told Mitch, Olivia is long gone!"

"Julian, you may be an expert at raising hell on the radio but I'm an expert on the human psyche, and I'm warning you that women like Olivia don't just go away! She'll keep coming back until she gets what she wants—or until one of you ends up dead! Is that what you want?"

"Whatever happens, happens."

"How dare you have such a selfish attitude! Did you ever stop to think about me? And what about Mitch? He's invested the past fifteen years of his life in you and your career! But the real question is, what's going to happen to Samantha? She's already lost a mother. Do you want her growing up without a father, too?"

I was speechless. I leaned against the counter feeling guilty and ashamed. I was so busy worrying about my reputation that I didn't think twice about how it was affecting the people in my life.

"You're right, baby. I'm getting way too caught up in this business—the money, the fame, the hype, everything! I promise you the next time I hear from Olivia I'll contact the police right away. Hell, I'll even call the FBI if you want me to." I looked deep into her brown eyes. "I've waited a long time to find this kind of happiness again, and I'm not gonna chance losing it—or you."

"Let's just pray that there won't be a next time," she said as she moved closer to me. "I don't want to lose you, either." Then we kissed.

I tried to pull away, but she wouldn't let me go.

"Julian, I think this is a good time to tell you something very important."

What is it, baby?"

"Well, you know I haven't been feeling well lately and—"

"Ooo, I saw that!" Samantha laughed while leaning her head in the door. "Can you two horny adults stop slobbering over each other long enough to open some gifts?"

"Where did you learn that word?"

"Chill out, Dad, I watch the Discovery Channel!"

She took me by the arm and dragged me into the living room where she had two boxes placed under the tree, one for me and the other for Terri.

"But it's not Christmas yet," Terri said.

"It's okay; this is a family tradition. Each person gets to open one gift before Christmas."

We took turns ripping the colorful paper off our presents. I went first. Samantha brought me Sade's *Best of Sade* CD. I gave her the Coach purse she had been begging for all year. She ran full speed into my arms, knocking me over.

"Thank you, Daddy, thank you, thank you!" she said while kissing me. "I promise I'll never lose it!"

"You got that right; you won't be wearing it out the house unless you're with me or an armed guard," I laughed. "Those things are expensive!"

Terri was still fiddling around with her box trying to get it open. She decided to stop acting cute and used her teeth to bite the tape off. When she finally got it open, she was speechless. She sat back on the floor and her eyes began to water. When I knelt down next to her I understood why. Inside the box was my old blue jean shirt, the one Carmen used to wear around the house.

"Do you like your present, Miss Terri?"

"Yes, sweetheart. It's the best present I ever had," she said with tears rolling down her face. "Come over here and give me a hug, girl!"

I was so moved I had to hold back my own tears. I held both of them in my arms and we rocked back and forth. It felt like old times again. Like family.

Chapter 39

IT WAS JUST after sundown on New Year's Eve when a yellow cab exited off Highway 288 onto Reed Street. After traveling two miles down the road, it turned into the parking lot of a raunchy building. The partially lit neon sign read THE SKYLARK MOTEL.

"You sure this is the place?" Eddie asked the driver.

"The address you gave me was 1803 Reed Street, mister," he replied in a strong Nigerian accent. "This is it, see?" He pointed at the crooked numbers over the door.

Eddie took a deep breath and stepped out onto the sandy lot. While the driver lifted his bags and camera equipment from the trunk, Eddie looked around in disgust at the area he found himself in. Across the street was a liquor store where bums were hanging out and begging for money. Next door was a run-down bar playing loud music. Dealers were selling bags of dope right out in the open. Eddie was no stranger to raunchy motels, but this was below even his standards.

"What the hell am I doing here?"

"I don't know, mister, but the fare is sixty-five bucks," the driver said.

Eddie slapped the money in his outstretched hand and then picked up his bags. It wasn't easy finding room 121 because the numbers on some of the doors were missing. Once he was outside the door, he checked the information one last time, hoping he had made a mistake. As he was reaching inside his coat pocket for the piece of paper, the door slowly opened.

"Hello, stranger," she said in a sexy tone. "Come on in."

"Olivia, you better have a good explanation for bringing me all the way from Chicago to this dump." Eddie dragged his bags into the dimly lit room.

The lamps had red lightbulbs in them and a strobe light was blinking in the corner.

"I love this Parliament/Funkadelic vibe you've got goin'," he said while taking off his coat, "but how do you expect me to take pictures in the dark?"

"I thought we'd try something a little different. That's why I chose this place; it has atmosphere."

"You got that right—*stank* atmosphere! Your face will come out blurred on the CD cover if I photograph you with these red lights in the background."

"I don't care about my face being seen. It's all about getting their attention!"

"Well, if you plan on wearing that outfit on the cover, you've got the problem solved."

Olivia had on a white halter top and a pair of cutoff blue jean shorts. Eddie stared at her ass while she walked over to the dresser. She bent over and pulled a bottle of Jack Daniel's from the bottom drawer, knowing damn well he was looking.

"You want some—whiskey?"

"Sure. Why not?"

She put two cubes of ice in a paper cup and began filling it to the top.

"Hey, that's enough! I've got to be able to focus."

She carried it over to him, then sat down on the bed and crossed her legs.

"So, how's Denise?"

"I wouldn't know. We broke up last month."

"I'm sorry to hear that. She was a nice girl."

"I guess this wasn't my year for relationships," Eddie laughed. "Oh, well, life goes on."

"Does it, now?"

"Excuse me?"

"Oh, nothing."

Eddie gulped down the rest of his whiskey, then walked over to the dresser to get a refill.

"By the way, thanks for flying me in to do this gig." Eddie was trying not to stare at her breasts. "Money was getting a little tight with me moving into my own place."

"Don't mention it." Olivia uncrossed her legs. "All I ask is that I get my money's worth."

Eddie gave her a sly grin as he stirred his drink with his finger, then he licked it.

"I haven't had a dissatisfied customer yet."

After another shot of Jack Daniels, Eddie began unpacking his camera equipment. Olivia went into the bathroom to change. When she came out, she was smoking a joint and wearing a sheer red gown with a matching thong. Even in the dim light, Eddie could see her erect nipples.

"I hope you don't mind if I smoke; it helps me relax," Olivia said.

"It's your dime, baby. Just save me a hit."

The photo session quickly turned into a scene out of a Cheech and Chong movie as Olivia lit one joint after another. The high from the weed enhanced the effects of the flashing strobe light and the red lightbulbs. Olivia's hazel eyes jumped out at the camera as Eddie shot one roll of film after another. And the more he smoked, the more aggressive he became. Instead of telling her what pose he wanted, he guided her with his hand.

"Now lift your leg over the arm of the chair." He rubbed his hand on her thigh. "Yeah, that's it!"

When he tried to touch her breast, she grabbed his wrist and stood up.

"Now let's change places." She snatched the camera out of his hand. "Take your clothes off!"

Eddie did a striptease as Olivia took pictures. Once he was naked, she pushed him onto the bed.

"Now, spread your arms out."

"For what?"

"Just do it!"

She quickly got undressed, then walked over to the dresser and pulled out two long extension cords.

"I knew you were a freak when I met you," Eddie said. "I could see it in those nasty eyes."

"You should've looked deeper," she said in a cruel tone as she tied his hands to the bedposts.

"Ouch, not so tight!"

"Shut the fuck up and take it like a man!"

Once his hands were firmly tied down, Olivia turned the volume up on the radio as loud as it would go, then disappeared into the bathroom.

"Hurry up, Olivia! I've been waiting a long time to get my hands on that round ass of yours!"

"Just a second, baby," she shouted from the bathroom. "I've got a surprise for you. Close your eyes."

Olivia came out of the bathroom with her right arm tucked behind her back. She took a sip of whiskey, then hopped on top of Eddie's chest. When he opened his eyes, she was staring down at him with an eerie expression.

"So where's my surprise?"

"Be patient, baby. I just want to ask you a few questions."

"Questions? Like what?"

"Like why you never asked about Julian. I thought you were supposed to be friends."

"Julian and I haven't spoken in weeks. Besides, I knew he wasn't serious about you. He just wanted to—"

"Go ahead and say it, he just wanted to fuck me, right? Just like you!"

"Look, Olivia. You called *me,* remember?"

"Yes, I did, and you came running like a horny dog."

"Hey! We're both adults, and I'm not committed to anybody!"

"That's right, you're the man who never makes promises." Her tone became more hostile. "Isn't that what you told Denise at Julian's house that night?"

"How did you know that?"

"I saw the pain in her eyes," Olivia went on. "I've felt the same pain a thousand times thanks to men like you and your fuckin' friend! Well, both of you can go to hell—and I'm sending you first!"

When Olivia brought her arm from behind her back she was holding a large box cutter.

"What the hell is this? Some kind of game?"

"That's right, *Fast* Eddie, and you're *it!*"

She slashed him across the face and neck. When her right arm got tired she used the left. Even after he stopped moving she continued to cut and stab. When it was over she calmly got up off the bed, picked up the camera, and took a picture of Eddie lying in the pool of blood.

"Happy New Year—playa!"

Chapter 40

I WAS PACING back and forth in my bedroom practicing my opening line for the show.

"'Good evening, ladies and gentlemen.' Naw, that sounds too white!"

I cleared my throat and tried again.

"'Whassup, brothas and sistahs?' Hell naw, that's *way* too black!"

After fifteen years in the radio business, here I was coming down with a case of the jitters. I tried to convince myself it was just another show, but I knew better. New Year's Eve was the highest ratings night of the year. It was also the first night the show was airing live in New York, Los Angeles, and Chicago. All my friends and family would be tuned in, not to mention all the haters from WTLK.

"You can do this, Julian!" I said while staring at my reflection in the dresser mirror. "Like Mitch said, it's your season!"

While I was getting all pumped up, I heard Samantha's knuckles tapping on the door.

"Are you butt *nekked*?" She laughed.

"Very funny. Come on in."

I was in a serious mood but broke into a smile when she walked in wearing Bugs Bunny slippers and pink pajamas.

"I came to tell you to have a good show tonight."

"Well, don't just stand there. Come and give your old man a kiss for good luck."

"Um," she groaned as she smacked me on the cheek. "Give them a show they'll never forget, Big Papa!"

"Are you sure you'll be okay until Juanita gets here at eleven?"

"I think I can take care of myself for two hours," she said with her hands on her hips. "I'm a big girl."

"Just remember what I told you—"

"I know, I know. Lock the doors, set the alarm, don't open the door for strangers, and call you on the hotline if anything happens—I got it!"

She took me by the hand and led me downstairs and then outside to my car.

"I'll call you after midnight to wish you happy birthday."

"Will you have my present when you get home from work?"

"Sam, you're getting too spoiled. Didn't I buy that expensive purse you wanted?"

"Yeah, but that was for Christmas. I want a present for my birthday, too." She pouted. "You told me if I got good grades we would go shopping."

"Okay, I'll make you a deal. If you get straight As on your report card I'll take you to the mall next weekend."

"But I showed you my report card already."

"I'm waiting on the official copy that comes in the mail. I remember how easy it was to change a D to an A." I laughed. "Now, let me go to work so I can afford you."

On the way to work, I checked the mailbox. It was full of junk mail, mostly catalogs and grocery-store coupons. Underneath my *Black Enterprise* magazine I saw the bright yellow envelope from Clover Junior Academy. I ripped it open and pulled out her report card. Sam had straight As except in her physical education class. "How in the world did that chile get a C in gym?"

I tossed the letter onto the passenger seat and sped off toward the studio. As I was driving down Highway 59, my cell phone rang.

"Hello?"

"Hey, baby, you miss me?"

"Who is this?"

"The love of your life; you just don't know it yet."

Then I recognized the voice.

"Olivia! How did you get this number?"

"I'm saving that surprise for later. Right now I think you better get over to the Skylark Motel. It's off Old Spanish Trail and Reed Street."

"I'm not meeting you anywhere!"

"Who said anything about meeting *me*? Your buddy Eddie asked me to call. He said it was a matter of life—and death!"

"You're full of shit, Olivia. Eddie's in Chicago!"

"Wanna bet?" she said bluntly. "He's in room 121. The door is unlocked." Then she hung up.

I immediately dialed Eddie's cell phone, but there was no answer. Then I called Denise, hoping she had heard from him. When she picked up I tried my best not to sound distressed.

"Hey, Li'l Sis!"

"Happy New Year, Julian! Whassup?"

"Oh, nothin'. Look, I was just wondering—have you heard from Eddie?"

"Yeah, he called me late last night talkin' crazy about getting back together for the new year."

"And?"

"And I told him to go to hell!"

"Did he say anything about coming to Houston?"

"He told me if I didn't want him he knew somebody in Houston who did."

"Thanks for the info, Li'l Sis. Talk to you later."

"Wait a minute. Is everything all right?"

"Sure! I just wanted to make sure he was listening to the show tonight, that's all."

"Well, you know I'll be tuned in. I'm your number one fan." She laughed. "Don't forget to give me a shout out!"

Now I was panicking. I checked the clock on the dash. It read 9:15. "Twenty-five minutes there, and fifteen to the studio," I calculated out loud. "I can make it!"

As I raced toward the Skylark Motel, I thought about the promise I had made to Terri. I told her I would call the police the next time I heard from Olivia. But there was no way of knowing what they would find at the motel. I wasn't about to take a chance on making a crank call on the most important night of my life.

"Sorry, sweetheart," I said to myself, "but this is one promise I'll have to break."

Chapter 41

THE MOMENT I pulled into the parking lot of the Skylark Motel I got a bad feeling. It was a filthy place. The windows were dirty, broken glass littered the ground, and it reeked of urine. I walked down the narrow corridor checking the numbers on the doors until I came to room 121. I could see a flashing light through a slit in the curtain. As I was about to turn the knob, I spotted a small brick lying in the dirt. I picked it up, then crept back up to the door. I was hoping to find him handcuffed to the toilet, like I did at the Park Avenue. That would have been a welcoming sight. "Here we go again," I said to myself. "One, two, three," then I opened the door.

"Oh—my—God!" I fell to my knees and started vomiting. My best friend was lying faceup on a blood-soaked mattress with his chest and face ripped to pieces. When I finally stopped throwing up, I stumbled around the room looking for the phone to call the police. When I found it, the cord had been cut. My cell phone was in the car, so I covered Eddie's body with a blanket and then went to use the pay phone that was outside the door.

"Operator, send the police to the Skylark Motel off 288 and Reed Street, room 121. Please hurry!"

"Calm down, sir, and tell me your name."

"What difference does that make? Just send the police, god-damnit! My friend is dead!"

I went back to my car and sat there trying to make sense out of what was happening. While I dried my eyes, I saw the message light blinking on my cell phone. I flipped it open and saw the studio number on the screen. It was a quarter to ten and I knew Mitch was worried about where I was. Just as I was about to return his call, the phone rang.

"Hello?"

"Fast Eddie's not so fast now—is he?"

"What the hell is wrong with you, Olivia! He never did anything to you!"

"He was a dog, and dogs sometimes need to be put to sleep!"

"He's not asleep, he's dead—you psychotic bitch!"

"It hurts, doesn't it? Now you know how it feels to lose someone. Now you know what *real* pain is!"

"The next person to feel pain will be you!" I said. "When I catch up with you, Olivia, your ass is mine!"

"Oh, I like the way that sounds. Can we do it doggy style?"

"We can do it any way you want," I was playing off her insanity. "Name the time and place."

"How about tonight at your place? Maybe Samantha can watch."

"You leave her out of this!"

"She's already in it, you dumb bastard! How do you think I got your home and cell phone number after you changed them twice? Do the math. Better yet, do your *homework*!" Then she hung up.

I reached inside my pocket for my car keys. I was so pissed, I fumbled them onto the passenger seat. They landed on top of the pile of mail. That's when I began to understand what Olivia meant by "do your homework."

The bright yellow envelope from Samantha's school was

the same as the one I picked up at Olivia's house. It had fallen on the floor with the electric bill. I recalled the clover symbol in the corner. Then I remembered the name that was printed on it, Olivia R. Brown, the same as on the business card she gave me at the hotel.

"Olivia R. Brown," I said over and over. Then it hit me. "Oh, shit, the R is for Randall. She's the substitute music teacher!" I sped out of the parking lot while dialing my cell phone. I called home, but there was no answer. I tried calling Juanita, but she wasn't home either. I was in a frenzy as I raced down the highway. I dialed home over and over, but Sam didn't answer. When I put the phone down to weave through traffic, it rang.

"Please don't hurt her!"

"Hurt who?" Mitch said. "Man, where the hell are you?"

"He's dead, Mitch! Eddie's dead!"

"What are you talking about?"

"Eddie's dead! Olivia killed him!"

"Calm down, Julian, you're not making any sense. Where are you?"

"I'm headed home. I think she's after Samantha!"

"I'll call the police and have them meet you there."

"No, don't! I'm gonna handle this myself!"

"That's what got you into this mess in the first place. Why do you—"

I hung up on him and stepped on the gas. As I swerved in and out of traffic, my mind flashed back to Eddie's mutilated body. I didn't know if I would get home and find Samantha in the same condition, or worse.

When I turned on to my block, I switched off my headlights and parked two doors down from the house. All the lights were out except for the one in Samantha's bedroom. I crept in the front door and made my way to the downstairs bathroom to get my pistol. When I felt underneath the stack of towels where I kept it, it was gone. I grabbed the pipe wrench from under the sink and moved quietly up the stairs. When I made it to her bedroom door, I put my ear to it, but there was no sound. I tried to turn the knob, but the door was locked. "Sam!" I yelled. "Sam, you in there?" When she didn't answer I said a short prayer, then I broke the door in with my shoulder.

I was relieved and distressed when I saw she wasn't there. But there was a box at the head of her bed. I opened it slowly, hoping not to see Samantha's head or another body part. When I pulled the lid off, I let out a sigh of relief. Inside was a letter and a royal blue pillow. I didn't recognize it until I turned it over and saw the embroidery on the front. It read *The Princess Is Sleeping*. It was the pillow Olivia gave me in the parking garage. She must have come back after our argument and pulled it out of the garbage. I tossed it across the room, then opened the letter.

I wish I could see the expression on your face. I bet you thought I was just gonna go away like some dollar-store 'ho. Well, you guessed wrong. I'm here until the end, until death do us part—isn't that in the marriage vows? Well, consider us married, and the reception is tonight at the studio.

Love,
Olivia

P.S. If I see any flashing lights or hear any sirens, your little princess will never see her eleventh birthday. See you at the party!

I ripped the letter into pieces, then dialed the studio to warn Mitch. It rang several times but he didn't answer. I tried his cell phone next, but still nothing. "Damnit!" I said as I slammed the phone down.

I went downstairs and got a butcher knife from the kitchen, then took off running back to my car. As soon as I turned on the ignition, I heard my voice over the radio.

"Welcome back to *Love, Lust, and Lies*. I'm your host, Julian Payne. We're talking about resolutions for the new year. Pamela from Hyde Park, what's your comment or issue?"

"Mitch, you're a genius!" He was playing a recorded show from WTLK in Chicago. But he still wasn't answering the studio line. That could only mean that Olivia was already there.

As I sped toward the radio station, I was praying that Samantha and Mitch were all right, but after seeing what she'd done to Eddie I didn't believe any of us would make it out of that studio alive.

Chapter 42

IT WAS ELEVEN THIRTY when I arrived at the studio. I parked in front of the building and ran inside. The lobby was unusually quiet. The only sound was a small radio at the security desk tuned in to WBMX. There were no janitors emptying trash or mopping, and Joe the security guard was nowhere in sight. I held my breath as I approached the customer service desk.

I leaned over the counter as far as I could, hoping not to see his body lying on the floor, when suddenly I heard keys jiggling.

"Can I help you with something, Mr. Payne!"

It was Joe. He was walking toward me buckling his pants.

"Joe!" I gave him a hug. "It's good to see you."

"It's good to see you, too, Mr. Payne. Sorry I wasn't at my post, but I had to squeeze the monkey, if you know what I mean." He winked. "Hey, how can you be here talking to me and on the radio, too?"

"It's a recording. I was running late and Mitch was covering for me," I told him. "Look, Joe, have you cleared anyone to go upstairs to the studio since you've been on duty?"

"No one except your sister and little Sam."

"My sister?"

"Yeah, your sister—Olivia. I signed them in about forty-five minutes ago. I didn't want to call upstairs and spoil the surprise."

"What surprise?"

"Samantha's birthday," he said. "They had a cake, balloons, presents, everything!"

"Damn!" I said.

"Is there a problem, Mr. Payne? You know I don't usually bend the rules, but I figured, what the hell, it's New Year's Eve."

"It's okay, Joe," I said while running toward the tower elevators. "Be careful tonight."

As I pushed the button for the twenty-fifth floor, I thought about going back and asking for help, but Joe was too gung ho. He would have gotten all of us killed, including himself. It was up to me to figure out a way to save my daughter and myself. How I was gonna do that with a dull-ass butcher knife was beyond me. I stared at my reflection in the elevator mirror as I pushed the knife down into my sock.

"You said you wanted to handle it—well, here's your big chance."

When the elevator doors opened, I could hear the station playing over the hallway speakers. I ran down the hall as fast as I could, staying close to the walls to avoid being seen by the security cameras. I knew the chances of her not watching were slim, but I needed every break I could get. Once I was at the lobby door, I punched the access code and went in.

The office was completely dark except for a dim light coming from inside the studio. It was the glow from my jasmine-scented candles. I crawled on my hands and knees toward the control room, which was about fifty feet away and next door to the studio. The door was slightly open.

As I crawled down the dark hallway, I heard a muffled sound coming from inside the control room. The closer I got, the more pronounced it became. When I made it to the studio I eased my head inside the door. The room was filled with balloons and there was a birthday cake with candles. I stayed down as low as I could and made my way over to the control room. The door was cracked open but it was hard to see inside. I had to find out where that humming noise was coming from, so I pushed the door open slowly and ducked my head in. "I'll be damned! Mitch!"

He was lying on the floor naked with his hands and feet bound with duct tape. He had a strip of it over his mouth and was bleeding badly from the head, like he had been pistol-whipped. When he saw me coming toward him, he jumped as if he was scared. But once he could make out my face, he let out a sigh. I sat him up in the chair and began taking the tape off his mouth.

"I had to open the door," he said, sounding hysterical. "She said she would shoot Samantha."

"Where is she now?"

"Right here, you son of a bitch!"

I didn't see her at first, then those hazel eyes gradually appeared out of the shadows. She was completely naked and holding a gun to Samantha's head.

"Put that tape back over his mouth and bring your ass in here!"

"Take the gun off her first."

"I'm running this show tonight!" She cocked the trigger and put the barrel in Sam's mouth. "Now do what I told you, or so help me God, I'll kill this nappy-headed little bitch!"

I put the tape back on his mouth and walked over to the studio.

"And you, get back down on the floor," she told Mitch. "The only reason I didn't shoot your ass is because you were nice to me at the party—but don't press your luck."

"Daddy, I'm scared!" Samantha cried.

"Don't worry, sweetheart. Everything is gonna be all right."

"Your father is lying to you," Olivia said while stroking her hair. "Everything *is not* gonna be all right, in fact, this is gonna turn out pretty fucked up, trust me!"

"Why don't you let her go, Olivia? You got me. Isn't that what you came here for?"

"I came here to bring in the new year and celebrate our daughter's birthday." She kissed Samantha on the forehead. "All we need now is for the guest of honor to arrive, and we can get this party started!"

"What guest of honor?"

"I'm sorry, Daddy," Samantha cried. "She made me call."

"Shut your mouth!"

Olivia tore off a piece of duct tape and covered her mouth.

"What are you up to, Olivia? This is just between us!"

"You just do what I tell you and your daughter *might* make it out of here alive tonight. Now pick up those boxes off the floor and get behind that console. We're going on the air in five minutes."

"Are you crazy?"

She moved in closer to me so I could see Sam's face as she began tightening her grip around her neck.

"Yes, I am crazy, which makes you a damn fool for arguing with me!" Sam's face was turning red. "Now, I'm not going to ask you twice!"

I picked the two small boxes up off the floor and moved behind the console.

"Good boy," she said. Then she stopped choking Samantha.

I stared down at the console. It read 11:40. It was obvious she was waiting for midnight to make her move. I began turning knobs and flicking switches on the panel, hoping she wouldn't know if we were on the air.

"Okay, speak into your mic so I can check the levels."

"Testing one two, testing one two," she said while clearing her throat.

I pushed a few more buttons and pretended to be preparing to go on the air.

"Are you ready?"

"Not yet—we're still waiting for our special guest," she said with a devious smile.

That's when I knew. Before I could react, the bell rang in the lobby. I looked up at the monitor and saw Terri punching in her access code. Olivia blew out the candles in the corner and stepped backward into the shadow, dragging Samantha with her.

"Don't try anything stupid."

When Terri walked into the studio she was wearing a sexy white dress and carrying a bottle of champagne.

"Surprise!" She rushed over and gave me a hug. "Happy New Year, baby!"

I wanted to cry as I hugged her back. I knew it was probably the last time I would feel her soft body against mine.

"I'm sorry," I said to her.

"Sorry for what?"

"Sorry that you were so damned stupid!" Olivia said as she walked out of the shadow.

"Oh, my God!"

"That's right, pray. You're gonna need him tonight. Now move over there and stand still, you booshie bitch." She directed Terri with the gun. "By the way—nice dress."

Terri set the bottle down and moved to the side of the console next to the tape rack.

"Now that everybody's here, we can start opening gifts! Why don't you open yours first, Julian?"

I pulled the top off the box and carefully reached inside. The light was too dim to see what it was, but I could feel a metal object with a strap attached to it. When I removed it from the box I recognized it right away. It was Eddie's camera.

"I thought you might want a souvenir." Olivia laughed.

"Fuck you, Olivia!"

"You already did, remember? That's what got you into this mess. Now pass the other box over to Miss Eve."

Terri took the box out of Julian's hand and set it down in front of her.

"Well, don't just stand there, *Doctor,* open it!"

Terri looked nervous as she reached inside the small white container. When she pulled her hand out she was holding a multi-colored rattle.

"You evil bitch!" Terri said with a hurt expression on her face.

"What's going on, Terri?"

"You mean you didn't know?" Olivia laughed. "This is too good to be true!"

"Know what?"

"Shut up, Olivia, I'm warning you!"

Olivia pointed the gun at Terri's stomach.

"No, I'm warning *you!*" she said. "I've already lost two babies—why would I give a damn about killing yours?"

"Olivia, please don't!" Julian pointed at the clock. "Look, it's almost midnight. I thought you wanted to go on the air."

"I'm not done with you yet," Olivia said to Terri. "Now hand me that last box!"

She walked up to the microphone and began adjusting it. While she was holding the gun to Samantha's head, she reached inside the box and pulled out two pieces of paper and a Walkman radio. She taped it to her naked waist then turned the dial to 102.3.

"I may be crazy, but I'm not stupid," she said while putting on her headphones. "Now, let's talk about love, lust, and lies—*for real!*"

I had no choice but to do what she said. When the last commercial was ending, I switched off the tape and went on the air live.

"Welcome back to the show. Tonight we're talking about resolutions. But, before we go back to the phones, I have a special guest in the studio who has a few thoughts she wants to share. Welcome to the show, Olivia."

"Glad to be here, Julian," she said in a sexy tone. "It's nice to finally meet the man behind the voice. You are even finer in person."

"Thanks," I said with an attitude. "So why are you here tonight?"

"I have a poem I'd like to read." She unfolded the two pieces of paper. "I want to dedicate this to all the women out there who have searched for love but found only misery and pain. I call it 'God's Gift to Women.'"

I laid down a jazz instrumental and adjusted the volume. Olivia closed her eyes, moved her head to the rhythm, and began to recite.

You say, I'm beautiful—sexy—classy,
and a little sassy
but most of all,
you love my honesty

all these things I possess
and yet—I am good enough for a night
but not good enough for a wife?

You ask what is wrong
what am I basing my opinion on?
like they all do,
he went on and on and on
pleading his case
meanwhile his sacks lay on my face

I'm tired of this shit
so now I'm gonna flip the script
remember the time I walked into the room
smelled the sweet perfume?
but it wasn't mine
but I'm the one you call crazy

and you want to know why I be hidden outside in the bushes
waiting fo' you to come out your 'ho's house
so I can bust you in the mouth—or cut your ass

or why you woke up and found
your four rims on four flats
how am I really suppose to act?
all I wanted was to have you back

again, I ask the question
I am good enough for a night
but not good enough for a wife?

and so precious man
you really thought you were God's gift to women
but the truth is—women are God's gift to you
If you weren't so busy strokin' on this cat
your arrogant ass would have realized that

I told you nigga
I wasn't afraid to pull the trigga
too bad you won't wake up from this sleep
rest in peace

There was an eerie silence. Terri and I stared at each other knowing she meant to kill us all. Her poem wasn't just an expression of her madness; it was a suicide note. I nodded my head slightly and shifted my eyes to signal Terri to tilt over the wobbly tape rack. Her eyebrows raised as if she didn't understand what I was trying to tell her. I tried to stall for more time.

"Well, that was very—interesting," I said, sounding cordial. "So, how long have you been writing poetry?"

"Don't patronize me, goddamnit!" Olivia snapped. "You know damn well that poem was meant for you!" She pointed the gun at me. "Now, get down on your knees and apologize for what you did to me."

"The only thing I'm sorry about is meeting your disturbed ass!" I said to her. "We had a one-night stand, and now my best friend is dead and you're holding a gun to my daughter's head, all because you can't separate your pussy from your emotions!"

"Well, how about I separate your head from your shoulders, smart-ass?"

She cocked the trigger.

"Olivia, please wait!" Terri said in a caring tone. "I know you still have emotional scars from being raped and losing your babies. There are millions of women like you who suffer in silence through their own private hell. But hurting innocent people won't make that pain go away. You're sick, and you need help." Terri slowly stretched out her hand. "Now please give me the gun."

Olivia burst out laughing.

"Now, *that* was some good shit, Doc! Did you hear that on *Oprah*?" She pushed Samantha aside and put the gun to Terri's forehead. "So, what's your philosophy on this, huh? You think you're so smart! You don't know the first thing about what I've been through. You sit in your cozy little office reading books about abuse, but I've lived through it every day of my life for thirty-five years." Her eyes filled with tears. "And there's no book or fuckin' pill that can make that pain go away. Some of us are just natural-born victims. Sometimes the only way to escape the pain of all the bad memories is through death."

"So why not just kill yourself?" I yelled. "Why Eddie—why me?"

She turned the gun back on me and aimed at my head.

"Because Eddie represented all the men in my life who ever hurt me. And you—you were everything good in a man that I knew I could never have." Then she gave me a wicked smile. "So, as the saying goes, if I can't have you, nobody else will!"

Just when she was about to shoot, Terri shoved the tape rack with her shoulder. Olivia shielded herself with her arm as it fell on top of her.

"Run, Sam!"

Terri grabbed Samantha and carried her out of the studio. I pulled the knife out of my sock and ran over to stab Olivia. She was buried underneath the rack, but the hand she was holding the gun in was still free.

Bang! Bang! Two shots rang out. The first one missed but the second hit me in my left side. It burned like hell.

"Gotcha, motherfucker!"

I rolled over on my back, holding the wound. Olivia pushed the rack off her and jumped on top of me.

"Like I told you, every dog has its day." She pointed the gun in my face and began to squeeze the trigger.

I closed my eyes and said a silent prayer, expecting to hear the pop of the gun. Then, from out of nowhere, Terri tackled Olivia, knocking her off me. The gun went flying across the room.

"That's for callin' me booshie, bitch!" Terri shouted as she punched Olivia in the face.

I crawled across the floor, trying to reach the gun. Just when I got my hand on it, Olivia reached over and pulled out the box cutter she had hidden in her purse. Terri was so busy punching her she never saw it coming.

"Terri, watch out!"

Olivia cut her across the shoulder, then she put her in a headlock and put the blade against her stomach.

"Throw that gun over here, right now, or you're going to witness your first abortion."

"Don't do it, Julian. She'll kill both of us!"

"Have it your way!"

Olivia pressed the blade into Terri's stomach. Blood gushed out, staining her white dress.

"Stop!" I screamed out. "Take it!" I slid the gun over to her.

"Here we are, just one big happy family," she said while waving the gun around playfully. "After I shoot you, I'm gonna go find your little princess and blow her brains out, too! What do you think about that?"

All of a sudden the studio door swung open. Mitch was standing in the doorway in his drawers pointing a .45.

"I think somebody else is gonna pick up all these damn tapes!"

Then he unloaded into her chest. The force of the shots sent her flying through the studio window. As Olivia screamed and kicked down twenty-five stories, Samantha ran over to the window and yelled out, "Don't forget to hold that note, Miss Randall!"

That's the last thing I remember before I fell into unconsciousness. When I came to, there were two paramedics hovering over me screaming into their radios.

"You chose one helluva way to bring in the new year, Mr. Payne," the paramedic said.

"Where's my daughter?" I asked while trying to sit up. "And where's Terri?"

"Please lie still. You'll only make the bleeding worse."

The radio station was on the twenty-fifth floor. I didn't feel strong enough to make it to the ambulance—let alone the hospital. The bullet had penetrated my left side and exited through my back. It burned like hell.

"Am I gonna die?"

They both paused, then looked at one another as if to seek the other's opinion. That terrified me. Once we boarded the elevator, they began broadcasting my vital signs into the radio. I didn't know the significance of the blood pressure and heart rate numbers, but judging by the urgency in their voices, I was in trouble.

"Where's my daughter? And where's Terri?" I asked again.

"Relax, Mr. Payne, your daughter is—"

He stopped in midsentence as the elevator doors opened on the lobby level. Suddenly, a wave of photographers and reporters rushed toward me. I was blinded by a barrage of flashing lights. Although my vision was blurred, I could see the outline of several husky policemen clearing a path.

"Julian, can you tell us what happened?" a reporter yelled out.

"Who shot the security guard?" another shouted while shoving a microphone in my face.

"Fuckin' vultures!"

I tried to lift my hand to shield my bloody face, but my arms were strapped down. The yelling was deafening—like a continuous roar. The paramedics tried to move faster, but it was no use. The lobby was packed with policemen, reporters, and nosy fans who had come to watch. The atmosphere was festive, like a circus.

"Get out of the way, please!" the paramedics yelled. "This man is in critical condition! Move, move, move!"

The paramedics fought through the main doors, but once we made it outside we came to an abrupt stop. The crowd was even larger. People were jumping up on the hood of their cars trying to get a better look. As the brisk night air blew across my bloody face, their loud voices suddenly faded—replaced by sirens and the humming of the helicopter blades. I could feel the blood soaking through the bandages.

It was obvious from the paramedics' expressions that we were running out of time. The ambulance was only a few yards away, but the crowd was out of control. When they continued to push, the cops pushed back—violently. People were knocked to the pavement and trampled.

"I love you, Julian!" a woman screamed as she struggled to get off the ground.

"I'm your number one fan!" another woman shouted as she lifted her blouse, exposing her breasts.

Suddenly a woman lunged toward me and ripped the sleeve off my blood-soaked shirt.

"*Aarrgh!*" I screamed.

"Now I'll always have a piece of you," she said. Her hazel eyes and deranged stare were all too familiar.

"Move back!" the cops yelled as they pulled her away. "Move back, damnit!"

They finally managed to get me over to the ambulance, but I was more concerned about Terri and Samantha. Just as they lifted me inside, I heard a faint voice screaming, "Get outta the way! I wanna see my daddy!"

When I lifted my head I saw Mitch fighting through the crowd with Samantha in his arms. Once she was close enough, she reached out for my hand and held it tight.

"Are you okay?"

"I'm fine now that I see you, Princess." I smiled. "Where's Terri? Did they stop the bleeding?"

"Don't worry about her; she's a tough old broad." Mitch laughed. "The paramedic said she's gonna be fine."

"What about Olivia, is she—"

"Dead as a doornail!" he said before I could finish. "The only way you're ever gonna see her again is in your dreams."

"You mean in my nightmares."

They loaded me into the ambulance and began wrapping my wounds with more bandages. Just as the paramedics were about to close the doors, I yelled out to Mitch, "Hey, Kato, I was just wondering—where did you get the gun?"

"I got it from Old Man Joe, the security guard. He was so charged up, he shot himself in the foot." Mitch laughed. "And how many times do I have to tell you, *I'm* the Green Hornet and *you're* Kato!"

Epilogue

Nightmares

Nine months later

IT'S BEEN NINE months, seven days, and thirteen hours since that terrible night. There's not a day that goes by that I don't think about Olivia and what she did to Eddie. Every night I wake up in a cold sweat thinking about those hazel eyes coming out of the shadow in the studio. Sometimes I have nightmares within nightmares where I wake up from one and she's the one tapping me on the shoulder telling me it's just a dream. Then she starts slashing me with that box cutter while screaming, "Every dog has its day!"

As for the baby, it's a boy—nine pounds, three ounces. We named him Edward, after Eddie. You should have seen Samantha's face light up when she found out she had a baby brother. I guess she'll have someone to beat up on after all. Terri and I haven't decided on marriage yet. Our love for each other is stronger than ever, but we don't feel the need to rush into moving in together. Everything happened so fast, we never had a chance to get to know each other, at least not in the way a husband and wife should. Besides, we're both still in therapy. If we make it through that hell, being married will be a piece of cake.

As for my show, *Love, Lust, and Lies* is still on the air. After New Year's Eve, the ratings went through the roof. The *New York Times* had a front-page story about the incident. CNN had a weeklong feature on stalkers. And the *Chicago Sun-Times* wrote an article titled "Fatal Attraction of the Airwaves." The only negative press was from some dumb-ass reporter in Houston who accused me of staging the whole thing just for ratings. The listeners didn't care one way or the other; all they wanted was their daily dose of drama.

The only positive thing to come out of that terrible incident was my inspiration to write this book. I've decided to dedicate it to all the arrogant men who think it could never happen to them. Maybe this will help them realize that a woman's emotions should not be toyed with. Maybe they'll learn that no matter what kind of understanding you have, their feelings can get out of control. All it takes is a combination of bad timing, low self-esteem, and the right person to come along to set them off.

I hope these so-called players read this book and take heed so they don't run into another Olivia Brown. Or maybe they'll just have to learn the hard way—like I did!

About the author

MICHAEL BAISDEN, a Chicago native, was born June 26, 1963. He redefined marketing in the book industry when he self-published his first book, *Never Satisfied: How & Why Men Cheat*. The controversial book of short stories about infidelity sold more than 50,000 copies during its first eight months and has since sold more than 300,000 copies, a staggering figure considering Michael had no experience as a book publisher. "Achieving success is all about determination, great customer service, and avoiding negative people."

In 1997 Michael self-published his second book, *Men Cry in the Dark*. It has become one of the most popular books ever among African American men and was adapted as a stage play by I'm Ready Productions in 2002. The play featured notable actors such as Richard Roundtree (*Shaft*), Allen Payne (*New Jack City*), Rhona Bennett (*Jamie Foxx Show*), and singers Christopher Williams and Monifa, and comedian Lavell Crawford from *BET Comicview*. In 1999, Michael self-published his third book, *The Maintenance Man*, which has also been adapted as a stage play by I'm Ready Productions in 2003.

In 2001 Michael decided to take time off from writing to pursue his lifelong dream of hosting his own nationally syndicated talk show. He got that opportunity when Tribune Entertainment choose him to host a daytime talk show called *Talk or Walk*. Unfortunately, it premiered during the week after the 9/11 attack and never had a chance to develop a following. It was canceled after only one season.

Michael saw the experience as an education about the television industry, and more importantly, about having control over his own destiny. "Money and celebrity mean absolutely nothing when the people you work with don't share your vision!"

Michael currently resides in Los Angeles and Houston, where he is working on several business ventures including event promotions, book publishing, and a website for singles called HappilySingle.com. Details can be found on his website (www.michaelbaisden.com).

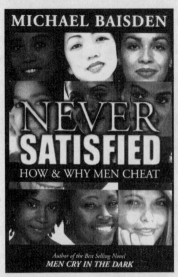